# I WAS
# YOUR FOOL

Also by Jacqueline M. Smith

I AM YOUR FOOL

Published by Urban Soul

# I WAS YOUR FOOL

Jacqueline M. Smith

URBAN BOOKS

http://www.urbanbooks.net

URBAN SOUL is published by

Urban Books
1199 Straight Path
West Babylon, NY 11704

ISBN-13: 978-1-59983-063-6
ISBN-10: 1-59983-063-9

First Printing: June 2008

10 9 8 7 6 5 4 3 2 1

Printed in the United States of America

# 1

Destiny sat in her Jag outside of Josephine's house, thinking about what had just transpired between them. She never meant to get herself entangled in a love affair that was so forbidden, but she had Josephine to thank for her current trouble. She didn't mean for things to get so out of hand between her and William, but Josephine had insisted that she leave him and move into her guesthouse until she prioritized her life. Destiny accepted the offer only because Josephine had been very good friends with her grandmother.

As Destiny sat in her car, thinking about what happened not even a month ago, she started to cry. "How could I have been so stupid? What the hell was I thinking to sleep with my therapist's husband?"

She was startled by the knock on her car window. "Why are you still sitting outside of my house?"

Destiny looked at Josephine standing beside

her car screaming at her. She wanted to get out and talk to her, but she knew that wasn't a good idea. She rolled her window down just enough so that her ex-therapist could hear what she had to say. "You were the one who got us in the predicament that we're in. You told me to leave my man, but yet you weren't being such a good woman to your own. You need to get away from my car, and leave me alone, because you don't own the damn sidewalk!" Destiny snapped back at Josephine.

"You trifling slut. You're a fool. All these years I've been helping you with your problems, you sleep with my husband. Is that the thanks I get for helping you?" Josephine screamed back.

Destiny was tired of all the nasty little things that Josephine was saying to her, and she looked up at her from inside her car. "Well . . . like I said, if you had been taking care of your own man instead of convincing me to leave mine, yours wouldn't have been all up in my grill! He's not good enough for you. Why do you put up with him? Remember all of that crap you said to me? Now here you are in the same boat that I'm in."

"You nasty heifer. I let you stay in my home to get yourself together, and you sleep with my husband? How much do you think you owe me for that?"

"Whatever I owe you, take it out of the money that I spent remodeling your dingy basement."

"It's not completed, you ungrateful person, if you don't move this piece of crap from—"

Destiny opened her car door abruptly and hit Josephine in the mouth. "I'm going to leave from in front of your house, but the next time you tell somebody to leave her man, make sure your crap is in order. I didn't come on to your husband, he came on to me. He forced himself on me, so what was I going to do?" Destiny said this, even though it was a lie.

Josephine let go of her bloody lip. "You should have come to me."

Destiny climbed back into her car and drove off. She didn't know where she was going. Maybe she'd go back to William and beg him to take her back. She was sorry for what had happened between her and Marcus. She drove until she found herself parked outside William's house. She pulled her car in the driveway behind his.

She dragged herself out of her car and walked up to the door. She rang the bell.

"Who is it?" William answered.

"Destiny."

"What do you want?"

"I want to come in."

"For what?"

"William, please, I don't want to go through this. Can I please come in?"

"Oh, now you don't want to go through this? You were the one who left, because your therapist said that I was no good for you, and now you want to come in?"

"William, please, I thought I was finally taking my life into my own hands when I left you."

"Destiny, now you're standing here saying that I was controlling your life?"

"I don't know what I'm saying, William. I know that I don't want to stand here at your door, looking like the fool that I am. Can I please come in?"

"What if I said no, I have company?" he countered.

"That's all you had to say," Destiny said. She turned to walk away, but William grabbed her by the arm and pulled her into his house.

"I don't have any company, Destiny, but I wanted you to feel the humiliation that I felt three weeks ago when you walked out of here."

"I don't know why I let Josephine tell me to leave you. She kept telling me that my grandmother didn't want me to date you. I did something so stupid."

"It's OK, baby. . . . It's OK. What you did wasn't stupid. You were trying to find out who Destiny is, and if it took you to leave me for a few weeks to find yourself, then that's what it took. I always knew that you'd come back, and Josephine has been calling here all day, but I didn't answer her. I know she left messages, but I didn't have time to check them."

"I can check the messages. I'm sure it's nothing."

"You think she wants you to come back?" William asked.

Destiny ignored him.

"I'll get your things out of the car while you check those messages and see what that crazy lady wants."

"Get them in the morning, baby," Destiny said.

Destiny felt so relieved when William said that he hadn't checked his messages. She checked them and was shocked to hear their content.

"William, this is Josephine. That tramp of yours has been sleeping with my husband." *Beep.* "William, answer your phone. This is Destiny's therapist, and she's been sleeping with my husband." *Beep.* "William, damn it, answer your phone. I'm trying to save you from a broken heart. Destiny's been sleeping with my husband." *Beep.* The rest of the messages all sounded similar.

Just as Destiny had finished listening to William's messages, he walked back into the room. "I was wondering how long it was going to take you to come back to your senses. Come here, girl." William stretched out his arms for Destiny to come into them. She rushed over and wrapped her arms around his waist.

"Three weeks. I was being stupid to think that a head doctor could actually help me resolve my issues, when she couldn't take care of her own." Destiny bucked her eyes at the slipup. *Damn, I hope he didn't catch that,* she thought.

"What do you mean she can't take care of her own issues?" William asked.

"Baby, I could see that she and her husband were having their own problems. They argued a lot, and he accused her of breaking people up—isn't that something?"

"I told you that night you decided to pack up your things and leave me that misery loves company. That's probably why she kept calling here. I don't have anything to say to that homewrecker, and she better not ever call my . . . I mean our house anymore, and I don't want you going to her anymore. Is that understood, Destiny?"

"Yes, baby, I understand. My grandmother thought that I needed the counseling after my first love was killed."

William held on to both of Destiny's arms and gently pushed her away from him. He stared her in the eyes and said, "Your what?"

"Honey, you know that was way before your time. He was my first love, and you're my forever love," Destiny said with a big smile on her face.

"That's what I'm talking about, baby. I'm not jealous of your past, but I like to think of myself as your first love."

"You are jealous. I can see it in your eyes."

"Yes, baby. I admit that I'm jealous, but the thought of you being with another man sets my soul on fire. Can't you feel the heat?"

"I don't know about your heat, but can you feel mine?" Destiny asked. Then she wrapped her arms around William's neck and pulled his mouth close to hers and kissed him. William pulled her up into his arms and carried her to the bedroom, where he made love to her for hours.

The last thing Destiny thought about before she closed her eyes was how friendly Josephine was toward her and other women. She thought about the night that they had decided to go out. Josephine had picked out the dress that she thought would look good on Destiny.

Destiny closed her eyes. She didn't want to think that Josephine had other motives for being so nice to women, and evil toward men. Just as Destiny had begun to drift off to sleep, the phone began ringing.

"Hello."

"I see you're back with William. Well, I will definitely make sure he knows that you are a homewrecker."

Destiny eased out of the bed and went to the room that William used for an office. "Josephine Riley, you may be a therapist, but if you call my man's house one more time, you'll be a *dead* therapist," Destiny hissed into the phone.

"I don't take kindly to threats. I will see to it that William finds out about your little escapades with my husband."

"Obviously, Josephine, you think that I'm afraid of you. Well, I'm not. Leave William and me alone, and don't ever dial this number again—unless you got ass to back up your fingers."

"I guess that's supposed to scare me?"

"Josephine, listen. If you don't want your fingers broken, stop dialing this number, or else put your ass up for collateral. If you call here one more time, I will either break your fingers or stick my foot so far up your butt, you'll wish you had let me break your fingers first." *Click.*

"I know that trifling little tramp didn't just hang up the phone on me," Josephine muttered.

Destiny had climbed back into bed. This time she turned the ringer off. She didn't know what to expect from Josephine, but she was willing to fight for her man.

Josephine lay in bed alone, furious with Destiny and with her husband, who, she guessed, was probably on the sofa in the basement, where he had fucked Destiny. She was going to have her revenge on Destiny if it was the last thing she did, and if Marcus wanted a piece of her, she'd hurt him too.

Destiny rose from bed early the next morning. She pulled the blinds in the bedroom to let in the sun rays. Had she looked out the window, she would have seen Josephine's Lexus pulling up in the driveway. She caught a glimpse of the sun shining on William's handsome face just before the chime of the doorbell awoke him.

"Who in the world could be ringing the bell this early in the morning?" William asked.

"I don't know, but I'll get it, baby," Destiny said as she grabbed her robe and went to answer the door. "Who is it?"

Josephine didn't answer. She just stood there, ringing the bell, even after she heard Destiny's voice.

"What do you want?" Destiny asked when she swung the door open.

"I want to talk to William," Josephine fumed.

"What do you want with me?" William asked.

"I got this, baby," Destiny said. She hadn't heard him come down the stairs behind her.

"Excuse me, William, I came to see you, not Destiny."

"Look, Josephine, William doesn't have anything to say to you."

"Hold on, Destiny. Let me hear what she has to say. It better be something good, since you've been calling my house like crazy."

"It is. Did Destiny tell you what her trifling ass did while she was at my house?"

"Josephine, wait a minute. Who do you think you are, coming over here this early in the morning and starting crap?"

"Destiny, I won't have you treating company like that. I don't care what time of the morning it is, you will respect this house," William said.

"Honey, I'm not even a patient of hers anymore, so why do you need to listen to anything that she has to say?"

Before William could answer, Josephine said, "Did she tell you that she was sleeping with my husband?"

William stood there in between Destiny and Josephine. He didn't know how to respond to what Josephine had said.

"Destiny, is what she's saying true?"

"Baby, I made a mistake. I—"

"Yes or no?"

"William, I didn't come here to start any trouble, but it's true," Josephine inserted.

"Destiny, did you sleep with her husband?"

"Baby, it was a mistake."

"Josephine, are you telling me the truth?" William asked.

"Like I said, William, I didn't come here to start any trouble. My son found them on the sofa in the basement, having sex."

"I bought that sofa," Destiny blurted out.

"Is that supposed to make what you did right?" Josephine asked.

"Get out! Just get out before I—"

"Before you do what, Destiny?" William asked.

Destiny was shocked at William. She wanted him to make Josephine get out of his house.

"William, why are you asking me that?"

"Because I want to know why she should leave."

"William, can we talk about this later? You're upset, baby, and there's more to this story than she's telling."

"If there's more to it than what she said, then maybe the three of us should sit down and talk. She's the therapist."

"Josephine I know what I did was wrong, but this just isn't the right time to be talking about something like this."

"William, if it's OK with you, I have all day to talk," Josephine said.

"I think we should talk. Don't you, Destiny?" William asked.

Destiny didn't know what to say. She followed Josephine and William into the kitchen and pulled a chair out from under the table while William made a pot of coffee.

"William, I may have been wrong for telling Destiny to leave you, but that did not give her the right to sleep with my husband. She complained about you not being there for her when her grandmother died. I suggested to her that maybe you were too busy to give her the attention that she needed."

"Josephine, you're lying. You didn't suggest anything. You told me to leave him."

"William," Josephine stated his name in a professional tone. "I can't tell my patients to leave their mate. I merely suggested to Destiny that if her relationship with you wasn't working out, she should give the two of you some air."

This time Destiny didn't try to hold back her anger. "You're lying," Destiny said as she walked around the table to where Josephine was sitting and grabbed a handful of her hair. Yanking Josephine's head down, Destiny pummeled her with her fist.

Josephine tried to get up from the chair, but Destiny had a good grip on her hair. William ran over to the table and grabbed Destiny's hand to try and loosen her grip, but he was causing Josephine more pain.

"Let her hair go, Destiny."

With rage in her eyes, Destiny looked at William. She started to repeat what Josephine had said to her, "'Leave him. . . . He's no good for you. Leave him. . . .'"

"But you were the one who said he wasn't satisfying in bed," Josephine managed to say.

"You told her that I didn't satisfy you in bed, Destiny?"

Destiny ignored William and kept on talking. "'Leave him. He only wants your money.'"

"Destiny, let her go now!"

Destiny still ignored William.

"'Leave him. . . . Your grandmother forbade you to be with him anyway.' Josephine, isn't that what you told me?" Destiny shouted as she pulled Josephine out of the chair and onto the floor, punching her all over her face and upper chest.

William grabbed hold of Destiny's hand and tried to free Josephine's hair.

"When I get up, I'm going to beat your butt!" Josephine screamed out in pain.

"I told you to stop calling here, but instead you came here starting trouble. Is this the collateral I told you to put up?" Destiny asked before she let go of Josephine's hair and started punching her in the face again.

"Collateral, you just messed up," Josephine said as she grabbed Destiny's hands and snatched her down on the floor with her.

William stepped in and broke the two women up. "Destiny, get your things and get the hell out of my house. Josephine, you can get out too."

"William," Destiny called out his name before Josephine hit her in the mouth.

"Familiar? Remember when you threw your car door open and hit me in my mouth? Payback is a motherfucker, isn't it?"

Destiny looked at Josephine and waited for her to blink, and when she did, Destiny cold-cocked her in the mouth. William ran and once more jumped in between the two of them.

"Josephine, get out of my house."

Josephine turned to walk toward the door and stopped in her tracks. "Can I still have that cup of coffee?" she asked, smiling at Destiny with her swollen face and bloody mouth.

Destiny picked up one of the coffee mugs that William had sitting on the counter and threw it at Josephine.

"You missed. Your aim isn't as good as you think it is."

"How could you have done something like that to me and to her?" William asked Destiny. "When you're done cleaning up the mess that you just made, I want you out of my house."

"William, baby, please don't do this to me."

"You did it to yourself."

Destiny picked up the broken pieces of the coffee mug. "I'm going to get her back, even if it takes me forever," she mumbled under her breath.

William sat on his bed, thinking what he should do. He didn't know if he could ever forgive her for sleeping with another man. It was one thing when she left him, but this was another.

Destiny stood outside William's bedroom door and knocked. "William, honey, open the door, please. Let me explain to you what happened."

William got up and opened the door. "Destiny, there's nothing to explain. You got money to do whatever you want. I suggest that you take some of it and get yourself a place to stay, because you can no longer stay here."

"William, let's not go through this. I love you, and that's all that should matter."

"Did it matter to you when you did what you

did? You told her that I didn't satisfy you anyway, so why do you want to be here?" William turned his back on Destiny.

Destiny walked up to him and grabbed his arm in an effort to get him to face her.

"Get your hands off me. Don't ever touch me again," William said as he snatched her hands away from him.

"William, please let's talk."

"Destiny, there is nothing to talk about. I want you to pack your things. . . . Oh, that's right— your stuff is already in your car and storage. So why don't you put on what you had on, and get out of my house!"

"William, please . . . baby, just tell me what to do to make it right?"

"Make it right? You want to know what you could have done when you walked through my damn door yesterday?" William asked as he turned to face Destiny. "You could have told the whole truth when you mentioned that you did something stupid. You knew then that it would come out. I guess you were prepping me."

"William, I didn't want to hurt you any more than I already have."

"So, then, Destiny, did you think that just because you left your therapist's house, she was going to let that ride?"

"I didn't think that she would come here and tell you like she didn't know that it wasn't going to hurt you, baby."

William closed his eyes for a moment to hold back his anger; then he turned to face her.

"Get dressed."

"Where are we going?"

"Just get dressed."

"Can I go to the car and get some clean clothes to change into?"

"No, I don't feel like waiting on you to do that. Put on what you had on yesterday."

She got dressed.

"Let's go," William said, walking out of the bedroom to the front door.

"Baby, you're not dressed."

William looked at her. "Don't you think I know that?"

Her heart sank when they got to the front door and William opened it. Destiny waited for him to walk out first, but he just stood there, numb.

"Honey—"

"Get out before I do something to you."

"William, please don't do this to me. Baby, we can get through this," Destiny pleaded with William, but she could tell from the way he stood there, not looking at her once, that he meant what he had just said.

"If you're not going to leave on your own, I'll just have to throw you out."

"William—"

William grabbed Destiny by the arm and flung her out his front door. He could hear her screaming to let her back in, but he ignored her and went back to his room and turned his TV volume up. The phone rang. He answered. "William, please don't hang up on me," Destiny said through sobs. "I left my purse. Can I come inside and get it?"

There was a long pause before William answered. "Look on the side of the house under my bedroom window. It should be lying on the ground." William dropped her purse out the window. Closing it, he plopped back down on his bed.

She picked up her purse and screamed up at his window. "William, all I want to do is explain to you how sorry I am."

William didn't hear her, his eyes were glued to the TV. He thought back to the night one month ago when he had pleaded with her not to leave him because her therapist had said she should. He remembered how he had held her and told her how much he needed her in his life. He loved Destiny, but he didn't think that he could deal with her sleeping with another man. William had tried unsuccessfully to get Destiny to see that something was morally wrong with Josephine inviting another woman to stay in her guesthouse, but Destiny wouldn't listen to him.

He had told Destiny on several occasions that a therapist's profession was to help a patient cope with what was going on in her life. Not convince someone to run away from it. Destiny had defied every reason that he had given her to keep her from moving into Josephine's guesthouse. It wasn't like she didn't have her own money to get her own place. What was she thinking? Only Destiny knew the answer to that question.

William turned the television off after he'd looked out the window and saw that Destiny was gone. He didn't want to end things the way he had. After all he had gone through to get her, it was surprisingly easy to let her go. Her grandmother who had raised her thought he was a pretty boy with a bunch of women, and that he was after her money. He wasn't; William wasn't the type to cheat. Because he didn't believe in that, he knew he would never have anything else to do with Destiny. He knew that she was going to try to come back to him, and that made him hurt more. He sadly thought about the engagement ring that he had planned to surprise her with when he took her out for lunch today.

Josephine smiled all the way home after leaving William's house. She backed her car into the garage, turned it off and climbed out. She didn't think twice about what she had done to ruin William and Destiny's relationship. "Who does that trifling little tramp think she is? Coming into my home and helping herself to my husband? I don't think so. Hell, I didn't get a chance to go through with my plans. That sneaky little tramp had a few tricks of her own," Josephine quietly said as she entered her house.

"Mom's back, Dad," Josephine's oldest son called out to his father, who was in the basement.

"What are you telling your father that I'm back for?" Josephine asked her son.

"Dad said to let him know when you get back."

"Is that right?" Josephine asked.

"Yeah, it is," her husband said.

Josephine whipped her head toward him like a cobra striking. She stepped up to him and hissed in his ear, "I suggest that you stay away from me for a while. Or *else.*" She put an emphasis on the word "else."

"Or else what?" he hissed back, when he should have been begging Josephine's forgiveness for what he'd done.

Josephine backed down. She wasn't afraid of her husband, but she knew that he didn't mind showing his natural ass in front of their two sons—although he did it in the most polite nasty way. At times when he was being this way, it turned her on. He showed his manliness instead of the whiny side that she hated the most.

"Marcus, I will not tolerate this in front of the kids, and besides, they need their breakfast. Skipping a meal can make a young boy grow into a whining old man," Josephine said, smiling.

Marcus knew what Josephine was trying to say, but he didn't give in to her. He didn't feel like arguing with her, because he was aware of her little games. He didn't want her that way this morning. He still had Destiny on his mind, and he was angry that his son had caught them, but deeply hurt as well. He didn't know how to face his son, but he knew that Josephine would take care of it for now. Later he would talk to him.

Destiny found herself sitting in her Jag, crying again. This time she was parked in front of a hotel. The only two men that she had ever loved were gone. Her first love was killed when some young boys mistook him for a gang member, and William was gone because she did the unthinkable. She would never be able to forgive Josephine for telling William what she had done. Destiny regretted what she had allowed herself to do, but if it took her forever, she was going to get even with Josephine.

Destiny wiped the tears from her face and looked in the rearview mirror. She was pretty, she thought. So how hard could it be to get another man? But would she fall in love with him the way she had fallen in love with William?

"Forget love, like Tina said, 'What's love got to do with it?' From now on, the world is going to meet the real Destiny Symone," Destiny said as she pulled one of her many credit cards out of her wallet and walked into the lavish hotel. She still looked good in her day-old outfit. She knew that, because heads turned when she walked.

"I would like a suite, sir."

"And how would you be paying for that, ma'am?" the clerk asked.

Destiny handed him the credit card. The clerk looked at it and asked, "May I see some ID, ma'am?"

Destiny handed the clerk her ID. He typed her information into the computer and checked for a room.

He assigned her a room and activated the key card; then he handed it to her, along with her ID and credit card.

Destiny swiped the card and went into her room. She needed to take a shower, order something to eat, relax and devise a plan to pay Josephine back. First, she needed to get her things out of the car. Destiny went back to her car, grabbed her clothes and returned to her room.

After Destiny finished eating the food she'd ordered, she lay across the bed and began to devise a plan to destroy Josephine. After thirty minutes of thinking devilishly, Destiny thought to hell with Josephine. She needed to think about finding an apartment.

She got up, grabbed her purse and went to get a newspaper. Once she made it back to her room, she looked through the paper and circled all the apartment ads that she thought would suit her needs. She wasn't ready to own her own home right now, because she didn't know what might happen after she'd paid Josephine back for her dirty little deed. Not that what she had done wasn't wrong, but she never thought that it would cause her to lose the man that she loved.

Destiny set up appointments to see three of the apartments over the next few days. After this was done, she began to think about William. She missed him. She wanted to call him, but she was afraid of being rejected again over the phone. Instead, she dialed Josephine's office. The receptionist told her that Josephine was gone for the day.

"Hmm," Destiny said to herself. "She knew that I was coming for her. Well, there's always tomorrow." Destiny couldn't help calling William then.

"Hello."

"Hello, I—"

"You what?" William shot back.

"I don't know why I called, but—"

"If you don't know why you're calling, maybe you shouldn't have dialed my number," William said, holding back the need to tell her to come back.

"William, I didn't call you to upset you. I just wanted to know if you're OK."

"Did you think about how I would feel when you were screwing your therapist's husband?"

"William, if you're going to talk mean to me, then we don't have to talk."

*Click.* Destiny heard the dial tone in her ear. "Damn, what was I thinking to say something like that?" She dialed his number again; his voice mail picked up.

It was by fate that she had met William. He was sitting in a booth at the "all you can eat" buffet, reading a paper. She'd fallen in love with him at first sight. He was much taller than her five-foot-five frame, and his dark caramel-colored skin reminded her of a piece of candy. His big brown eyes set off everything. Destiny wanted those eyes to be the eyes that she looked into every night before she fell asleep, and every morning when she awoke. William was the most handsome human creature she'd ever seen.

When Destiny saw William push his empty plate to the edge of the table and slide out of the booth, this was her cue to meet him. She covered her plate of food and walked over to the salad bar, where William was making himself a salad. Destiny accidentally bumped into him, causing him to drop his fork. "Oh, excuse me. I'm sorry. Let me get you another one."

"That's OK, I can just grab one on my way back to my table," William said. He got a good look at Destiny and changed his mind about that. "On second thought," he said, "why don't you grab that fork for me, that way I can get me something to drink."

"Sure," Destiny said, smiling. She fixed herself a small salad, grabbed two forks and hurried up to William. She was silently thinking what he actually said next.

"Why don't you get your things and join me."

Destiny smiled and said, "Sure." She felt a little embarrassed, because all she could get out was a "sure." She hoped he didn't think her vocabulary was small. Destiny went to the table where she had been sitting and retrieved her things. She sat across from William and found it hard to eat her food. The effect that William had on her was overwhelming. The way he chewed his food looked sexy to her. All she could think about was feeling his lips on hers.

"Aren't you going to eat?" William asked Destiny.

He'd caught her somewhat off-guard. She was staring right at him, but in a trance. Destiny finally realized what she was doing and said,

"Oh yes. I was just thinking about something and got caught up in my thoughts."

"If you ask me, I think that whatever you were thinking had something to do with me. By the way, my name's William Benjamin, and yours?"

"Destiny Symone."

"That's a very pretty name. It fits a very pretty woman," William said, smiling at Destiny.

"Thank you. My grandmother named me," she said, smiling back.


Destiny wanted William back, and she knew that in order to get him back, she had to do something quick. Otherwise, she had lost him for good. She had three things on her "to do" list: one, find a way to get her man back; two, find an apartment; three, get revenge on Josephine. Destiny chuckled at her list. It was number three that made her laugh the most. She knew that Josephine was probably at home having a blast over her and William's breakup. Destiny picked up the phone and called Josephine's home.

"Hello."

Destiny knew that this was one of Josephine's sons on the phone, so she politely asked if she could speak to Josephine. She could hear him calling his mother.

"Hello," Josephine said in a relaxed voice.

"I see it didn't take you any time to get back to normal after what you did this morning."

"Ah, Ms. Symone. What exactly can I help

you with now? You do know that I charge for my time? Of course you knew that," Josephine said, snickering.

"Ah, Mrs. Riley. When I'm done paying you back for breaking up my relationship, you're going to wish that you never met me."

"Hmm, Destiny, you sound so hostile, dear. How about you come lie on my sofa and we talk? Oh no, I forgot—that's where you screwed my husband."

"Obviously, you seem to think that this is funny, but rest assured, Josephine, that ass of yours just bought a cake that I'm going to frost," Destiny said, laughing into the phone.

"You know, it's silly little girls like you that make a woman like me sick. Destiny, whatever you think you got for me, I'll be waiting for it. Now I'm not going to be rude and hang up the phone on you, so I'm saying good-bye."

"Oh, Josephine, before you go, tell Marcus that I said he was the best sex a girl could wish for, and why you don't want it is a mystery, unless—"

"You slut—you dirty little slut. If I ever catch you near my husband again—"

"You'll what, Josephine?"

"I'll—"

*CLICK!*

"Marcus . . . Marcus, come in here right now."

Marcus came to see what his wife wanted. He could tell that she was very upset. "What do you want?"

"Marcus, if I ever catch you in Destiny's face again, I'll kill the both of you."

"Is that what you called me in here for, Josephine?"

"Yes, it is. Do you know what that trifling tramp just said to me?"

"No, but I'm sure you're going to tell me."

"She said your sex was real good. Well . . . if you want to keep that dick of yours, I suggest that you keep it in your pants."

"Right now it would do a lot of good in your mouth. All you do is talk crap, Josephine. Work all got damn day. Go out with your clients, and I guess you say to hell with your husband. When are you going to spend some of that time with me, Josephine? Huh? Maybe then I can keep my dick in my pants. You think!" Marcus snapped at his wife.

"Is that it, Marcus? You think all I do is go out with my clients? If it weren't for me, most of those women that I counsel would have committed suicide by now."

"My dick wants to commit suicide."

"Do you think your dick is more important than me saving a life?" Josephine asked.

"Do you think that my dick doesn't need to be saved from time to time? If you had been a wife to me, I would have never cheated on you with that girl," Marcus said, shifting the blame for his cheating onto his wife. "I never asked you to stop helping your clients either, Josephine. I just need you sometimes too. I know that what you do means a lot to you, but, baby, you can't keep neglecting me. I'm your husband," he said in an attempt to make her believe that it was her fault for his cheating.

Josephine fell for Marcus's tricks. "You're right, baby. I can't keep neglecting you, and I understand why you did what you did. Destiny is a very attractive woman, and she probably did seduce my man. I hope that you're never going to do that to me again. Speaking of again, Marcus . . ."

"Yes, baby."

"Have you ever cheated on me before Destiny?"

"No, baby."

"Marcus, are you lying to me?"

"No, baby. I've never cheated on you before. I promise you that I haven't."

# 2

A week had passed since Destiny had last talked to Josephine. Destiny felt like she had won round one. She knew that Josephine was furious with her for telling her something that she already knew.

She hadn't talked to William in a week, so she called him with the hope that this time they would be able to talk without getting angry at one another.

"Hello," William answered the phone.

"William, you know who this is. Can we please talk?" Destiny asked.

"Yes, Destiny, we can talk. You can say everything that you need to say."

Destiny knew that what she'd done had hurt William really bad. She could tell by the sound of his voice that he was feeling down. She knew that she had to choose her words carefully so that she wouldn't upset him further.

"William, I never meant to hurt you. When we first met, I knew that you were the man that

I wanted to spend the rest of my life with. There were times that I would feel like you weren't there for me when you were gone for long periods of time."

"Destiny, my job requires that I travel for short or long periods of time, and you knew that before you got involved with me. I even told you that I was going to travel less so that I could spend more time with you. That's when you began to think that I was suggesting that we live off your money."

"Honey, I didn't suggest that. Josephine did."

"When are you ever going to grow up and be your own woman, Destiny? Are you gonna go through life blaming other people for what you do and say?"

"I'm not doing that."

"Yes, you are," William snapped. "You just said that Josephine suggested that I wanted your money. Did you not?"

"Yes, I did, but—"

"There are no buts."

"OK, William, I don't want to upset you. I called to talk things out."

"OK, then start by accepting the fact that you are a grown woman and you've made whatever decisions that you made on your own. You are twenty-seven years old. You're not a baby."

The way that William was talking to her made her cry. The tears stung her eyes and the emotional pain choked her up. "William, I—I am to blame for what I did. I had no right sleeping with Josephine's husband. I was the one who listened to her when she suggested all those things about you. I knew that you would have never done anything to hurt me, but what I was trying to get from you, and the way that I did it, backfired on me."

"What did you want from me, Destiny, that I wasn't already giving?"

"I wanted you to ask me to marry you."

"You're right, you went about it the wrong way. First, you leave me, because your therapist told you to. Second, you sleep with her husband. Who told you to do that? Was that an attempt, too, to get me to marry you?"

"William, nobody told me to sleep with her husband. I was stupid to think that I could even get away with it. I don't know what I was thinking, but I wasn't thinking that I would lose you."

"You didn't? That's right, I forgot just that quick—you can't think for yourself."

"William, I'm trying to say that I'm sorry, and if you'll give me just one more chance, I promise not to ever let you down."

"How many times did you sleep with him, Destiny?"

"William, that's not important, baby. What's important is that we get through this."

"How many times did you sleep with him, Destiny?"

"Two."

"Two?"

"Yes, just two."

"You say that like two doesn't matter no more than one."

"Baby, I just answered your question."

"OK, can you give me two reasons why you slept with him two times?"

*Why is he doing this to me?* Destiny thought. "William, please, I don't want to do this, baby."

"Two reasons, Destiny."

"I don't know. I just did."

"You don't know, and you just did? OK, let me explain two things to you then, and maybe you'll figure things out. One: I do know that I could never trust you again. Two: we're done for good. It's over. I didn't think that you'd be able to answer that question, not that it would have made any difference to me. I just wanted to see if you had a reason for doing what you did. Don't dial my number ever again."

"William, baby, *nooooo* . . ."

"Are you done talking to me, Destiny?"

"No, I'm not. William, please tell me that you're not leaving me. I can't live without you. I love you so much, baby," Destiny said, sobbing.

"We're done. We're over. Stop calling my house, Destiny. I have nothing more to say to you—ever."

"But why?"

"Because I just don't." William hung up his phone and finished packing his suitcase. His job was sending him out of town to close a business deal.

Destiny cried until she could no longer tolerate the headache that she had developed. *When I get my hands on Josephine, I'm going to do some damage.* Destiny knew that she had lost him forever. She didn't even know why she had slept with Josephine's husband, but she regretted it deeply. For every ounce of pain that she felt, she was going to make Josephine feel double.

It hurt William even more that he had talked to Destiny. Hearing her voice brought back all the love that he had for her, but what she had done to him was unforgivable. She couldn't even give him two reasons why she had slept with the man.

Destiny found the perfect apartment close to the downtown area. It had two bedrooms, a living and dining room, a spacious kitchen and bath, and lots of closet space. She spent part of the day shopping at various stores to furnish the apartment, and just before the storage facility closed, she went there and picked up her clothes and shoes.

She got back to the empty apartment, and for the first time she realized that she was alone. All of her life she'd lived with her grandparents. They provided her with everything that she needed. Destiny sat on the hard floor of the apartment and thought about what she was going to sleep on. She hadn't even been in the apartment long enough to think to purchase her furniture before she found the apartment, because she wasn't used to doing things for herself.

She remembered passing a department store and now she hoped that it was still open so that she could get an air mattress, sleeping bag, sheets and toiletries. She grabbed her purse and keys, then rushed out of her apartment in

an attempt to catch it open. Just as she locked
her door, and dropped her keys into her purse
without looking up, she bumped into someone. "I'm sorry," she said as she looked up into
a pair of sexy brown eyes.

"It's OK. I wasn't paying attention either,"
Eric said.

"Oh, let me help you with that," Destiny said
as she began to help the man pick his groceries up from the floor.

"I got it. You look like you were in a hurry,"
he said.

"Oh, it's not a problem."

"By the way, my name's Eric." He stuck out
his hand for her to shake. Destiny was beautiful and Eric felt an instant attraction to her. "I
live right down the hall in apartment 2D."

"I'm Destiny, and I live right here," Destiny
said as she pointed to her apartment door, 2A.
After helping Eric pick up his groceries, Destiny went on her way. She had noticed that he
was very handsome, but she brushed it off.

Before entering his apartment, Eric turned
to look at Destiny as she walked away. She was
nice enough to help him pick up his groceries
after bumping into him. Maybe he could invite
her over for dinner one day, he thought.


Eric would occasionally run into Destiny
coming or going from her apartment. After a
month of bumping into one another, he finally
asked her if she wouldn't mind joining him for
dinner.

Destiny was flattered. "I don't want to bother you and your girlfriend or wife," Destiny said, picking Eric for information.

"I said *me*, not *us*. You could say it's like I'm welcoming you into the neighborhood, neighbor."

"I could have gone out for something to eat," Destiny said, blushing.

"Perhaps you could have, but you won't find a steak like mine anywhere in Chicago," Eric said, smiling.

"OK, you win, but first I need to change clothes."

"That's fine. I'll be waiting for you."

Destiny closed and locked her door. She thought about how handsome and polite Eric was. *This is definitely the beginning of the new Destiny. If I can't have the man that I want, why not sample them all until I find one just like him?* She walked into her bedroom, picked out a pair of jeans and a loose-fitting shirt to change into. She dug in another bag for some underwear; then she decided that she didn't need any. A few minutes later she was knocking on Eric's door.

"It's open."

Destiny turned the knob and walked in. His apartment was built the same as hers. He had a really nice leather living-room set, with glass tables and nice lamps. In his dining room he had a leather pit, and a giant-screen television set encased in an expensive cabinet, plus a stereo system.

Destiny went to the bathroom to make sure she looked all right. On her way to the bathroom, she couldn't help noticing that his bedroom door was ajar. She peeked inside. He had a gorgeous Valencia bedroom set, with a beautiful piece of African art hanging above his bed.

"I got that at the African-art store in the mall."

Eric had startled Destiny. She didn't know that he had walked up on her while she was admiring the picture. "I'm sorry. I was supposed to be going to the bathroom, but I couldn't help noticing the picture. It's beautiful."

"Thank you. Dinner will be ready in a little while."

Destiny walked into Eric's bathroom, and she wanted to cry. William liked lighthouses, and everything in Eric's bathroom had a lighthouse on it, from the shower and window curtains to the rugs on the floor. Out of curiosity she opened the medicine cabinet door to see if it had the same things in it that William had in his, but it didn't. She looked at herself in the mirror and saw that everything was all right, and then she turned on the water to wash her hands.

"There are towels in the linen closet," Eric said aloud.

Destiny took a hand towel from the closet and dried her hands.

"I'm in here," Eric called out from the kitchen when he heard the water go off in the bathroom.

Destiny went to the kitchen. "It smells really good in here."

"That's because I am a great cook."

"Is that right?"

"If I may say so, it is."

"So where do you want me to sit?" Destiny asked.

"Wherever you'd be the most comfortable."

"Are you always this nice to strange women?"

"Only the very pretty ones."

"I bet you're serious too."

"No, I'm not. I was just joking. It's not every day that I bump into someone that I can have dinner with, and especially in my apartment building. You can't trust everybody, but with a beautiful face like yours, you're certainly not a serial killer or madwoman. Are you?" Eric asked, joking.

"Not unless you want me to be," Destiny said.

"Well, I guess you know the answer to that?"

"I guess I do."

Eric fixed his and Destiny's plates. "Would you like a glass of wine?"

Destiny blushed, then asked, "Do you have something a little stronger?"

"Sure. What would you like?"

"A shot or two of cognac on ice would do."

Eric got up from the table and went to one of the cabinets. He took out a glass and then the cognac. "You want a double?"

"Yeah, why not?"

Eric poured the drink and handed the glass to her.

"You forgot the ice."

"My fault," Eric said.

Destiny ate and drank. She and Eric ended up in the dining room after dinner, listening to his dusties collection and drinking the cognac. They laughed and talked into the wee hours of the night.

"I better get home," Destiny said as she stumbled to her feet.

"I wish you didn't have to go," Eric said as he stumbled to his. "I was really enjoying your company."

"I enjoyed you too, Eric."

"Maybe we can get together for dinner again?"

"I'd like that, but next time it's my turn."

"Hey, before you go, I have a question."

"What's that?" Destiny asked.

"What kind of dessert do you like?"

"I like ice cream."

"I'm sorry about dessert, but the next time we have dinner, I'll have a dessert."

"I'd like that too, and before you ask, any flavor," Destiny said; then she walked out his door.

Eric caught up with her and walked her to her door.

"Thanks," Destiny said as she turned and opened her door, disappearing inside.

Eric stood there for a moment, hoping that she would open the door and invite him in, but she didn't. He walked back to his own apartment, with his head hung low. *There's always tomorrow,* he thought.

Destiny unfolded the sleeping bag and climbed inside. She laid her head on the pillow, but could not fall asleep. *Ice cream,* she thought. *Hmm . . . Eric could definitely be a scoop of dark-chocolate ice cream.* Destiny licked her lips. *Like I said, if I can't have the man that I want, why not sample them all until I find one like him?* Just as she thought about what she had wished for, she could hear her grandmother's voice inside her head. Of course she knew this was only the good side of her conscience telling her that she was dipping her feet in hot water. "Whatever," Destiny said aloud. Then she pulled the covers over her head and fell asleep.

Destiny heard a light tapping at her door. "Aw, damn, who could that be at this time of morning?" She was feeling the effect of the alcohol that she drank the night before, and her head was pounding. She dragged herself over to the door. "Who is it?" she asked.

"I'm sorry to bother you so early in the morning, but I just wanted to check on you to make sure that you were OK."

Destiny smiled. It was Eric, and he sounded even sexier to her than he had yesterday. She opened the door and allowed him in.

"You can't hang with the big dogs?" Eric asked, holding a plate of food wrapped in foil and a glass of something to drink.

"What time is it?"

"It's twelve."

"You're kidding me. I never sleep this late," Destiny said. Then she ran her fingers through her hair and blew out a breath of air. "Oh, excuse me," she said as she ran to the bathroom and brushed her teeth. Her own morning breath had almost knocked her out, and she was sure that she was going to find Eric passed out on her floor from it. "Sorry 'bout that, but I had to brush away the dragon."

Eric smiled at her and said, "Here, you better eat this before it gets cold." He handed her the plate and she accepted.

"What's in the glass?" she asked.

"It's something to help you with your headache."

Destiny took the glass and drank it down. Immediately it began to take away the headache.

"Look, I have to make a quick run. I'll be back shortly if you need help with anything today."

"You're very thoughtful, chocolate."

"What did you call me?" Eric asked.

"Sorry, that part wasn't supposed to come out."

"Well, it did, and I guess that means you like my chocolate-colored skin?" Eric said, smiling.

"I guess I do."

"Well, I better get going. See you when I get back."

Destiny closed her door after Eric had left. She pulled the foil off the plate, and the aroma of the food made her realize how hungry she really was. She was grateful for a neighbor like Eric, but was he after something—like she was? Destiny knew that she was just playing a game, and she didn't really want to fall for anyone— that is, unless he made her feel the love that she felt for William. Thinking about William brought on her turbulent feelings. She found it hard to swallow the food that Eric had brought, but she knew that she had to eat. She couldn't let her breakup with William keep her down, and she knew from experience that life did go on.

Destiny finished the food on the plate and washed it down with a glass of cold water. An hour later she was up doing some housework and unpacking the few things that she had left in some boxes in the hall closet. Destiny jumped when she heard the knock at her door. "Damn, I guess I got to get used to that too." She walked over to the door and opened it without asking who it was.

"What if I had been some stranger coming to harm you?" Eric asked.

"I know your knock, chocolate."

"So, is that my new nickname?" he asked.

"Yeah, if you don't mind."

"Naw . . . I don't. It's cute."

"I was wondering if you wouldn't mind going with me to the mall where you purchased your African art. I want to buy a few paintings for my apartment."

"I don't mind. Just knock on my door when you're ready."

"Will do," she said; then she closed her door. After taking a hot shower, she thought about what she was going to wear. She picked out a pair of dress slacks and a silk blouse. "Why am I getting all dressed up to go to the mall on a Saturday morning?" she asked herself. She put the slacks and shirt back, and chose a pink jogging suit instead. She pulled out her gym shoes, some pink ribbon and ponytail holders. "This one always did make the men do a double look," Destiny said, deciding that this was the perfect outfit to wear today. She got dressed, pulled her hair into a ponytail and was ready to go.

She tapped on Eric's door.

"You always look that good in pink?" Eric asked when he saw Destiny standing there. The way she had fixed her hair made her look younger than she did the day before.

"Destiny, how old are you?"

"Should a woman tell her age?"

"If she doesn't have anything to be ashamed of."

"I'm twenty-seven. How old are you?"

"I'm thirty-two."

"Why are you still single?" she asked.

"Why are you single?" he asked her.

"Technically, I'm not. My boyfriend is just mad at me right now for allowing another person to come between us," Destiny said, wishing that those words were true.

"That's why I'm single. She couldn't keep other people out of our business, and, technically, you are very single too."

"Why do you say that?"

"A woman who isn't single wouldn't rent an apartment that has a year's lease if she had a man, technically."

"How 'bout I like to think of my situation as such?"

"What would be the point? You're a very beautiful woman, and I'm sure you already know that, and I wouldn't be wasting my time trying to get to know you if I didn't think so."

"There you go again. Are you looking for a relationship? Because if you are, I'm not the one."

"Did I say that I was looking for a relationship? If I did, I apologize. Everything takes time, and I have plenty of that. Besides, I'm still healing from the last one. I don't see anything wrong with having a beautiful friend to help me heal, and perhaps I can do the same for you."

"You got good game," Destiny said, smiling at her new friend.

"Maybe you're right. I got good game, because I don't plan on getting my feelings involved with another woman anytime soon."

"OK, chocolate, I'll keep that in mind. Are you ready to go? I got a lot of shopping to do."

"I'm ready only if you promise to have dinner with me tonight."

"That depends."

"On what?" Eric asked.

"That you allow me to do the cooking this time."

"I like you, it feels like I've known you for a very long time. My ex would have been very jealous of you."

"Your ex?"

"That's what I said."

"I wouldn't want to run into her then," Destiny said.

Eric helped Destiny pick out very nice paintings at the mall, and he'd promised to help her hang them when she returned home from the grocery store.

Destiny had turned heads inside and outside of the store, and she liked the attention that the men were giving her, especially from this tall, slim, light-skinned brother. He wore his hair in layered braids, and they made him look sexy. Destiny followed him to the aisle where the dog food was.

"Can you recommend a good puppy food for my puppy?" she asked the man.

"What kind of puppy do you have?"

"Um . . . it's . . . I mean, she's a golden retriever."

"Well, I've always used Puppy Chow. It's great for the teeth and coat."

*Mmm, he sure does have nice teeth, and no ring on the finger,* Destiny thought. "Do you think that maybe I could give you my cell number, and you could maybe call me later to recommend your vet?"

*She's even better than me,* Hakim thought. *I'm going to have to use her pickup line.* "Um . . . sure, I'll just put the number in my phone." He took his cell off the clip and entered her number, then saved it. "By the way, my name's Hakim, and yours?"

"Destiny."

"That's a very pretty name. Unique, but pretty," he said, showing his pearly whites.

"Thank you," Destiny said as she left the dog food aisle.

"Hey, you forgot the Puppy Chow."

Destiny placed her hand on her chest and said, "Oh yeah, that's right." She grabbed a small bag of the puppy food and walked away. "Put my foot in my mouth this time. Who's going to eat this damn dog food?" she mumbled. *Josephine,* she thought.

Destiny took her items to the checkout counter and paid for them. She took the things to her car, then sat in it and watched the exit door to see what type of vehicle Hakim was driving. Hakim walked out of the store with a short, medium-build female by his side. She was yapping at the mouth, but it seemed like Hakim wasn't paying her much attention. Perhaps he was looking for Destiny. Hakim pushed the cart close to a Land Rover. He pressed the button on the key chain, and the woman climbed into the vehicle. Destiny put her car in drive and drove past him, mouthing, "Call me." Hakim winked at her and mouthed, "I will."

# 3

Destiny had done a little grocery shopping, but she changed her mind about cooking dinner. Instead, she wanted takeout. She put on a CD and pressed the fast-forward button until she found the song that she wanted. "Al, I'm tired of being alone too," Destiny said as she snapped her finger to the beat of the music and drove to a Chinese restaurant that wasn't far from where she lived. She ordered a large pepper steak with rice, two egg rolls and some almond cookies for dessert. After receiving her order, she climbed in her car, turned the stereo back on and turned it way up. She bobbed her head up and down to the music as she sang the song in her version of what it meant.

She took her bags to her apartment, threw the dog food in the pantry, grabbed the bag of Chinese food and went to Eric's. She could hear music coming from his apartment. "He must be in a good mood." She knocked on his door.

"Who's there?" Eric asked.

"Destiny. I brought dinner."

Eric opened the door. He looked sexy standing there in a pair of jeans with no shirt. "Come in," he said.

"Chinese," Destiny said as she held the bag out for Eric to see.

"My favorite. Why don't you take the bag to the kitchen, while I go find a T-shirt to put on."

"I liked the view. Why cover it up now?"

"Why tease you, when I'm coming up short."

"It's like that?" she asked. She was ready to try out her "new girl" persona.

"Come on, Destiny, you don't know me like that."

"It's not like we just—and I didn't say that I wanted to have sex—I was just admiring your chest."

"Oh, forgive me for jumping the gun. You know where my head's at?"

*I wish between these thighs,* Destiny thought. "That's OK, I started it."

*I want to finish it,* Eric thought. He wanted Destiny underneath him the moment he laid eyes on her. The things that he pictured himself doing to her made him become erect. If he had never had a one-night stand before, he damn sure was tonight. He wanted Destiny, and he guessed the same about her. She still had on that pink jogging suit. The pants fit so well; they accentuated her body. He knew that she knew, and she wore them on purpose.

He joined her in his kitchen, where she'd already set two plates out. "Oops, I forgot the drink. I'll be right back," Destiny said. She rushed to her apartment, grabbed a fifth of Rémy Martin and hurried back to Eric's.

"What took you so long?" he asked, joking.

"I was gone all of two-point-five seconds."

Eric smiled at her and bit his bottom lip playfully. "Let's eat." He watched Destiny as she fixed their plates. *Mmm . . . mmm . . . mmm,* he thought while he watched her curvaceous body move around his kitchen from the table to the cabinets. When she finally sat down to eat, she'd made him rock hard. He knew that she was a tease, but he liked the show that she put on for him. He didn't know how he was going to make it happen, but Destiny was going to be his by the end of the night.

They ate heartily and drank more than half of the fifth of alcohol.

"I think I've had too much to drink, Eric," Destiny said. "Do you mind if I use your bathroom before I leave?"

"No, I don't, if you'll allow me to join you," Eric said, making a move on her.

*It's the alcohol making me see things,* Destiny thought. *His chocolate ass is superfine.* He was so fine to her that he looked like he was shining. She imagined his clothes to be the wrapper on a chocolate candy bar, and she was peeling it off. *I'm definitely feeling the effects of the alcohol,* she thought again. "Yes, I do mind," she answered. She looked at Eric, and she could have sworn that his head turned into the wolf from "The Three Little Pigs." *I'll huff, and I'll puff, and I'll let him blow me down,* Destiny thought, *but I better pee and go home.*

"What the hell is wrong with me?" Destiny asked herself under her breath.

"Did you say something?" Eric asked.

"No."

Eric felt like a fool when he'd asked her if he could join her in the bathroom, so he decided to try a new tactic.

"Do you mind if I come over to your place for a while?" he asked when she emerged from his bathroom.

*This is my chance to run. The wolf is about to peel off that sheepskin that he's been hiding under,* Destiny thought. She wanted to run out his door, to the safety of her own apartment, but she stayed because she knew what Eric had been trying to imply by asking what he had. She didn't want to blame the effects of the alcohol on what she was feeling for Eric, nor did she want him to think that she was easy. However, the attraction toward one another was mutual.

Eric didn't have to ask any more questions. He knew that when she didn't leave, she wanted to be with him as much as he wanted her to be. He went to the bathroom and ran a hot bath for them. When it was ready, he invited her in the bathroom.

"Destiny, you can come in now," Eric called out to her.

Destiny walked slowly to the bathroom. She didn't know what to expect, but when she opened the door, she was surprised by the soft glow of candles that surrounded the tub, which was full of bubbles. The scent was mesmerizing.

"I apologize for asking such a dumb question earlier. I didn't want to come right out and ask you if you wouldn't mind staying over tonight."

"I accept your apology. I was thinking a little crazy myself."

"I drew a bath."

"For who, Eric?"

He didn't answer, but he grabbed her and pulled her close to him. He undressed her, and then he undressed. Destiny closed her eyes and let Eric take control of her. He held her and kissed her passionately on the mouth. At first, she imagined him as William, but that was too painful for her. She knew that it was time to let go of any hopes that she and William would ever get back together again. She gave in to Eric and soon she began to relax. Destiny rested her head on Eric's chest, once they were in the tub. Eric redid her ponytail so that it wouldn't be in his way when he kissed her on the neck.

After that, he nibbled on her ears and caressed her firm breasts. It felt good being in a man's arms. Destiny only wished that it were William, but he was gone, and she needed to move on. She could feel her eyes burning from the tears that she wouldn't allow herself to shed. She didn't need William to be happy. She was done with relationships, but Eric made her feel different about that.

"This is so romantic," Destiny said in a whisper.

"I thought so too," Eric said as he stood and helped her up so that he could bathe the two of them. He took the washcloth that he'd placed in the tub and rubbed soap all over her; then he washed himself. After doing this, he pulled the plug from the drain and turned the shower on to rinse the soap off. Under the spray of water Eric pinned Destiny up against the shower wall. He kissed her passionately on the mouth again.

Destiny wanted to stop him before things went any further, but she realized that she wanted him just as much as he wanted her. She kissed him back, allowing their tongues to touch and explore one another's mouths. She began to see how easy it was to fall for another man, but at the same time she was scared. "Eric, no strings," she whispered in his ear, fearing that things wouldn't work out between the two of them.

Eric didn't like what she had said, but he knew that she had been hurt in her last relationship, just as he had been. He knew that things would change for them over time if she trusted him. Eric turned the shower off, stepped out of the tub and helped Destiny out. He picked her up and carried her to his bedroom; neither one of them thought about drying off first. He laid her on the bed and took a condom out of the nightstand before joining her.

She had been wrong to think that no other man could make her feel the way that William had.

After their lovemaking ended, Destiny lay in Eric's arms, and, to her surprise, he wanted to talk. She had never been with a man who wanted to hold a conversation after making love. This was different.

"Why did you and your guy break up?" he asked her.

"Because I didn't trust him enough to take his word over my friend's." She called Josephine her friend, because she didn't want Eric to know that she'd been to a therapist. "Tell me why you and your friend broke up."

"She did what you did, I guess. She was always listening to her friends, and one in particular that I really didn't like. She seemed to have a great influence on her, and eventually she moved out."

"Just like that?" Destiny asked.

"Yup, just like that. A friend of mine said that he'd seen her almost every weekend going into this gay bar across from where he worked."

"Do you think that she's gay?"

"I don't know, and I don't care. I just hope that whatever she is, she's happy."

"You're not mad at her?"

"Off and on. I have to accept that if she's gay, she didn't want me in the first place. It's hard on the ego."

Destiny laughed. "I guess you're right, but if she passed up all of what you just gave me for a woman instead, she has got to be crazy."

Eric sucked in his bottom lip, looking even sexier to Destiny. "You want some more?" he asked.

"If it comes with no strings," Destiny replied.

"Why do you say that? Are you afraid of falling

in love again? I didn't think that I would ever fall for another woman until that day when you knocked my groceries out of my hand."

"I just want to take it one day at a time with you," she said. "So what do you do for a living?"

"I'm a lab technician and I'm a premed student. After drawing blood for so long, I decided that I wanted to become a doctor, and now I have one more year of medical school. What about you?"

"I'm an accountant. I used to work for my grandparents. They owned a Laundromat, but they passed away."

"So what happened to it?"

"I sold it."

"It wasn't the same after they passed ?"

Eric sensed that it was time to end their conversation. He didn't want to spoil the mood by making her think sad things over the passing of her grandparents. After putting on a fresh condom, he pulled her close to him and made love to her again.

Hakim finally decided to call Destiny, after keeping her number in his wallet for two weeks.

"I thought you had forgotten all about me," Destiny said into the phone. She was stretched out on her bed.

"Naw, I didn't want to seem like I was sweating you."

"So you made me wait for two weeks on a call?"

"I'm sorry. I'll make it up to you if you let me."

"You can't, plus you already have a woman."

"You don't have to worry about her, she doesn't bite."

*She looks like a dog, though,* Destiny thought. "Why is that? She is your girlfriend, isn't she?"

"No, why?"

"I just asked."

"Why would that be any of your concern when you just told me that I couldn't make it up to you?"

"You're right. So maybe we should end this conversation and you might want to lose my number."

"Wait, not so fast. I was just thinking that maybe we could just be friends?"

"How many friends do you have now?" Destiny asked. She really wasn't concerned with the amount of friends that he had, she just wanted to see where Hakim was going with the conversation.

"A few. I kind of like, I guess you could say, to be able to have a list of them to choose from. I'm not ready to be tied down with a wife and kids just yet. And the one that you saw me with that day? She's married, but we have an understanding."

"So you mess around with married women?"

"They like to get their freak on too."

"You're a trip."

"No, I'm telling you what's real. I don't have a problem with dating a married woman. That way, when it's over, it's over. No strings attached."

"Is that how you see it?"

"It's reality, baby. I don't know a married

woman that left her husband for another man, and I sure as hell haven't met a married brother who's left his wife for the mistress. I don't always date married women, but from time to time I run into one who isn't satisfied at home."

"So what about her husband? Does he matter at all to you?"

"Yes, he does, but look at it like this. I'm not trying to take his wife from him, I'm just helping him out. What he's not doing for his wife, I do."

"Well, I guess you have a lot of friends, then?"

"You could say that. I don't mind sticking around, and being the other man."

"Why?" Destiny asked.

"I already told you why, but if you didn't understand, let me put it this way. I ask that you don't get offended, it's just my way of putting it. I'll be single till I die. I have no particular reasons why. I love my freedom, so I don't get serious about anyone."

*He's shallow,* Destiny thought. "I guess you're entitled to your opinion."

"So when can we get together?" Hakim asked.

"Never."

"You got a man?"

"Why?"

"I just asked."

"Why would you want to know after I said we can never get together?"

"You didn't seem to have one the day at the store. What kind of puppy food should you feed your puppy? Remember that? I looked at you and could tell that you didn't have a puppy."

"Oh."

"Baby, looking as good as you look, you're the type who takes care of everything except puppies. I know that if you had a puppy, you would already have a vet. I like your pickup line, though."

"Yeah . . . yeah . . . yeah . . . whatever."

"So, can I get up with your fine ass?"

"I don't think so."

"You playing hard to get?" Hakim asked.

"I'm not playing anything, but you are."

"Hey, baby, if that's what you think, I don't mind."

"Well, I have to go, and I do mind if you call me again, so don't," Destiny said.

"Stuck up too, ain't you?"

"Good-bye, Hakim, and please lose my number," Destiny repeated again.

"Wait a minute, Destiny, maybe we got off on the wrong foot. I'm not some kind of dog going around looking for women to dog out. I just enjoy their company. One date is all I'm asking for, and if it doesn't go well, then we'll quit."

Destiny was beginning to enjoy the fact that she and Eric had grown closer, but she had stressed "no strings attached" to Eric. She didn't see any harm in one little date with Hakim, so she agreed to it. After finally getting Hakim off her phone, she went to her bedroom to pick out something to wear. She wanted to look nice, but still a little sexy. She didn't know exactly what she was going to wear. She picked through her closet until she found a denim skirt, with splits on both sides, and a white lace halter top. She picked out a pair of white sandals that had a two-inch heels and straps that tied up the legs.

"You looking good," Hakim said to Destiny.

"You look good yourself."

"So, is there anything special that you want to do?" he asked.

"I thought maybe we could have a scoop of ice cream and ride over to the lake."

"Sounds good," Hakim said. "And then what else do you want to do?"

"I don't know yet. I'm sure we'll come up with something else."

"That sounds good too. A little boring, but I guess we'll figure it out eventually."

"As long as you don't figure that it'll be sex."

Hakim just laughed and led Destiny to his car, where he opened the door for her.

"So what do you do for a living?" Destiny asked as she sat across from Hakim in a booth at the ice-cream parlor.

"I'm co-owner of a construction company," Hakim said; then he licked his ice-cream cone.

"Who owns the other half?"

"My dad."

"What about your mother?"

"What about her?"

"I don't know."

"She's around. She and my dad divorced

after thirty-five years of marriage. She got herself a younger man, one who looks like he's my age."

"Does that have anything to do with the reason why you're the way you are?" Destiny asked.

"I think so. What about your parents?"

"I never knew my father. And my mother, she left me when I was about two. I was raised by my grandparents."

"Do you ever hear from your mother?" Hakim inquired.

"She used to visit me at my grandmother's once a month until I turned sixteen. I didn't see her again until my grandfather's funeral, and again after that until my grandmother passed. She came around for the reading of the will, and I haven't seen her anymore since she asked me for half of what my grandmother left me. I told her no, and she said that's the reason why she didn't love me anyway."

Hakim felt like holding Destiny in his arms. He felt sorry for her, and her mother. "Why didn't you give her what she wanted?"

"Because she walked out on me."

"You look like you need a hug."

Destiny didn't think so.

"I think it's time for that stroll on the lake. You ready to go?" Hakim proposed.

"Yeah," Destiny said. She threw the rest of her melted ice cream in the garbage can on the way out the door.

"You seem a little angry," Hakim said as he opened the door with the keyless remote.

Destiny opened her door before Hakim could do it for her. Hakim didn't say anything to her when she did it. He waited until he got in the car and said, "Just because I asked a question about your mother that made you angry doesn't mean that I can't open and close the door for my date."

"Sorry if that offended you. I am an independent woman."

"It's that type of woman that I like to get with the most, because she thinks that she knows everything, and she thinks that she doesn't need anybody in her life."

*Is he talking about me?* Destiny thought. "What do you mean that she thinks she knows everything?" she asked.

"Do you think you're an independent woman, Destiny?"

"I do, but I've never thought that I knew everything, and I definitely don't mind a man opening and closing a door for me. And if talking about my mother gets me upset, so what."

"OK, you are entitled to get upset at whatever you want to get upset over. I'm an independent man who doesn't really mind spending a little time with an independent woman, because, like I said, I'm single for life. That's a good way of not having anything or anyone to get me upset over anything."

"You're single for life because you haven't met the right woman yet."

"Is that right?"

"I think so."

Hakim and Destiny walked along the lake-shore, hand in hand, until the sun began to set.

"So who's the new guy?" Eric asked Destiny. They were sitting at her kitchen table eating some leftover Chinese food.

"His name is Hakim. He owns his own construction company, and no, I didn't give up the bootie to him."

"I don't recall asking you if you did. Remember this is a relationship with no strings attached?"

"So who's the new girl?"

"Camille, she's in one of my classes. She's not the new girl, she's a study partner for a class assignment."

"You said that with attitude."

"I don't have an attitude. I just got a lot of studying to do because school isn't easy."

"Doesn't having a study partner make it easier?"

"Hell no, it doesn't."

"She must have some good kitty, because you look like you're smitten by the love bug."

"Come on, Destiny, I'm not sleeping with her. Why are you nit-picking? You were the one who went out on a date." Eric was annoyed that Destiny didn't seem to mind asking him questions about Camille when she had just come in from a date with another man.

"I was just kidding with you."

"I'm in no mood to kid around. What you did humiliated me."

Destiny was just playing around with Eric about Camille, and his attitude hurt her feelings. "You sound like William on the day we broke up."

"By the way, what actually did happen between you and William?" he asked, trying to humiliate her the way she had belittled him.

Destiny took a deep breath, then asked, "Do you really want to hear about that?"

"I asked, didn't I?"

"Long story short, I slept with another man. I was seeing a therapist who suggested that we didn't need to be together anyway."

"Destiny, my ex was seeing a therapist also, and her therapist told her that she didn't need to be with me. To be exact, the therapist told her that she didn't need a man who didn't have enough time for her."

"She left you, because of that?"

"Yes, she did, but I was tired of trying to convince her that when I was done with school, I'd have more time to spend with her. I'm tired of talking about old relationships and school— let's go out this weekend and have some fun."

"I don't have anything new to wear."

Eric chewed and swallowed the piece of egg roll that he'd stuffed in his mouth, cleared his throat and said, "You got a closetful of clothes. It isn't going to be hard for you to find something to wear."

"I guess I can wear something that I already have."

Eric took Destiny to a nice club in the downtown area, where a live band performed. Destiny had never been into live bands at clubs, but tonight she really enjoyed the music. They stayed until it was time for the club to close. Destiny liked the band so much that she suggested they come again the following night. Once they made it home, Destiny decided that she wanted Eric to spend the night with her. She thought about the way that she had joked with him about his classmate, but in reality she did so out of jealousy. She didn't realize she had felt that way until she had seen Camille leaving his apartment more than once. Maybe Eric was feeling the same way she was, when he had asked about Hakim.

Eric awoke before Destiny. He looked at her lying in his arms. They'd only known each other for a short period of time, but their friendship was a bond that he would never let anyone take from them. If she and Hakim got together, he would still be there for her emotionally. He kissed her, slipped his arm out from under her and slid out of bed.

"Where do you think you're going?" Destiny asked.

"I was going home. You were awake the whole time, weren't you?"

"Nope, I woke up when you kissed me."

Destiny grew to love the special feeling that came over her when Eric kissed her before leaving.

"Liar."

"Eric, get back in this bed. I got something

under the cover for you," Destiny said, smiling seductively at him.

Eric couldn't resist her smile. It was one of his weaknesses. He eased back in her bed and into her arms. He held her for a long time before he made love to her again. Their love-making was different. It wasn't casual-type sex. It was as if they both put feelings into the act. Both were unwilling to admit that they had deeper feelings for one another, but nonetheless they liked things just the way they were—or so they thought.

"It's late, baby . . . I mean Destiny," Eric said, quickly correcting himself. "I got some homework to finish before I go back to work. See you later."

Destiny smiled up at him and said, "OK, honey. Oops, I meant Eric."

"What's with you? Are you mocking me?" he asked.

"Am I? Did it bother you that you called me baby?"

"No, not really. I just didn't want you to think that I was getting all googly over you."

"Whatever," Destiny said; then she threw a pillow at him.

Eric caught it and threw it back. "Come on, get up and lock the door. I'll see you later."

Destiny got up and walked him to the door. He leaned down and kissed her passionately on the mouth before exiting her apartment. "Have a good day," he said as he walked down the hall to his apartment.

When Eric left her apartment, Destiny missed

his presence. She went back to her room and climbed in her bed. It felt empty and cold, and it made her miss William. It had been more than a month since she'd last seen him. She missed him a lot. She couldn't help the way she felt. Letting her curiosity get the best of her, she called him just to see how he was doing.

"Hello," William said, answering his phone.

"Hi, William."

He recognized her voice. "Hi, Destiny."

"Hey, I was just thinking about you, and I guess I wanted to know how you were doing."

"I'm doing great, and you?"

"I'm doing OK."

"That's good, but um, I don't think that you should be calling me anymore. I thought that I made that clear to you when you called the last time."

"I apologize. You don't have to worry about me calling your house anymore," Destiny said.

"Thank you," William said. Destiny had hung up her phone before he even recognized that she had. All he could hear was silence, and he felt once more the emptiness that he had experienced the moment that she walked out of his life. Destiny wasn't angry, nor was she hurt by William's attitude. Although she wished that he had given her a chance to make things right between them, she had no more regrets about what had happened to break them apart. What was done was done, and she couldn't change it—no matter how much she wished that she could.

\* \* \*

"You look like crap," Eric said to Destiny the next morning. He was on his way to class, and she was on her way for her morning jog.

"I know. I didn't sleep well last night," she responded. He hair was up in a scraggly ponytail, her clean face had no makeup, and the jogging suit that she wore didn't look anything like her pink one. The pants were too big and wrinkled, and the top was just as wrinkled.

"Why?"

"I just didn't. I had too much on my mind."

"You called William, didn't you?"

She looked up at him pitifully and shook her head yes.

"Why, when you knew that he was going to say something to hurt you?"

"I don't know. I just thought that by now he'd at least talk to me so that I could have some closure."

"Maybe one day you'll learn how *not* to set yourself up to be hurt, and maybe you should think about how *he* felt when you did what you did," Eric said. Then he left for school.

Destiny walked behind him. "Thanks for the advice, Eric," she said. She was angry with him for no reason at all. Eric had told her to just stop calling William and to move on with her life, but for some reason she always felt that that one last call was going to be the one to bring them back together. She was wrong each time she called, though. She stuck her middle finger up to the back of Eric's head before they exited the building.

A few days had passed since Destiny last called William. She and Eric spent more time together doing things that a couple did—with the full understanding that they were nothing more than friends. Eric was glad that she was starting to move on with her life, but for some reason he felt a little confused at the way Destiny had said that their relationship was just a friendly thing. One minute he felt like they were in a relationship, and the next moment Destiny was adding stipulations for them. He hadn't given her any reason to believe that he wanted more than friendship from her, even though he did. He had to overlook her and the feelings that he had about the way she put things, because it was clear to him that she was still hurting over William.

When the weekend came, Destiny was knocking on Eric's door to let him know that she was ready to go. They had plans to go back to the club where he had taken her.

"You look nice," Destiny said.

"You look nice yourself," Eric said, laughing. He grabbed Destiny's hand and they were on their way to the club. This time Destiny drove them to the club. The club must have been packed, because the only park they could find was a block away.

Once inside the club they had to find a place to sit. They found two seats in the rear of the bar. Destiny didn't complain, because it was close to the dance floor, but before she even thought about dancing, she needed to get her drink on. She ordered a double shot of Rémy on the rocks, and Eric ordered a Sex on the Beach.

"Why a Sex on the Beach?" Destiny asked.

"I heard that they taste good and I wanted to try one."

"Whatever. I'm drinking what I know is good," Destiny said. She smiled at Eric, and then said, "I wouldn't mind having sex on the beach."

"Can you keep your mind out of the gutter for a minute? We came here to have a good time."

"I could if you didn't order things pertaining to sex, and the beach."

"Destiny, look over there," Eric said, holding his hand down and pointing a finger so no one could see him.

"Over where, and for what?" she asked.

"Over to your right. That's Aleesyia."

"Who is Aleesyia?" she asked.

"That's my ex that I told you about."

"Which one is she, Eric?" Destiny asked. She wanted to see what this Aleesyia character looked like.

"The one in the hoochie skirt and beige top."

"OK, I see her. Is she with that man standing next to her dressed in that pin-striped suit with the Dobbs hat?"

"Would a man have breasts?"

"Some of them do."

"Well, that one has nice-sized tits, and that suit she/he has on is really nice," Eric said.

"It isn't Versace. It's cheap, but it's nice," Destiny said.

"How do you know if it's Versace or not?"

"Eric, I know clothes. I'm a fashion queen."

"Look at that crap," Eric said. "That no-good ass—you-know-what left me for a woman?"

"Calm down, brother. Remember we're here to have some fun—not get mad at your ex," Destiny said before she took a sip from her glass.

Eric picked up his drink and drained the glass. He burped and said, "Fun, my ass, I want to get up and walk over to her and cuss her out. That—"

"Eric, stop that crap. Order another drink."

"Yeah, I need one," Eric said as he motioned for a waitress.

"May I take your order?"

"Yes, let me have two double shots of Rémy on the rocks."

"OK," the waitress said; then she turned to Destiny and said, "Would you like another drink too?"

"No, I'm OK." Destiny took another sip from her glass.

"Just bring three doubles of Rémy," Eric said, "just in case she finishes that one before you return."

The waitress walked away after taking Eric's order.

"I think she was giving you the eye."

"Eric, don't get me twisted. I don't have

anything against people and their sexual preferences, but I don't get down like that, and if you don't want me to act a damn fool up in here, I suggest that you walk your happy ass over to the bar and get the drinks from now on. Just because you spotted your ex with a woman doesn't mean that everybody in the bar is gay."

"I got a better idea. Why don't you go to the bar and get them? Look over there at the end of the bar by the DJ booth."

Destiny looked and she spotted Aleesyia sitting alone. "So what do you want me to do? Go over there and strike up a conversation with her?"

"Did you leave your brains at home? What else did you think I suggested it for? Did you think that I was asking you to go over there and strike up a threesome with her and her date?" Eric countered sarcastically.

"OK, excuse me, Mr. Attitude," Destiny said to Eric. "I got you."

"For the record I don't have an attitude. Now go on over there and do your thang."

"Where did the wo-man she came in here with go to?" Destiny asked.

"She's in the DJ's booth spinning records."

Destiny got up to go to the bar just as the waitress came back with their drinks. "Who's paying for these?" the waitress asked.

Destiny stuck a hand deep inside her bra and peeled off a hundred-dollar bill. She handed it to the waitress. "Give the change to Mr. Attitude, I have to go."

The waitress looked at Eric like he was going to run off with Destiny's change. Destiny ignored her and walked off. The waitress changed the bill, then laid the cash on the table in front of Eric. She walked off.

Destiny walked over to where Aleesyia was sitting and accidentally bumped her. "Ooh, excuse me. I didn't mean to do that."

"It's all right," Aleesyia said, staring at Destiny. "You don't come here that often, do you?"

"No, it's my second time," Destiny said, staring back.

"You like it?" Aleesyia asked.

"So far I do."

"Good, tonight is gay night. By the way, my name is Aleesyia, but everybody that I know here calls me Desire, and your name is?"

Destiny had to think quick. She didn't want to give Aleesyia her real name, "Star," Destiny said.

"Is that your real name or the name you want to go by in here?"

"Yes, that's my real name. My mom said I was going to be a star when I grew up," Destiny lied.

"Are you here alone, Star?" Aleesyia asked.

"Um, no, I'm with a friend. Are you here alone?"

"No, my girl is spinning the music."

"When she's done, how about the two of you join me and my friend?"

"That would be cool," Aleesyia said, hoping that she and her friend could get together with Star and her friend after the party.

"Great, when your friend is done, I'll come back over to get you."

"You don't have to, just point to where you're sitting. I'll find you."

"Over there in that corner," Destiny said, pointing.

"What the hell is she doing?" Eric mumbled under his breath.

Destiny turned to walk away, and Aleesyia called out her name. "Star, didn't you want to order something?"

"Oh yeah. I almost forgot."

The bar attendant asked Destiny what she needed. "Give me two tonic waters, please."

"You and your friend are drinking tonic water?" Aleesyia asked.

"No, he ordered three doubles instead of two and a tonic water."

"Oh, well, me and my girl should be over there in about twenty minutes. The regular DJ will be here in fifteen."

"Sure, we'll be waiting on you," Destiny said. *Eric is going to kill me,* she thought as she walked nervously back to the table with the two glasses of tonic water.

"Destiny, what did you just do over there?" Eric asked.

"The name is Star. I just invited her and her girl to our table."

"Star, Destiny, whatever your name is now, what am I going to do when she comes over here?"

"I didn't know—just act natural. You know why it's so packed in here tonight?"

"Do I have a choice? No, why?"

"She said that tonight is gay night, and she is known as *Desire*," Destiny informed, putting an emphasis on "Desire."

"Desire? What in the world is going on in here?" Eric asked.

"The hell if I know. This is your hangout."

"It wasn't like this a few months ago."

"How long has it been since you've been here?"

"A few months ago."

"Well, you may as well enjoy yourself, maybe you'll attract some of the men in here," she said, sticking out her tongue in a playful gesture.

"I wouldn't do that if I were you. Somebody might drop a pussy on your tongue, so you should keep it in your mouth, duh," Eric said, laughing.

"It would take somebody like you to say some dumb crap like that."

"It made you put your tongue back in your mouth. Didn't it?"

"Whatever, Eric. When we get home, I got something for your ass," Destiny said, shaking her head up and down.

"I hope it's something good, because I could use that. If it's bad, keep it to yourself, honey," Eric said; then he gave her the two-snaps-and-a-circle gesture.

"I think you've been in here too long, you're starting to act like them," Destiny said.

"Gay bashing, I dare you."

"Eric, shut the hell up. Here comes your ex, and her lover."

"Oh, wow. I guess I better think of something to say to her, I mean them."

"You better make it quick."

"Hmm, let me think."

"Think quick, they're almost over here."

"Call me Sonny," Eric said, and then he burst out into laughter.

Destiny was laughing too. "I guess we can be Sonny and Star," she said as she burst out laughing again. "I guess she just forgot your name because she's with a woman now?"

"I guess so," Eric said in a high-pitched voice.

"What's gotten into you? It's not like you're really gay."

"Damn, Des . . . I mean Star, you're right. I don't have to change my voice."

Destiny and Eric downed one of the double shots of Rémy just before Aleesyia and her friend made it to the table.

"They making you nervous?"

"You just downed your drink too. Are they making you nervous?"

Before she could answer, Aleesyia and her friend were at their table, seating themselves. "Hi," Aleesyia said to Eric. She frowned when she noticed who it was.

"Hey, how have you been since I last saw you?" Eric asked.

"I've been fine. Eric, this is David and that's Star."

"Honey, you know them?" David asked.

"Yeah, he's an old friend."

"You two come here often?" David asked.

"I used to before they changed the place," Eric answered. It was clear to him that David was really a woman, but if she wanted to be called David, who was he to dispute that?

"So what brought you two out to this club tonight?" David asked.

"We were here another weekend and thought that it would be fun to come tonight," Eric said.

"Well, we're meeting a few more friends here tonight. You two can join us if you like," Aleesyia said.

"Aleesyia," David called out to her. "I like to get to know people, but we don't associate with everybody. When I see something that looks as good as you two, then I want you in my circle of friends, but how do you know that they want to join us?" David was flirting, but at the same time she didn't like the fact that she didn't know anything about Eric.

"Oh, it's fine. You two can go ahead and meet up with your friends. Eric and I are going to finish up here and leave soon," Destiny said.

"I really didn't mean anything by that. It's just that my friends are particular about new people," David said.

*This bitch gone get a beat-down up in here tonight,* Destiny thought. "No offense taken. We know how it is when you're meeting new people for the first time," Destiny said. She sensed that David was probably feeling a little threatened that Eric and Aleesyia were old friends.

"There's a few of our friends now. We better leave you two alone so you can finish your drinks," Aleesyia said, waving her hand in the air to let her friends know that she had seen them.

Before Aleesyia and David got up to leave, Eric asked Aleesyia, "How long you've been coming down here?"

"Just a few months, and I love it."

*Just a few months. Just the same damn few months ago that you left me,* Eric thought. He wanted to hawk the biggest hunk of spit in Aleesyia's face. He couldn't believe that she had left him for a woman. Another man wouldn't have hurt so bad, but a woman.

Destiny saw the look of anger come across Eric's face, and she interjected, "Eric, that's my favorite song. Let's dance."

"Destiny, I've had one too many drinks. I think we better be going before I throw up on something," Eric said, waving his hand like Aleesyia had done whenever she spoke.

"Why do you have to allow her to spoil our night out?" Destiny asked, pretending that she was angry with Eric.

"Girl, let's get the hell out of here. Now take me home before I piss my pants and throw up!"

"I'm really sorry that you two have to go," Aleesyia said. "Tomorrow they'll be jumping. It's talent night. So why don't you two join David and me. We'll be sitting right here waiting."

"I don't think so," Eric said.

When they got to Destiny's car, Eric gave her the keys. "Here, you drive. I'm too upset. That bitch left me for a woman. I couldn't have been that bad of a man," Eric said as he climbed into the car.

Destiny gave Eric the same advice that he'd given her a few weeks back. "Eric, why don't you just get her out of your system, and move on with your life."

"I'm all right, Destiny. I just don't understand what she sees in a woman. What happens when one is on her period and the other isn't? Do she wait or do she cheat?"

"I don't know, Eric, and I will never know. But if bumping pelvis bones is her cup of tea, then so be it."

"You're right, boo, I'm always on you about William, and here I am acting like a bitch over one. Let's get something to eat before we get home."

Destiny liked the sound of that. It reminded her of coming home to William. She smiled at the thought, but she let it go. She and Eric might have a chance of being more than friends. "What do you want to eat?" she asked.

"Let's go to that Polish stand and get two fat, greasy Polishes and two pops," Eric said.

"Did you have to say it like that?"

"It ain't like you're eating on this Polish," Eric said, pointing to his crotch.

"Don't get no ideas either," Destiny said, smiling. Then she thought about what it would be like to taste him.

"Your mind is in the gutter again, isn't it? You just passed up two park spaces back there."

"Sorry, and no my mind wasn't in no gutter. I didn't want to park by all those people."

"You're lying. Just park here, and I'll jump out and get the food."

He brought an extra sandwich just in case they didn't get full. On the way home he asked Destiny what she thought about Aleesyia. She told him that she could understand that it hurt him to see her like that, but maybe Aleesyia had been looking for her inner self.

"I guess she found it then, huh?" Eric asked.

"I guess. Either that or she was like that before you two started dating."

"I guess so. It would have been nice if she would have left me alone before I fell in love with her."

"Eric, shut up and come on."

"I can do that. My place or yours?"

"Mine's closer," Destiny said.

"Yeah, by a few doors."

After eating the sandwiches, Destiny and Eric showered and brushed their teeth together to wash away the smell of the onions. Neither put on any pajamas. They climbed into Destiny's bed. Destiny's curiosity had gotten the best of her. She wanted to know what Eric tasted like. She licked her lips as she thought about a scoop of chocolate ice cream, and she slid under the covers and took her chocolate man in her mouth.

Eric's eyes almost popped out of his head when he felt the warmth of her mouth engulf him. He reached under the covers and gently held her face in his hands as she moved her mouth up and down on his chocolate stick. Destiny could feel his heartbeat getting faster, and his chocolate stick getting stiffer. She knew that he was ready to explode, so she pulled up and climbed on top of him. He pulled her down close to him and kissed her passionately on the mouth, again and again, until they both came.

# 4

Destiny had remained friends with Hakim, even though he thought that they could be more than just friends even after she had made it clear to him that they wouldn't be anything more. She told him all about her relationship with Eric, and she told Eric all about Hakim. Hakim told her that it sounded like she was falling for Eric when she talked about him. Destiny denied that, saying she and Eric were just close friends. Hakim doubted that they were *just friends* and asked why she hadn't introduced him to Eric, since Eric had requested that on several occasions.

Eric hadn't hesitated to introduce Camille to Destiny when she'd asked him. When he did so, he told Destiny that he had told her the truth about who Camille was.

She eventually did introduce Hakim to Eric. When she did, it eased all of Eric's suspicions about Hakim because Hakim didn't seem to mind whenever Eric was around. Destiny knew that Camille had some feelings for Eric, because whenever Destiny came over during their study sessions, Camille's attitude would change. Destiny proved to be right about Camille. When Camille came over to study with Eric one night, she told Eric that she didn't think it was best for them to continue studying together if he was going to be friends with Destiny.

Eric didn't see what Destiny had to do with the two of them studying. He felt that Camille was wrong, because he hadn't given her any reason to believe that they would ever be more than study partners. He'd walked her to his door and told her good-bye and thanked her for the time that they had studied together. Camille was upset with him, but it was her own thinking that led her to believe that she and Eric were going to be more than what they were.

Eric couldn't get over the eerie feeling that he had thinking about how much Destiny and Hakim resembled each other. They could pass for brother and sister. He often teased them about it, but they'd just laugh right along with Eric. One day Hakim did tell Destiny that she favored his sister a lot, but Destiny had told him that everybody had a double. Hakim wanted her to meet his sister one day, but they both seemed too busy to get around to it. Hakim had invited her to a party hosted by one of his sister's friends, but the party was canceled. Both Destiny and Hakim were glad, and so was Eric, because he wanted to take Destiny to a play that night.

\* \* \*

Marcus had been feeling guilty since Josephine found out that he had cheated on her with Destiny. As her husband he needed to find a way to show her that he was sorry for his actions. He decided to have the basement turned into an office where Josephine could counsel her patients instead of being out of the home so much. This way they could have more time together when he wasn't working and the kids would see their mom more. He wanted the basement partitioned off into three rooms: her office, where she would see adult clients, the waiting area and a room that was suitable for children who needed therapy.

Marcus had thumbed through the phone book and came across D and H Construction and Home Remodeling Company. He called and made an appointment for them to complete their unfinished basement as a surprise gift to his wife. Josephine hadn't been in the basement since he and Destiny had been caught.

Hakim arrived at the Rileys' home early the next morning. He went through the basement, writing down the instructions that Marcus had given him. Then he wrote down the measurements of the floors and doors, and quoted Marcus a price. Marcus requested that the job be completed within the next few days, before his wife returned from the convention that she was attending.

Hakim returned the next morning with his crew and they started the work on the basement. Hakim and his crew had completed the work in a day and a half. That left Marcus three days to furnish the rooms. Marcus went shopping and purchased furniture for all three rooms.

When Josephine returned home from the convention, she loved what Marcus had done to the basement. She immediately forgave him for what he'd done—extracting a promise that he would never hurt her that way again.

"Marcus, baby, I love you. This means so much to me. I didn't think that I would ever set foot in this basement again," Josephine said as she went from room to room.

She had often dreamed of having a home office, and Marcus had made it a reality, out of guilt. Josephine was so happy that she no longer had to practice outside her home that she called her regular clients personally and notified them of the change. She had her office notify those she didn't see on a regular basis. Once she was done calling her patients, she phoned some friends to invite them over for a special party.

Josephine held her gathering two weeks after Marcus had the basement finished. The first one went so well, she planned a second one. Josephine and all of her guests were so impressed by the work that the remodeling company had done that she recommended their services to all of her friends who needed some type of repair or remodeling work done. Hakim and his crew went out to inspect the houses that Josephine recommended. Upon arrival at one of the houses that Josephine had recommended, the guy that Hakim had sent out had more in common with the homeowner than just business.

Josephine postponed her second party to a later date, but Marcus wasn't aware of this, because Josephine didn't want her husband to attend this party. This party was for her special friends—the ones that Marcus knew nothing about. When Josephine had told Marcus that she was canceling the party in order to take the kids to Disney World for a vacation, Marcus saw this as a way for them to spend some quality time together. Marcus wasn't aware that she had not planned to meet them later in Florida, nor did he know that it was all a lie.

Josephine had sent out invitations to her friends behind Marcus's back. Marcus never suspected a thing, because he was excited about taking the trip. Josephine had packed her suitcase, along with theirs, but she had never planned on joining Marcus and the kids at Disney. Josephine had explained to the kids and her husband that she had some very important business to take care of from the old office, so she couldn't make the flight with them. She promised that as soon as she tied up the loose ends, she'd be on the next flight out to join them. On the day that they were leaving, Josephine dropped Marcus and their two sons, Kyle and Tyler, off at the airport, kissed them good-bye and made sure they boarded the plane.

\* \* \*

Josephine's guests arrived on time. The majority of her guests were her clients—women whom she'd convinced to leave their mates. She'd been intimate with almost all of them behind Marcus's back, and she would have persuaded Destiny—but Destiny had plans of her own.

The guests that she'd invited to her party were gay men and women always looking for someone new to dig, and Josephine enjoyed watching her friends perform as much as she liked them watching her. She noticed a new guest on the arm of one of her old and trusted friends. He piqued her curiosity. She went over to where they were standing so that her friend could introduce her to this new guest.

"Josephine, this is Randy. You recommended him to me."

"I did?" Josephine said.

"Honey, you did. He's from that construction and remodeling company."

"Oh, I see. You two sure did become friends pretty fast."

"You know me, baby. Whatever I desire, I get," Josephine's friend Byron said, laughing.

"How come you didn't bring the rest of the crew?" Josephine asked Randy.

"Um, I don't think that they're into this kind of party."

Josephine hunched her shoulders up at Randy and said, "Their loss. More fun for us." Then she walked off and joined Aleesyia and her friend, who were engaged in some weird sex act.

"Man, this is some freaky stuff," Randy said to Byron. He'd never been to an orgy before, and here he was at a swingers' bash, where they were sharing sex with whomever they wanted.

"Yeah, it is, and we usually all get along so well," Byron said.

Randy decided that this kind of party was a little too much for him to handle. He was gay, but he didn't believe in sleeping around with different people, and definitely not any that he was meeting for the first time at a party. "Man, I can't stay here and watch this. Your lady friend is really something. Where is her husband while she's over there sniffing in another woman's twat?"

"I don't know, but let's get out of here if you're not comfortable with what's going on," Byron said. He and Randy stepped over men with men, and women with women, and walked quietly out of Josephine's basement.

"Does the door lock by itself?" Randy asked. "I don't think that she'd want anybody else just walking up in her house while she's having that kind of party."

"Yes, it does," Randy's date answered as they walked toward his car.

"Byron."

"What's up?"

"If those kind of parties is something that you like to attend, then maybe I was wrong for thinking that you and I could get to know one another."

"I do apologize for inviting and bringing you with me without explaining to you what type of party I was attending. I must have misunderstood a few things that you said the other day when we were talking."

"Maybe you should drop me back off at my place and we can talk later."

Josephine was so busy doing what she was doing that she hadn't noticed that two of her guests had left. But one of her guests noticed, because he had his eye on Randy. After Josephine's guests were done changing partners, and were exhausted, they began their session of telling who did what and how they felt about it, and who and what they should try next time. These were the kind of therapy sessions that Josephine liked the most.

The guest who saw Randy and Byron leave looked at Josephine, who was still recuperating from her sexcapade with Aleesyia and her friend David. "What in the hell was going on with the two big handsome hunks that left this bomb-ass party?" he asked.

"Who left?" Josephine asked.

"Byron and one of the most handsome men I have ever seen," he replied.

Josephine got up from where she was lying on the floor and walked over to the light switch. She turned the light on bright. "I hope that Byron's friend doesn't tell anyone he works with about this party."

"Why?"

"Because he works for that construction and remodeling company that did the work on my basement. They may turn down other jobs that I recommend them for because of this."

"Business is business," Parnell said.

"Don't be silly or naïve, Parnell. I'll call Byron tomorrow and make sure that that won't happen. Now let's eat," Josephine said.

"I hope it's food because I really worked up an appetite," Aleesyia said.

Josephine licked her lips and said, "Of course it's food. Dessert comes later." Josephine and her thirty or so guests got up from where they were sitting or lying. They helped themselves to the lavish setup of food that she had catered for the party. After eating, some of her guests engaged in more sexual activity. Others sat around naked and had another therapy session with Josephine. Josephine talked a lot after these parties, believing that as a therapist she had to counsel her friends on what a wonderful thing it was to be open with one another, and how her parties relieved sexual tension.

# 5

Josephine was busy cleaning the area in the basement where she'd thrown the party, when her office phone rang.

"Hello."

"Good afternoon, Josephine."

"Same to you, Parnell."

"Josephine, did you handle that business with Byron?"

"Parnell, don't you have anything else to do other than worry about things unnecessarily?"

"Josephine, come on now. Did you talk with Byron about his friend?"

"Baby, you know I did. I know that you have to keep things on the down low. So do I. Just like you, every time I have one of my parties, I risk losing my family or my license as a therapist. But thanks to your being such a great lawyer, I don't have to worry about that."

"Money talks, bullshit walks," Parnell said.

"Yeah, and you got a lot of mine too."

"It's the price you have to pay when you live

the lifestyle that you do, and when you have a friend who has access to court documents that can disappear when you need them to."

"One has to really admire a crooked lawyer who also enjoys the type of lifestyle that I do. Nonetheless the money that I paid you to get rid of those documents from that suit, which could have cost me my license, was well worth it."

"I know. By the way, did Byron mention why he and his friend left?"

"No."

"Too bad he didn't stay. We could have used some fresh meat up in there."

"We could have, and your colleague Romel would be the perfect piece to start with—with his sexy ass."

"Romel loves women just as much as you do, so you can forget about him."

"He's a man, and any man can be made to do whatever as long as the price is right. You should know that."

"I do, and like I said, you need some fresh meat up in there."

"Bring your wife next time. I'm sure I can show her a really good time."

"I can do the same for Marcus."

"Good-bye, Parnell. I can see that this conversation is getting out of hand."

An hour later, after Josephine had come up from the basement, she was enjoying some of the leftover food when the house phone rang.

"Hey, hon, when are you coming? Me and the boys are expecting you soon," Marcus said.

"Honey, I'm sorry, but I didn't hear you. We must have a bad connection or something."

"I said, me and the boys—"

"Honey, I can't hear you. There's a lot of static on your end. Call me later," Josephine said. Then she hung up the phone. *I don't feel like listening to him or being with him and his sons in Disney World or anywhere else. When he calls back, I'm just going to tell him that I was tied up with so much to do that I couldn't make it. They'll be fine,* she thought. "They'll get over it. I got another party to plan," she said aloud.

Josephine picked up the phone to call Michelle, her receptionist, who was off from work. "Girl, what happened to you? My party was the bomb."

"Leon was tripping. He wanted me to stay at home with him. I told him that I was going to help you move the stuff from the office to your new office at your house, since it would have been considered overtime pay. He said that I didn't need the money and he needed to spend that time with me. He gets on my last nerve at times," Michelle said.

"I told you to leave him."

"Josephine, you tell everybody to leave their man if you think that you're going to replace him," Michelle replied.

"Well, you're part of that everybody, but I don't like you like that."

"That's because you met Aleesyia. Speaking

of her, I saw her at the club one night. She was sitting at the table with Destiny and some man."

"How come you didn't go and find out who he was?"

"How come you didn't come to the club, you could've met him yourself?"

"You know that me and Destiny don't get along," Josephine said.

"Well, that's between you and her."

"You are such a smart-mouthed person," Josephine commented.

"The last time I checked my birth certificate, it read, 'Michelle Griffin born to Michael and Sonja Griffin is a grown woman and can say whatever she wants to say, whether the person likes it or not.'"

"I guess you didn't read the fine print at the bottom. It reads, 'Leon James is her real daddy, and he tells the grown woman what she can, and cannot, do.'" Josephine burst out into laughter.

"I don't find that funny, Josephine."

"Then why are you laughing at it?"

"To make you feel good."

"Whatever. Are you coming to my next party?"

"I thought you had decided to go to Florida with your husband and kids."

"Well, you thought wrong. I'm having another party."

"I just thought that since you had told Marcus that you were joining them in a day or two, you weren't going to have another party."

"Are you coming or not?"

"I'll be there."

"What if Leon won't let you out of the house again?"

"I'm grown."

"Michelle, you're still confused. You were grown when I threw last night's party, but you weren't there."

"Yeah, whatever you say, Josephine. I guess you want me now? Did Aleesyia disappoint you when she started seeing David, or Davita, or whatever she calls herself?"

"Not really—since I had them both last night."

"You're never going to change," Michelle said, and then she burst into laughter.

"Bye, Michelle."

"Hey, Josephine."

"What?"

"What are you going to tell Marcus when he calls you back?"

"That I messed up the computer that I keep the clients' info on, and I had to have someone come out and fix it, so I could download each file again, one by one."

"You're going to get your ass in a whole lot of trouble when that man finds out that you are a down-low sister."

"I won't tell, if you won't."

"My lips are sealed. Hey, are you moving the stuff from the office today?" Michelle asked.

"Girl, please! I hired a moving company for that. I have another party to plan."

"OK, I'll talk to you later," Michelle said. She really was confused about who she was and her sexuality, but at the same time she loved Leon. This was going to be the last time that she attended one of Josephine's parties. She had to make up her mind, whether or not she was straight or gay. If Leon found out what she had been doing with Josephine, and some of her clients, he'd probably kill her and Josephine. In the meantime, while Leon was at work, she had some shopping to do, and a few lies to think of to tell him.

She called Leon at work and told him that she was going to hang out at Josephine's house on the weekend to help her set up her new office. Leon told her that it was fine, because he and his friends were going to a sports bar to watch a baseball game that day. *That son of a biscuit eater gets to go wherever he wants to go, and when he wants. I got something for his butt, though,* Michelle thought. She grabbed her car keys, went into his stash of money, which he had tucked away for a rainy day, and peeled off two hundred-dollar bills.

The night of the second party was finally here. Josephine called the catering company and ordered a large shrimp platter, crab legs, butter sauce, forty small lobster tails, a garden salad with a variety of dressings, a large cheese-and-veggie platter, spaghetti with sauce and dinner rolls.

"Would that complete your order, Mrs. Riley?" the store clerk asked.

"Um . . . let me see. Did I leave anything out?"

"Are you asking me that question?" the clerk asked.

"Yeah."

"Last week you ordered the variety fish platter," the clerk said.

"Oh yeah, I sure did. Give me that too, and good looking out."

"You're welcome, Mrs. Riley."

Josephine reset the phone and called Parnell. "Parnell, can you take care of the drinks for me? I'll pay you when you get here."

"If I didn't know any better, I'd think that you are getting to be one lazy person, since your husband had that basement turned into your office/orgy palace."

"If I didn't know any better, I'd uninvite you from my party."

"Bye, Josephine. Do you want me to get the same drinks that you had last weekend?"

"If you don't mind, can you pick up a few bottles of something else too?"

"Sure. I hope you ordered some chicken this time. You know, you women have a natural fishy odor, and that mixed with all that seafood you had last weekend was too much for a brother to handle."

"I didn't think you'd mind, since you're always wishing you had what a woman has."

"This time I'm for real. Bye, Josephine."

"Typical of your male wannabe," Josephine said.

"Typical of a wannabe man. Butch."

Josephine started laughing. "But I still love you, though."

"I love you too, baby girl. I mean boy."

"Bye, Parnell. See you tonight," Josephine said; then she hung up the phone.


Hakim and Destiny had become good friends. They shared a lot of things together, such as personal experiences with other people. Hakim had called Destiny and told her about a job that they had done, which led to his discovery that one of his crew members was gay. Hakim had told her that he'd stepped out of his office and overheard a conversation that Randy was having with someone on the phone. Hakim really didn't think much about it, nor was he trying to eavesdrop. However, when he heard Randy tell the person how angry he was that his friend wanted to attend a gay party, while they had agreed that they were going to be monogamous, Hakim knew that something was wrong with his coworker.

Hakim told Destiny that at that point he couldn't help eavesdropping. He knew exactly where the party had been held and who had thrown it. He even knew that there was another one going on tonight. Destiny was floored when she put two and two together and found out that Hakim had been to Josephine's house to do the remodeling of her basement. She asked Hakim to come over to her house when he got off work so they could talk. She didn't want to tell him that Josephine was the therapist that she had told him about. This was her chance to get even with Josephine. Hakim had some stuff on her that Destiny knew would bring her perfect little world tumbling down.

Destiny just had to figure out a way to get Hakim to attend the next party that Josephine was having. She would do anything to get Hakim to do this one thing for her. She couldn't wait for Eric to come home so she could tell him the good news. As soon as she knew Eric would be walking to his apartment, she opened her door and snatched him by the arm.

"I know you must have something good for me, the way you just yanked me into your apartment," Eric said.

"Eric, sit down, because what I'm about to tell you is going to knock you off your feet."

"I hope you're not going to tell me that you're pregnant, and it's my baby."

"Naw, it's better than that," Destiny said.

"OK, Mommy, what is it that you have to tell Poppy?"

"Eric, Hakim called me today and told me that one of his crewmen went to a party at Josephine's."

"So what's wrong with her giving parties?"

"Just shut up and listen, will you?"

"Bossy today, aren't you?"

"Come on, Eric, let me finish the story."

"OK, boo, go ahead, finish."

"Well, that depends on the type of parties that she gives."

Eric's eyes got wide with curiosity. "The type? What type of party was it?"

"If you shut the hell up and let me finish the

damn story, I can tell you what type of party it was."

"I'm sorry, go ahead and tell me the story."

"Hakim said that he overheard the conversation of one of his crewmembers, Randy. He heard how Josephine gives gay parties in her basement, and Randy was obviously upset with the person that he was talking to. She's giving another party at her house tonight."

"Get out of here. You got to be kidding. Josephine . . . I know that name. That's the name of the therapist that Aleesyia was seeing," Eric said.

"I thought you said Josie?"

"I did know that it started with a *J*, didn't I? So that's why Aleesyia left me. Josephine was doing some serious therapy on her, and I guess I was no match for her," Eric said, shaking his head.

"I asked Hakim to come over here when he gets off work, so I can try to talk him into going tonight."

"What makes you think he's going to go for that?"

"I don't know that he will, but all I can do is explain to him who Josephine is and what I'm trying to do," Destiny said in desperation.

"What do you want him to go for?"

"Think, Eric. If he goes, then he can get some dirt on her, and I can use it against her."

"Oh, sorry. I guess my brain doesn't work at times. I wouldn't mind going to get even with that low-life woman."

"What about Aleesyia?"

"What about her?"

"Don't you think she's going to want to know what you're doing there?"

"It isn't her business. For all she knows, I could be coming to have a little fun too. I know this guy at school who's really into photography, and I bet he has the equipment that we can use to get this party on tape," Eric said.

"Do you think that he'll let you use it?"

"Yeah, we're pretty cool."

"I can't wait to bring Josephine down to her raggedy knees," Destiny said.

"I second that, Ms. I Spy."

"Whatever. Get the door."

Eric frowned at Destiny, then went to answer her door. He opened it without asking who it was. Hakim was standing there. "What's been up with you?" he asked.

"Man, you don't want to know. It might make you sick," Hakim said.

"Man, Destiny already told me."

"Hey, Hakim," Destiny said as she joined Eric and Hakim in her living room.

"Hey, Destiny. So what's up?"

"Hakim, I know that you didn't want to find out the way that you did that Randy was gay, but I need a serious, serious favor from you."

"If it has something to do with the woman who gave that party, you can forget it," Hakim said.

"Eric, get the man a double shot of Rémy on the rocks. I can see that this is going to take some time."

"Time for what, Destiny?"

"Hakim, remember when I told you about my therapist who made me leave my man?"

"Yeah. I remember."

"Well, that was her that you did the work for."

"Get out of here."

"No, Hakim, that's who broke me and my man up."

"And don't forget she made my woman leave me too," Eric said from the kitchen.

"You two have got to be kidding me?"

"No, we're not kidding you," Eric said, handing Hakim his drink, then Destiny.

"So what do you want me to do, Destiny?"

"I want you and Eric to go to her next party, take pictures and film it for me."

"How are we supposed to take pictures and film something like that without being noticed? And how are we going to get invited?" Hakim asked.

"Eric said he has a friend at school with the right equipment for that, and I know you're going to think that I am crazy, but I will pay you to do this for me."

"You're serious about this, aren't you?" Hakim asked.

"Hell yes."

"So what else do you want me to do?" Hakim asked.

"Go to Randy, tell him that you overheard his conversation on the phone and you sympathize with him. Make it seem like you're offering him your support."

"Destiny, I don't know about that."

"Please, Hakim? You don't know how important this is to me."

"What do you think I'd do to Randy if he came on to me?"

"I'm sure that for ten thousand dollars you can come up with something to keep that from happening, and get me the stuff that I need."

"You're going to pay me ten thousand dollars to do this for you?"

"I'll pay you fifteen if I have to."

"What do you want me to do, Destiny?"

"It's got to be real soon because the party is tonight."

Destiny, Hakim and Eric devised a plan that would get him and Eric into Josephine's party. Hakim was going to talk to Randy and convince him that he was offering his support and at the same convince him that he should go to that party with his friend. The only catch was, Hakim had to pretend that he, too, was gay and that he and his lover—who would be Eric—were looking for parties like that to get into.

"Thank you, Hakim. You are so sweet," Destiny said; then she got up to give him a hug.

"Wait a minute. What about me? I think I deserve a hug and a kiss too, since I have to pretend to be gay," Eric said, and then he laughed.

"Man, you're crazy," Hakim said; then he finished his drink.

"I thought it was all men's fantasy to see two women getting down," Destiny said.

"Naw. I would rather be the one getting

down with a woman. I don't want to kiss one that's been eating what she has," Hakim said.

"I second that motion. I ain't hanging if it's swinging, but if it's an ocean, I'm in motion," Eric said.

"Shut up, Eric," Destiny said, laughing.

"So, Eric, you get the stuff that we need, and we'll meet at Josephine's house if Randy falls for our plan."

"Got you."

"Destiny, I'm out of here. I got to meet my dad for dinner. He's signing on some big company that needs a big job done. I'll talk to you guys later." Hakim finished his drink and got up to leave.

When Destiny locked the door behind him, she turned to Eric. "I could have used a big brother like him."

"What you need is another drink."

"I'll take it if you're having one with me."

"I can. I don't have any homework or class tomorrow, but I do need to call my guy and ask him if I can borrow that stuff that we're going to need."

Destiny playfully slapped Eric on the shoulder.

"You know touching leads to other things, so I suggest that you keep your hands to yourself," Eric told Destiny.

"So what are you trying to say?" she asked.

"Let me make the phone call first, and let's finish our drinks, and I'll show you," Eric said. He downed the Rémy, called his friend and asked if he could borrow the things that he needed to record the party.

\* \* \*

Hakim called Randy and started talking about the job that they had done at Josephine's and how nice it was for her to have recommended her friends to them. After thirty minutes, Hakim changed the conversation about Josephine to how many failed relationships he'd been in, and finally he'd told Randy that he had overheard his earlier conversation. Hakim tried to make Randy feel comfortable enough to open up to him about things. Randy eventually began to talk. He wouldn't have done this if Hakim hadn't approached him, but he was glad that Hakim had. The burden of holding it in had become too great for Randy.

He told Hakim that it was really hard for him to hold in the fact that he was gay and to not have many friends that he could talk with about it. An hour into the conversation, Hakim mentioned that he would like to go to the party that he'd heard him talking about, and he used Destiny's phrase. He told Randy that it had been a fantasy of his to see two women together.

Randy confided in Hakim that he wanted to talk to him once before about being gay. He told Hakim that since they had been coworkers for so long, he felt that he could be someone that he could confide in. Randy mentioned that he really didn't feel comfortable enough to talk to his family about it because he was afraid that they wouldn't accept him as being gay. Hakim knew that he was jeopardizing his work relationship with Randy, once Destiny got what she wanted, but he could use the money that she offered. Whatever happened between him and Randy, he'd deal with later. Hakim didn't have a lot of time to get ready for the party, but he needed to call Destiny to let her know that he was on his way there.

Destiny and Eric went by Eric's friend's home to pick up the equipment. By the time Destiny and Eric made it home and into her apartment, her cell was ringing. It was Hakim calling to see if Eric was ready to go as well.

"Hey, we just got back from picking up the stuff that Eric needed. What's up?"

"You owe me big time for this, Destiny."

"OK, I got an idea."

"What's that?"

"Why don't I buy lunch for you and your entire crew for doing the work on Josephine's house. If you hadn't, I wouldn't be this excited."

"That would be nice. We don't want hamburgers or cheeseburgers for the mess you're putting me through, and don't forget that ten grand. What I'm about to do is going to get you what you want, and at the same time cause some friction between me and Randy," Hakim said, joking.

"I hope not, but this is important to me, and once I have that film in my hands, I'll write you that check."

"Good. See you after the party?"

"I'll be waiting."

# 6

Destiny gave Eric a thumbs-up after he got dressed for the party. He had on a wife beater and a pair of dress slacks that fit a little tighter than he liked.

"I think I'll go by the name Chad when I get there."

"Where in the hell did you come up with a name like Chad?" Destiny asked him.

"It fits this ridiculous outfit that I have on."

"You look, like, nice to me, Chad."

"Destiny, I already don't feel like doing this. Do you think you can cut the jokes short?"

"I'm sorry, Eric. I'll stop," Destiny said. She turned her back and giggled under her breath.

"I hear you, slick."

"All right, I quit for real this time."

"How about I take this ridiculous outfit off and put on something more casual and dress you up to make you attractive to the same sex?"

That made Destiny laugh out loud. "I'm

sorry, Eric, you made me laugh, and you're right. I'll stop with the jokes."

"Forget you, Destiny. What time did Hakim say to meet him? Did he give you the address?"

"No. He should be pulling up soon. I didn't think that you two needed to be in separate cars."

"Destiny, how do I really look?"

"Like a talk show, Chad."

"I figured you got me looking like a damn clown, but that's fine, because you owe me big-time too."

"And, baby, I'm going to pay you everything that you've earned." Destiny kissed Eric on the mouth. "That's Hakim out there blowing, baby. You got everything?"

"Yeah. I'll see you when the party's over."

"You're staying that long? You're going to get poked."

"Destiny, shut up and lock your door."

"What's up, Eric?" Hakim asked.

"Nothing much, man. I hope this works, because Destiny got me looking like a clown in this wife beater and tight slacks."

"Well, if your ex wasn't going to be there, you wouldn't have to dress for the men."

"Not you too, man?"

"Hey, it's better than what Destiny called you."

"Don't tell me that she called your cell before I got down here?"

"You know she did. She said you looked like a talk show, Chad."

"You two are going to pay for this."

"Man, take that up with Destiny," Hakim said

as he laughed at Eric. "Say, you got the camcorder from your friend?"

"Yeah, right here." Eric held the tiny camcorder up so that Hakim could see it.

"Hey, this is cool. I'd like to have one of these for myself," Hakim said.

"I'll ask where you can purchase one at. So how long do you think we'll be there?"

"Long enough to get some of that freaky stuff on tape, take some pictures and eat."

"I don't know why I let Destiny talk me into this, but that's my girl. I want to get in and out before I get approached."

"I feel you on that one, man," Hakim said.

By the time Hakim and Eric made it to Josephine's house, Byron and Randy were pulling up. "Glad you made it," Randy said.

"Me too," Hakim said.

Hakim introduced Eric to Randy as one of his friends who was looking to have a little fun too.

"Ah . . . baby, I see that you've come back," Josephine said to Hakim. "Ready for fun, not business?"

"And my, oh my, don't you look nice," Hakim lied.

"Thanks for the compliment. So who's the new guy?"

"This is Eric."

Eric had forgotten to tell Hakim that he wasn't using his real name, but it didn't matter much, since Hakim had already introduced him.

Josephine extended her hand to Eric and

said, "You must be good friends with Hakim and Randy?" He took her hand in his and kissed it lightly. He wanted to throw up, because he pictured her hands being stuck up one of her friends' twat. "Eric, darling. I hope that you and Hakim enjoy the fun tonight."

"I'm sure I will, but I'm more of a watcher than a participant."

"I hate that you're not joining in on the fun, but I guess it's just as pleasurable to watch. Perhaps the next time you come, you will join in on the fun."

"I'm sure we will. This is a beautiful place, hon . . . ," Eric said.

"Oh, thank you."

"Is the party in the basement?" Hakim asked, trying to make it seem like he was comfortable with the whole setup.

"Oh, darling, I see you're coming out of that shell of yours," Josephine said to Hakim. "What about you?" she asked, pointing to Randy. "You left early the last time you were here."

"I had a few things to attend to. I apologize for that," Randy said.

"Well, I think all of my invited guests are here. Let's go party." Josephine walked to the entrance of the basement. "Don't be shy, honey," she said to Eric. "Come on, the party is this way."

Eric followed her and Hakim to the basement.

"Guys, we have newcomers. This is Eric and this is Hakim," Josephine said, pointing to the men. "Now let's get this party started." Josephine dimmed the lights a little in the basement, and everybody except Eric and Hakim got undressed.

Eric looked around the room until he spotted Aleesyia. She was naked and doing someone other than the girl that she was at the club with. Eric took the tiny camcorder out of his pocket and began filming the scene, while Hakim took snapshots of the party guests in various positions. He wished that he had gotten his digital camera instead of having to use the disposable that Eric had brought along. Nobody seemed to care that they were being watched by Eric and Hakim, nor did anybody know that they were being filmed.

Eric felt sick to his stomach watching Aleesyia getting down with another woman. He wanted to go over and snatch her up, then beat her down for leaving him for a woman.

Hakim eased over to where the food was set up on a table. Eric saw him and rushed over to where he was. "I don't know how you can eat with all of this funky sex, moaning and groaning going on. What if they put something in that food?" he asked.

"Damn, man, you sure know how to spoil a brother's appetite, but those lobster tails were smelling good," Hakim said.

"Yeah, but if they're laced with something, I might have to pull you out from under one of these men," Eric said, laughing.

"Man, let's get the hell out of here. We can go to a seafood restaurant and order some lobster tails," Eric said.

Both of them eased out the door, and once

again everybody was so wrapped up in what they were doing, no one noticed that they were leaving.

"Man, all that moping and groping going on up in there is ridiculous," Eric said.

"I take it that you saw your ex?" Hakim asked.

"Yeah. She was the one with the blue velvet dress on."

"What was up with that dress?" Hakim asked Eric.

"Hell, I don't know. She started acting weird when she hooked up with Josephine. Maybe she thinks that she's some kind of rock star or something."

"Well, maybe next time you won't be so quick to let another one of your girls go to a female shrink."

"You got that right. Let's get the hell away from here before the whole butt-naked party come after us," Eric said as he climbed into Hakim's car.

"Yeah, let's go to that twenty-four-hour drugstore and develop this film first," Hakim said.

"They were so into what they were doing that they didn't know that you were taking pictures while I filmed them," Eric said to Hakim.

"Yeah, but I know that when I get to work Monday morning, Randy will probably want to know why we left. Plus, when this stuff gets out, I know he's not going to trust me ever again or attend any more of Josephine's parties with me. So I hope we got good pictures and video."

"I do too, because seeing Aleesyia made me

want to kick her ass, and I know if I see her like that again, I will."

"That'll get Josephine all the attention that she don't want from the cops."

"She isn't that stupid to call them out to her house," Eric said.

"Forget Josephine and her parties. That was the second, and the last, time that woman—or whatever she prefers to be called—will ever see me again," Hakim said as he drove to the store. They developed the film on one of those do-it-yourself machines in the store, and the pictures came out perfect. They got a shot of Josephine just before and then after she had hooked up with another woman.

"Let's get this over to Destiny," Hakim said.

"Yeah, she's blowing my cell up right now," Eric said.

"Mine too."


Destiny rushed to the door as soon as she saw Hakim's truck pull up in front of her apartment building.

"Let me see! Let me see! I can't wait any longer. You two could have answered your cell phones."

"For what, so you could bug us every five minutes like you did?" Eric asked.

"Whatever."

"I'm going home. You two can look at that by yourselves."

Destiny thumbed through the pictures. She looked at each picture carefully to see if she recognized any of the people. She shook her head at the pictures as she looked at them. "Ooh-wee," she said as she looked at each picture.

"Ooh-wee, what?" Eric asked.

She showed Eric the picture of two men. "This guy right here," she said, pointing at one of the men in the picture. "He's a lawyer, and he's married with kids."

"Get the hell out of here," Eric said, shocked.

"I'm not lying. He works in a family-practice law firm downtown."

"What do you think his wife would say if she saw those pictures and that video?" Eric asked Destiny.

"I don't know. Wait . . . wait, you got this on video too?"

"Yeah. Was I supposed to just film Josephine in a lewd act?"

"Ooh, yes. Eric, do you know what we got ourselves here?"

"Trouble."

"That too, but just imagine what I could do with these pictures and that video," Destiny said.

"I know that look. You can't do bad things to innocent people, Destiny," Eric said.

"Aw, there you go spoiling my moment. I'm not trying to get even with any of these people. I want Josephine, remember?"

"I do, but did you listen to what you just said?"

"Yeah, but I'm not that mean, Eric. I don't want to break up that man's family. He's going to do that in due time, himself. How long do you think he can lead a double life without getting found out?"

"Not long, as another brother on the down low," Eric said, shaking his head at what he'd just found out about the man. "Do you know anybody else in any of the rest of the pictures?"

Destiny turned up the corner of her lip at Eric. "You know I do. Josephine used to have these group sessions, where all of her clients would meet at least once a month. I attended one of them. Come to think of it, I remember seeing Aleesyia there, but she wore her hair shorter back then. That's why I didn't recognize her at the club. Her hair was longer."

"I guess she let it grow back, since she's the woman in her new relationship."

Destiny burst out laughing. "I think you're just jealous."

"Suppose you and William were a hot item, and you just knew that your relationship was going somewhere with him, and you later find out that William is gay. What would you do?"

"Kick him in the balls hard enough to crack them, and I bet you he won't be able to use the bat for a long time," Destiny said, laughing.

"You got mad issues, Destiny."

"And that means what, Eric?" she asked.

"Why would you want to hurt him just because he turned on you?"

"Why are we talking about William anyway? I'm not thinking about him, but you are," Destiny said to Eric.

"You're right. Forget about William, let's look at the video."

"Pop some popcorn first," Destiny said, joking.

"You don't have any. Come on, hook the thing up to the television and let's see what we got."

Destiny got up and plugged the cords into the jacks on the side of the television. She turned to Eric and said, "How do you know there's no popcorn?"

"Because I popped the last pack."

"When?"

"The last time that I slept in my own bed and watched a horror movie. That's when."

"That bag was laced with cyanide, and you're going to die slowly," Destiny said, smiling at Eric.

"And you're going to miss all of this," Eric said, pointing to himself. "Now get your skinny butt out of the way, and let's see what's on the video. I made sure that I got Aleesyia and both her women."

"For what?" Destiny asked.

"Just like you want to pay Josephine back, I want to pay her flaky ass back."

"Gay bashing, are we?"

"No . . . no, I didn't mean flaky like that, but she could have told me that she was leaving me for a woman, who thinks she's a man. Now, isn't that a mess? Eve and Ava."

"Where did you come up with those names?"

"Everybody always says 'Adam and Steve,' so why not 'Eve and Ava'?"

"Man, turn the television up, and let's watch the video."

Eric used the remote and turned the volume

up. He frowned at what he had to watch for a second time.

"Ooh, turn that crap down. I can't take all that moaning and groaning. I could if it had been heterosexual sex, but how good could it feel to have another man poking you in the butt?" Destiny complained.

"Oh, are you gay bashing, Destiny?"

"Naw, baby, this stuff is disgusting."

"Maybe it's disgusting to us, but to them it's what they like."

"I guess you're right."

"You want to look at it another time?" Eric asked.

"Naw, let's get it over with now. Ooh, Eric, look," Destiny said, pointing to a female in the video.

"Who's that?"

"That's Josephine's receptionist, Michelle. Her boyfriend is so damn jealous, and if he got hold of this bit of info, he'd probably kill her ass."

"Then we know that he's never going to get hold of it, right, Destiny?"

"I didn't say all that."

"Right, Destiny?"

"I couldn't stand her skinny smart-mouthed ass. She was right there rooting Josephine on when she talked about William like a dog one day, and she can't even go to the corner store without Leon sniffing her funky panties when she comes back."

"How do you know all of that? Mmm, hmm,

they done turned your ass out too. You just don't want to admit it," Eric said, joking.

"You must be crazy. Josephine got in everybody's business, and she didn't mind sharing it, and now I know why she did that."

"Why?"

"She was feeling the women out. She makes you comfortable, and then she pounces."

"Who made you a philosopher?"

"Think about it, Eric. She tells you somebody else's business, and things that person has said about you. Then once you're all mad and ready to get even, she calms you down by becoming more than just your therapist. She makes herself your friend right away."

"That doesn't mean that she's trying to get next to you, Destiny."

"Come on, Eric. Look at how she used to come in the bathroom while I was in the tub or showering, and to make matters worse, I was renting her guesthouse and she had no business doing that. A real woman doesn't sit in the bathroom with you while you're washing your ass, and she definitely isn't going to stick around until you get out of the tub! The lady is a freak. Pure and simple."

"OK, baby, I get your point. Hey, I got to get going. I got some studying to do for a test Monday, so I'll see you tomorrow," Eric said. He got up to leave Destiny's apartment.

"Monday is two days away," Destiny observed, pouting.

"My test is very important."

"OK. I'll see you tomorrow then." Destiny walked Eric to the door and gave him a hug.

"I want my surprise for risking my sanity and my life making that video for you."

"Your life? How did you risk your life?"

"I could have gotten attacked by all those manly women and womanly men in that place."

"You're stupid."

"I'm gone before I change my mind," Eric said.

"I don't mind," Destiny said seductively.

"I know you wouldn't. Lock the door. I got to study. See you in the morning." Eric left.

Destiny sat alone in her apartment and watched the video. She got a notepad and wrote down as many of the participants' names that she knew. She knew about thirteen of the twenty-five guests that attended Josephine's orgy. She didn't know what she wanted to do with the info just yet, but she was sure some good stuff would pop up in her head. Oh, she wanted to call Josephine so bad, it hurt her. She had some shopping to do tomorrow. She needed a computer, a printer, lots of ink and paper. She wanted the high-tech stuff, because she was going to make several copies of the video and plenty more of the pictures.

She turned the video off. It was making her sick to see the people who, she knew, had wives, husbands and children. She could only imagine how devastated they would be to find out that they had been betrayed.

\* \* \*

After Hakim had made it home, he called his sister, Jasmine, to see how she'd been. Hakim had told Jasmine all about Destiny and how they had met. He told her that he wanted her to meet her one day, because she was a lot of fun to be around. Jasmine joked with him the way she usually did about him wanting her to meet his female friends. She asked Hakim if he'd warned her of his "three *F*" rule: find them, freak them, forget about them. Hakim had laughed at his sister when she asked him that, but he told her that the "three *F*" rule didn't apply to Destiny because they were just friends. Jasmine said that she'd like to meet her one day, and maybe then he wouldn't mind hanging out with her and her friends, since he'd have someone to bring along. She said that she didn't know when this would occur, with so much going on at the hair shop. Hakim told her to call him whenever she was ready to meet Destiny.


Destiny did as she promised. She wanted to show her appreciation to Hakim's crew, because without them she wouldn't have found out about Josephine and the type of lifestyle she was living behind her husband's back. She went to a steak house and ordered six of everything. She ordered steaks, well done, and big baked potatoes with sour cream and chives. Corn on the cob and garden salads with ranch dressing. For dessert she ordered six pieces of chocolate cake. After packing everything in her car, she stopped at a corner store and got a few six-packs of grape soda. She would have gotten them some expensive wine to go along with the food, but they were at a work site.

When Destiny made it to the work site, she called Hakim from her cell phone. "Hey, it's me. I'm at the entrance."

Hakim told her to pull in and drive to the gray trailer. Destiny did as told. He helped her get the food out of her car and take it in the trailer, where his crew and his dad were waiting. He introduced her to his crew and his father. His dad, Derrick, spoke first. He got up and shook her hand. He told her that he'd heard a lot about her, and what did he owe for such a nice gesture? Destiny smiled at Derrick and said, "I've heard a lot about you too. You don't owe me anything. I just promised Hakim that I'd bring lunch down for you guys."

"This was nice of you Destiny," one of the crewmen said.

"Yeah, it is nice—for what I had to do for her," Hakim said. He and the whole crew burst out into laughter, and they said they could figure it out on their own.

Derrick fixed himself a plate and went off to his little office to eat his food. Something seemed familiar about Destiny, but he couldn't put his finger on it. Suddenly he thought that it was her eyes that reminded him of a friend. She was very attractive, and he didn't understand why his son didn't want to date her. He ate his food and cleaned off his desk. Destiny made him think about a friend from long ago. That friend was someone he'd dated long ago.

"I better get back out there, enough for reminiscing. I got work to do," Derrick said to himself. He was puzzled that Destiny's eyes brought back memories that he had long since forgotten.

He walked past Destiny and his son, who were now standing off in a corner, talking. He heard Hakim telling her that she would really enjoy meeting his sister, Jasmine. Derrick didn't know why Hakim wanted her to meet the rest of the family if they were just friends, but that wasn't his business. He'd seen a lot of different women come and go in his son's life, so why waste his and her time introducing her to the family?

Derrick put his hard hat back on and went to supervise the group of men that he was responsible for. When he saw Destiny drive off the site, he radioed for Hakim to meet him. When Hakim walked over to where his father was standing, Hakim was concerned about the look on his father's face. His dad looked worried.

"What's up, Pops? You look like you're worried about something."

Derrick looked at his son with tired eyes. "I'm worried about you, son. You've invited that girl to meet your sister, but yet you say that there's nothing going on between the two of you. I don't remember you ever inviting one of your friends to meet your sister. You do know that she's busy running that beauty shop?"

"So what are you saying, Dad? Are you saying

that Destiny shouldn't be allowed to meet your precious daughter?"

"That's not what I'm saying, Hakim. I'm just saying that your sister is very busy with her beauty shop."

"Dad, when Destiny walked in that trailer, you looked like you saw a ghost. Do you have something that you want to tell me about Destiny?"

"Hakim, are you insinuating that I know Destiny?"

"I don't know, Dad. Why don't you tell me what's up?"

"Hakim, your friend reminded me of someone that I knew a long time ago, and when I first saw her, I thought that my past had come back to haunt me. I realized that it was just her eyes."

"So, you're telling me that you've done some things in the past that I don't know about, Dad?"

"Son, there's a lot of things that you, your sister or your mother didn't know about, but we can discuss that after work," Derrick said to his son. He dropped his head like he had a lot to be ashamed of. He was acting like he had a lot of guilt on his shoulders.

Hakim looked at his father's hard hat and said, "Dad, whatever it is that you have to tell me, I promise not to think otherwise of you. I love you, Pops." Hakim turned to walk back to the trailer.

"Hakim," his dad called out to him. Hakim turned around. "Son, I love you too."

Hakim smiled at his dad and winked one eye. "How about you come over to my place for dinner, and we can talk about whatever it is that's got you so down now."

Derrick looked at his son and said, "That sure would be nice. See you around seven, after I go home, shower and change."

"See you at seven, then." Hakim walked away.


Before Derrick met up with his son, he needed to relax his mind. After getting cleaned up, he poured a stiff drink and sat down on his sofa. His head hung low and his shoulders were heavy with guilt. Hakim had brought another one of his many women around, and this time he wished that this one had been left a million miles away. He often wondered why Hakim brought them around, when he had no plans to settle down with any one of them. Destiny had brought back some deep, dark, buried secrets that he had forgotten about over a period of over thirty years. She brought back memories of his infidelity that his wife, family or friends knew nothing about. Destiny looked so much like his old friend that it spooked him, but he knew that there couldn't have been any connection between the two. It was just that she had beautiful eyes, just like his friend had.

Once he started, he couldn't help thinking about his old friend, and how much he had loved her back then. That love had ended abruptly, when she started seeing another man. She had found out that she was pregnant, and had told him that he was the father of her unborn child. He refused to believe that the baby was his, and he ended the relationship, never looking back. He had felt bad for leaving her, but he couldn't accept the fact that she, too, needed someone in her life. He had a wife and two kids and he wasn't about to leave them on a whim, when his friend's unborn child could have been the other man's. Derrick raised his glass and said, "To my old friend, wherever you are." He drank the contents of the glass in one big gulp. "Whew, that burned." Derrick wiped the corner of his mouth with his sleeve, got up from the sofa and grabbed his keys. He left to meet his son for dinner, and a long, much needed talk.

Derrick pulled up in front of Hakim's house, parked and got out of his car. He took a deep breath before walking up to the door. He rang the doorbell. Hakim opened the door, and the aroma that came from inside made Derrick's feet seem like they had lifted off the ground and carried him inside.

"Hey, Pops."

"Hakim, what's for dinner? It sure smells good."

"Thanks, Dad. I made your favorite dish."

"Oh yeah," Derrick joked. "You made steak and eggs?"

"That's not your favorite dish," Hakim said. Then he laughed.

"Just checking," Derrick said.

"Come on, Dad, you know I know that your favorite dish is smothered chicken, with onions, gravy and rice. Would you like a beer before we eat?"

"Nope, I'm hungry. You didn't say what kind of vegetables you made."

"Corn. I know that that's your favorite vegetable. Come on in the kitchen, Dad. Let's eat."

Derrick walked behind his son to the kitchen. "Tell me that you made some of your mother's homemade biscuits?"

"Man, you know I did." Hakim chuckled.

"Hey, Hakim."

"Yeah, Dad."

"After we finish eating dinner, I want to tell you something that has been on my mind for a long time."

"Is that what you were talking about earlier today?" Hakim asked.

"Yeah, but let's not spoil dinner. Let's eat first, then talk."

"Sure, Dad," Hakim said. Then he and his dad took seats at the table and fixed their plates, eating in silence.

"Hey, do you have any more biscuits?" Derrick asked.

Hakim nodded his head yes and got up from his seat. He went to the oven and pulled out a pan of biscuits wrapped in foil and handed them to his father. "I made extra, just in case you wanted to take some home."

"Thanks, I'm sure glad that you did, that way I won't have to cook anything for dinner tomorrow," Derrick said as he spread some butter on the biscuit.

After cleaning up the kitchen, Hakim offered

his dad a beer. Derrick twisted the top off the beer and said, "Well, I guess it's time for that talk."

"Dad, you don't have to do this if you don't want to."

"No, son, it's time that I got rid of this heap of guilt and burden that I've been carrying around with me for a long time now."

"You sure?"

"Yes, I'm sure. In 1974, I met and fell in love with someone. I loved your mom a great deal also, but things just weren't so great between us anymore. Your mom started drinking heavily, and blamed that on me. I let her, but I should have stopped her. She just had some issues that she refused to allow me to help her with. My friend came into my life just when I could no longer deal with your mother's drinking. She was there for me mentally, and physically—"

"Dad, what was Mom going through that she couldn't tell you?" Hakim asked.

"She wanted out of our marriage. She felt that it had been forced on us by our parents when she got pregnant with you."

"Is that the reason she left you as soon as we were able to care for ourselves?"

"Yes."

"She never knew anything about your affair?"

"No, she never knew a thing."

"All right, so what happened to this friend? And why did you choose to tell me about her now?"

"Um . . . when your lady friend, Destiny, walked in the trailer today, I looked at her and it was as if I was staring right at that old friend again."

"What happened?"

"I was selfish. I had a wife and two beautiful kids, and everything belonged to me. She wanted me to leave your mother, you and your sister, but I told her that I could never do that. She knew that your mother didn't want to be married anymore, and she felt that she and I would be happier together. I just couldn't leave my two babies. She met a man, and I'm not sure of how long she'd been seeing him, but I knew that things between her and me were not the same. She didn't tell me about him. I had to find out on my own. When I confronted her about him, she just told me that she was tired of sleeping alone every night when I was going home to my wife and kids. This hurt me deeply, and I pleaded with her to give me a little time to settle things at home, and that's when she told me that she didn't have time, because she was pregnant."

"So what are you trying to say, Dad? That you may have a child out there somewhere?"

"No, Hakim, that's not what I'm saying."

"Oh."

"Anyway, I told her that the baby couldn't be mine, because she had started sleeping with another man, but she tried to make me believe that he had never touched her. I didn't believe that, and I left her. I never looked back."

"So you don't know what she had?"

"I ran into her old landlady about twenty years ago, and she said that she believed that my friend had a son. I asked her about that guy that she had been with, and she told me that she thinks that they got married and moved out of the state, but she wasn't sure."

"So Destiny's eyes reminded you of that old friend?"

"Yeah, they did."

"You know, Dad, you could have a son running around here somewhere. I really wouldn't mind finding out if I got a little brother. It sure would make things a lot easier than trying to hang with my sister, but I told her about Destiny. She said that now I don't have an excuse not to hang with her and her friends, since I have someone to bring along."

"You know Jasmine's busy—"

"Yeah, too busy for her big brother. That's why if I had a little brother we could hang out and do guy stuff together."

"That would be great except . . . I don't think he's my son, and I'm not sure if my friend's parents are still living, but we could go by their place one day this week and check. Just maybe I can find out about her child and if it's mine."

"You up for that, Dad?"

"I think so. It's about time I got that burden off my shoulders."

"I might imagine so," Hakim said.

"How do you think your sister would feel about all of this?" Derrick asked.

"I don't think she'll be angry with you, but with Jasmine, you never could tell."

"Well, I guess I'm just going to have to tell her, and see what she thinks," Derrick said.

"You mean 'feels,' don't you?" Hakim asked. He and his dad finished another beer before Derrick left with the leftover food that Hakim had made.

Hakim didn't know what to make of what his dad had just told him. He didn't understand why his dad held that in for so long. He wasn't the only dad who made the mistake of falling for another woman. Now he was worried that he may have a younger brother somewhere in the world that didn't know his family. He was relieved that his dad didn't say, "Son, Destiny is your sister." Eric had mentioned that they favored. Hakim was full from the dinner, and drowsy from the beer. He went to his den and stretched out on the futon and turned the television on.

Destiny waited patiently for Eric to finish with his studies so that he could go to the store with her to purchase a computer and some other things.

Eric told her that he'd be on his way as soon as he put away his books, showered and got dressed.

While Destiny waited on Eric, she decided to call Josephine.

Josephine answered the phone without looking at the caller ID. "Marcus, got damn it. For the last time, I said that I had too much business to take care of, and that's why I couldn't make it down there." Marcus had called her several times questioning her about why she hadn't come to Florida to meet them. It was too late now, because they were on the way home.

"This isn't Marcus. This is your worst nightmare."

"Oh, Ms. Destiny, lost child," Josephine said casually.

"Is that what you think I am?"

"You don't have a mother. Oh, and let me see, or a father, and your grandparents died on you too. Ooh, and last but not least, your man kicked you out on your sorry ass. So that makes you a lost child."

Destiny smiled to herself, but she kept her anger in. "Josephine, honey, when I'm done with you, you're going to wish that you never met me, not to mention that you're going to regret that you did."

"My . . . my . . . my. You have jokes to tell so early in the morning?"

"Yes, I do, and guess what? The joke's on you."

"Destiny, let me give you a bit of advice, dear. If you were going to do something to me, you would have done it by now. So my advice to you is, get on with your sorry, miserable life and stay out of mine before I find you and kick your sorry little ass again."

"We'll see when I'm done with you, you—"

"I *what?*"

"You whatever it is that you do when your husband isn't around."

"What do you mean? Destiny . . . Destiny," Josephine screamed into the phone, but the line was dead. Josephine looked worried. She wondered what Destiny meant by that last comment she had made. Josephine picked up her phone and dialed *69. The call wouldn't go through; Destiny had blocked her number.

Josephine dialed the operator. "Hello. I'm sorry, but I seem to have gotten disconnected from the last call that was made to my phone, and the call was life-threatening. I was wondering if you could reconnect me, sir."

"I'm sorry, ma'am, but that's not possible. I can't reconnect your call," the phone operator said.

"What do you mean, you can't reconnect my call?" Josephine asked angrily.

"Ma'am, I can connect you to another department. Maybe they can help you."

"I don't need to be connected to another department. You are the operator, aren't you?"

"Yes, ma'am, but I can't reconnect a call for you. Why don't you hang up and try the number again."

"If I had the number, do you think that I would be trying to get you to reconnect me to it?"

"Ma'am, all I can do is transfer you to another department, and maybe they can help you with that."

"What good are you if you can't reconnect me to a dropped call?"

The phone operator became annoyed with Josephine, disconnecting their line.

"I know he didn't hang the damn phone up on me," Josephine said. She dialed 0 again, and this time she got a different operator. Josephine tried to get the operator to reconnect her call, but the operator told her the same thing that the first one had. Josephine was frustrated. She didn't know how to get in touch with Destiny, and then she thought about William. She dialed his number, and when he answered, Josephine asked him if he had seen or heard from her. William told her no, and asked her politely not to ever call his home again.

*If that trifling heifer thinks that she's got me afraid of her, she better think again.* Josephine put Destiny out of her mind temporarily. She had to clean up the mess in her basement before her husband and kids came home. She went to the basement and the memories of the night before were very vivid in her mind.

She reminisced about the events that took place. Her mind went back to Hakim and Eric. Why hadn't she paid more attention to them?

Josephine thought, what if Michelle had mentioned something to Destiny about the parties that she threw? She knew that Destiny and Michelle had been kind of friendly when Destiny would come in for her sessions. Josephine tried to remember if Michelle had ever said anything about her and Destiny ever going out together, but she couldn't recall. Josephine called Michelle. She was still asleep. She tried to get Leon to wake her, but he refused.

*Today just isn't my day. What in the hell have I done?* She started throwing out the plates that were left on the table. She picked up empty beer bottles and threw them in the trash. She doubled two plastic garbage bags and threw the leftover food in them.

She got the vacuum cleaner from the storage room and bent down to plug it in a socket by the stairway. Josephine noticed a small box. She picked the box up and her eyes almost popped out of her head when she read: *Disposable 35mm Camera.* She tried hard to remember which one of her guests had been taking pictures. She threw her head back and closed her eyes. She had made it clear to her elite little clique that no one under any circumstances could take pictures of any kind or film the events. She had made her guests leave their cameras and video recorders in their cars.

She called Parnell's cell phone.

"Parnell, somebody brought a camera in here last night. Did you see who it was?"

"How in the hell do you know somebody brought a camera there?"

"I was getting ready to vacuum the floor and I found an empty disposable camera box."

"Are you sure you didn't leave it down there?" he asked.

"Yes, I'm sure. I haven't taken any pictures of anything lately."

"Maybe Marcus had one to take on the trip, because I didn't see anybody taking any pictures."

"Oh yeah. Maybe he did. He could have thrown the damn box in the garbage," she said, feeling relieved.

"Next time think before you call me and scare the hell out of me. If somebody took pictures last night, do you know what that could do to my reputation?"

"What about mine?"

"What about it?"

"Bye, Parnell."

"Bye, Josephine. Oh, Josephine?"

"What?"

"That party was a great one," Parnell said.

"I know. I can't wait to have the next one."

"I bet you can't. I got to go before Sasha hears me on the phone. It's Sunday, you know. I don't do business on Sundays."

"Talk to you tomorrow." She hung up the phone and thought nothing more of the empty box. She finished cleaning the basement in time to pick her husband and kids up from the airport.

When Marcus got in the car, he didn't say a word to Josephine. The boys had been so excited about going to Disney World that it hadn't mattered to them that their mother never showed up. Josephine knew that Marcus was angry with her, but she'd find a way to make it up to him later. She hated that they had returned, and wished that they had stayed one more week, because she would have given another party. When they got to the house, Marcus took the suitcases in and went to the family room. Josephine came in to try and talk to him, but he still refused to speak to her.

"Suit yourself. Stay angry forever if you want. I told you that I had a lot of work to do. I had to reboot my computer and put all of my clients' information back in it, and I had a ton of paperwork to finish, along with a million other things that had to be done."

After Eric finished with his studies, he was ready to take Destiny to the store to buy a computer and whatever it was that she was trying to get.

"What kind of computer are you trying to buy, and why?" Eric asked while he drove her to the store.

"Something to make copies of that video on, and one with a printer so that I can make a lot of copies of those pictures," Destiny said.

"Destiny, don't do anything to anybody that didn't do anything to you. There are consequences and repercussions for hurting innocent people," Eric said.

"Eric, you're right. I'm not trying to hurt anybody else, and from this point on, I'm going to stay focused. I just think that it's a shame that those people, like Parnell and Michelle, are deceiving their mates."

"It is, but that's not your problem. Eventually what they're doing is going to come to light, but not because you had something to do with it. OK?"

"I hear you. I'm glad to have a friend like you, because at times I feel like I don't have anybody," Destiny said.

"Why don't you try to at least get in touch with your mother and make things right between the two of you?"

"Eric, she left me. I would love nothing more

than to have my mother in my life, but not if it's got to have anything to do with my money."

"I feel you on that one, but you need to at least give her a chance."

"I can do that, but right now I don't think that I'm ready."

"Well, when you are, I want you to do it. I'll be by your side—no matter what."

Destiny looked over at Eric, and she truly was grateful for having a friend like him. He made the hard things in her life seem so simple.

"What are you looking at me like that for?" he asked.

"Why you want to know?"

"Because you're looking at me. That's why."

"Drive, why don't you, and don't worry about why I'm looking at you."

"Anybody ever told you that you got a smart-ass mouth at times?" Eric asked.

"Quite a few people, but like I told them, I'll tell you the same. Would you rather I have a dumb-ass mouth? Which, by the way, my ass has nothing to do with my mouth."

"Girl, one of these days you gon' make me pop you right in the kisser."

"With what?"

"With this." Eric stopped the truck and kissed Destiny on the mouth.

"I like it when you pop me like that."

"I like popping you like that too."

Eric pulled into a parking space, and he and Destiny got out of his truck and went shopping for the things that she wanted. After purchasing the items, Destiny took Eric shopping and bought him some clothes, shoes and other accessories.

"What's all of this for?" he asked.

"For my friend."

"You don't like the clothes that I wear?"

"I didn't say that, now did I?"

"No, you didn't, but you didn't answer the question either."

"Yes, Eric, I like the way you dress. I just thought I'd do something nice for you, since you did something for me."

Eric put the bags in the back of the truck with the rest of the things.

"Let's go to the ice-cream parlor and get some ice cream."

"How about we go to the food court and get something to eat?" Destiny suggested instead.

"We can do that."

They ordered sandwiches and chips for lunch. Eric carried the tray to the table. Destiny was putting some extra mayonnaise on her sandwich. When she finished, she picked it up to take a bite, and her eyes fell upon William, who was sitting two tables over from her, with a woman. Destiny lost her appetite. The woman that he was with was talking and laughing, and teasing him with a French fry.

Eric saw that Destiny had put her sandwich down, and he asked her why she wasn't eating.

"I just lost my appetite all of a sudden," she said.

"Are you OK?"

"I'm fine. I just feel a little sick all of a sudden," Destiny said. She looked past Eric and watched

as William allowed the woman to hand-feed him.
If Destiny had any hope at all of them ever getting back together, that hope was shattered by
what she was witnessing now. She didn't have anything in her stomach, but she felt something
coming up her esophagus. She swallowed hard
to keep it down. She held back all of her feelings
of pain to keep from stopping Eric from finish-
ing his sandwich, which he seemed to be enjoying. It seemed like it took him forever to eat the
last bite and drink the rest of his soda. She
watched William pick up the food tray and empty
it in the trash bin, and he and the woman walked
toward the entrance, hand in hand. Destiny felt
tears swell up in her eyes and she grabbed a
napkin, faking a sneeze.

"Damn, you got to sneeze that hard that it
made you cry?" Eric asked.

"Excuse me. I guess I'm allergic to all these
people in here," she lied.

"Well, let's get the hell out of here before
you start screaming. Do you want this soda?"
he asked her.

"No. I don't want that sandwich either," she
said in a daze.

Eric couldn't help noticing that her mood
had change even more. "What's the matter
with you, Destiny?" he asked, concerned.

"I don't want to talk about it."

"When are you ever going to learn how to
open up and talk?"

Destiny was starting to feel annoyed with
Eric, but she kept her cool and asked, "How's
that unhealthy, Eric?"

"Look at what keeping things from your last man got you."

Destiny looked at him as if he knew that William had just been sitting two tables away from them. She didn't know what to say, so she turned and started walking toward his truck, with him following her. Eric caught up and grabbed her arm and turned her toward him.

"What the hell is wrong with you? First you're hungry as hell, and then you lose your appetite. Now you're acting like something is stuck up your ass, and you don't want to talk?"

Destiny moved closer to him and put her head on his chest and cried. Eric wrapped his arms around her, like he had to protect her from something.

"Destiny, please tell me what's wrong with you."

"Eric, I'm sorry that I'm acting this way. When we were sitting at the table, I looked up and William was sitting two tables away from us. I guess seeing him made me feel sick to my stomach."

"Now, was that hard to tell me?"

"Naw, I just didn't want to bring him up, that's all."

"It's OK, baby, that's not the only time you may run into him, but you have to get over him, and live again. Remember, life goes on," Eric said, and kissed her on the forehead. "Let's go home."

As usual, Eric had made her feel better. She climbed into the truck and they talked about setting her computer up when they got back home. Destiny didn't tell him the real reason why she had bought him all those new things, because she wanted to surprise him and ask him if he wanted to take a trip with her when he went on summer break from school. She had planned on sending Hakim and his friends on a trip of their choice for getting those pictures and video of Josephine's party.

She glanced over at Eric and wondered what it would be like to be in love with someone as special as he was. She smiled at the thought, but she had made it clear to him that they would never be more than just friends.

# 7

Josephine never did ask her husband about the empty camera box, and he never showed her any 35mm pictures. The only pictures that he brought back were those that had been taken professionally while in Disney World. One week later, Josephine was in the kitchen making lunch for her husband and kids. She was in a good mood. She had turned the portable radio on that sat on top of the refrigerator, and she was singing along to a song. She didn't hear her doorbell ring, nor did she know that her husband was signing for a special delivery package addressed to him. Josephine was singing and cooking, and Marcus was opening the package.

Josephine was setting the table, and Marcus was ripping the package open. Josephine made orange juice from concentrate, and Marcus was opening the DVD that was in the package. Josephine placed drinking glasses by each table setting, and Marcus turned on the television and DVD player in the family room. Josephine sang the words to another song, and Marcus listened to the moaning and groaning going on in the video. Josephine called her family down to the kitchen to eat, and Marcus called his brother to let him know that he was coming over for a few days.

"Marcus . . . Marcus, honey, your plate is fixed, and we're waiting on you to come eat with us," Josephine called out to her husband. "Marcus," she screamed out louder, "your plate is fixed. Now come join your family, dear. We don't have all afternoon to wait on you."

Josephine went back to the kitchen and sat at her place, waiting for Marcus to come to the kitchen and join them. She heard his footsteps coming down the stairs, and when he approached the entrance to the kitchen, he stood there with his suitcase in his hand.

"What the hell is going on, and where the hell do you think you're going?" she asked. "Boys, leave the table. You're excused," she quickly added.

"I got a special delivery package while you were in the kitchen cooking lunch, and I opened it. Inside were two DVDs—one for me to keep, and a copy for you, along with two letters, one for me and a copy for you," Marcus said.

"Marcus, what are you talking about? Who are the DVDs and letters from?"

"If you get up off your ass, you can see for yourself," he said.

"I know you're not starting a fight with me after we just made up, and I've fixed you lunch," Josephine snapped back.

"Josephine, I'm leaving you. When you get through eating your lunch, I suggest you watch this DVD and read the letter that came along with it."

Josephine tried to stop Marcus, but he pushed her to the side and walked toward the door.

Josephine ran after him. She stopped him and asked what was going on. Marcus pushed her out of his way and opened the door. Josephine kicked the suitcase out of his hand, and stood in front of him. Marcus pushed her out of his way again, but Josephine was persistent. This time Marcus slapped her so hard that the impact sent her falling to the floor. She lay there, holding her face and crying, as she watched her husband walk out the door.

Josephine got up, closed the door and rushed back to the kitchen and snatched the DVD and letter off the table. She ran to the family room and closed the door. She read the letter before she put the DVD into the player.

*Hey, Marcus,*
*We missed you at the party, and we wondered where you were, but since you couldn't attend, we filmed it for you to see how much fun we had. I hope you enjoy the video.*
*Sincerely,*
*Your Friend*

Josephine felt her heart start to beat fast as she walked over to the player, put the DVD into it and pressed play. Her heart sank. She fell to her knees and began to cry. She watched herself performing different sex acts on a woman that Marcus had met several times. She watched the rest of her guests doing their thing. She didn't see Hakim or any of the guys that came with him in the video. She knew that Destiny had something to do with this, but she couldn't prove it. If she could, what was she going to do about it?

"Oh, my goodness. What have I done?" she cried out. "I'm going to kill that bitch if she had anything to do with this. What am I going to do? Why is this happening to me?"

Josephine's sons heard her crying and rushed to the family room. "Get out! Get out," she screamed at the boys. The video was still playing when they rushed into the room. She knew that they had caught a glimpse of it, because their mouths fell wide open. Her two sons ran out of the room, ashamed of what they had seen on the television screen, and now they knew why their father had left.

Josephine didn't know how she was going to explain to her ten- and twelve-year-old that their father had left her. She was ashamed that her sons had burst in and had seen her on a giant-screen television performing sex on another woman. Josephine pulled herself together. She needed to explain things to her sons first to make sure that they were emotionally sound.

Josephine stepped out of the room, and her eldest son was looking at her with malice in his eyes. Marcus hadn't looked that evil when he walked out on her. Josephine knew that she needed to explain to him right away what had been going on, in a way that he would understand.

"Kyle, honey, Mommy has done some very undesirable things, but, honey, I love you and I want to explain some things to you."

Kyle folded his arms across his chest and narrowed his eyes at his mom. "I don't want to live here with you anymore. I want my daddy," he said in a shaky voice.

Josephine could see clearly that her son was upset and she had to choose the right words to say to him to calm him down. She knew that this issue was a lot for her young son to handle, and maybe even harder for her younger son. "Kyle, Daddy and I were having some problems anyway, but once I talk to him, he'll come back home. Just wait and see," Josephine told her son.

"I don't believe you, Mom. Dad's not coming back. Every day while we were in Disney World, he called you, because he kept saying how much you would enjoy being there with us," Kyle said, and then he ran upstairs to his room.

Josephine had to face her younger son, who was more aggressive than his brother. "Tyler, I know that you heard the conversation between me and your brother. I know that you and your brother are upset with me, but Mommy is going to make everything right again."

"I hate you. I hate you. . . . You're gay. You're not my mother. My mother wouldn't sleep with women behind my dad's back. You are the bitch that he says you are."

"Where did you learn such language, Tyler?"

"That's what I hear Dad saying about you all the time."

Josephine wanted to slap her son, but she didn't want to make the matter worse than what it already was. He'd only repeated what he had heard his father saying. "Honey, Daddy didn't mean those things that he said about me." Josephine reached out to touch her youngest son, and he pulled away from her.

"Don't touch me," he cried out.

"Tyler, I'm not going to have you talking to me in that tone of voice or saying the things that you have already said. I am still your mother," she said as calmly as she could.

"Leave me alone," Tyler said; then he ran to his brother's room.

Josephine ran after him, but she wasn't fast enough to catch the door before he slammed and locked it.

"Open this door, Tyler. . . . One of you had better get up and open this door. Mommy just wants to talk to you."

"Go away, Mommy. I don't want to talk to you. You made Daddy mad and now he's gone," Tyler said to his mother.

"Boy, if you don't open this door, I'll kick it in," Josephine snapped.

"And I'll call 911," Tyler said through the door.

Josephine ran back to the family room, and when she saw the door to the DVD player open, she knew that her son had taken it. She ran back up to his room. "Kyle, please, honey, don't look at that video. Mommy can explain everything," she sobbed. Kyle didn't say anything to her, but she could hear him talking. "Kyle, open the door for Mommy, please?" She could hear her son on the phone talking to his father.

"Dad, please come get me and Tyler. Don't leave us here with Mommy. I took the video that Mommy had that made you mad."

"Kyle, are you and your brother sure that you want to be away from your mother?" Marcus asked his son.

"Dad, if you don't come get us, we're going to run away from here," Kyle cried into the phone.

"Son, I'm on my way back to get both of you. Stay in your room and I'll pack your things when I get there. I'll be there, OK?"

"Yes, Dad."

"You're talking to your father on the phone? Kyle, open this door right now."

Kyle ignored his mother and waited on his dad to come back and pack some clothes for him. He emptied the dirty clothes out of the suitcase that they had brought back from Disney World. He huddled up with his brother on his bed.

"Kyle, why won't you open the door for Mommy?"

"Because I don't want to talk to you, Mommy."

"Boy, you better open this door. I'm still your mother."

"You already said that. I don't know who you are."

When the boys heard their father's voice thirty minutes later, they jumped up from where they were, flung the door open and sprinted toward their dad.

"Where do you two think you're going?"

"With Daddy," Tyler snapped at his mother.

"Boy, if you and Kyle don't get back up to your rooms and unpack, I'll—"

"You'll do what, Josephine?" Marcus asked. He stood there waiting on an answer from her. "You'll do what, Josephine? If you put your hands on my sons, I'll call the Office of Professional Standards and expose you, and I bet your lawyer friend won't be able to save you this time from losing your license. Then I'll call child protective services up on you and tell them what you've exposed our sons to. Now get away from them."

Josephine felt like she was losing control. She didn't want Marcus to call anyone up on her, so she stepped aside and allowed him and the boys to return to their rooms to pack some clothes. She hadn't exposed them to anything. She had made the mistake of leaving the video in the DVD player while she talked to Tyler, and Kyle went in the family room and took it.

"Give me back the video before you leave, Kyle."

"I left it in my room."

"You had no right taking it, Kyle," she said.

"I took it because it made Daddy leave and I wanted him to come back, Josephine."

"Don't call me Josephine, boy," she snapped at her son.

Josephine ran out the door behind them and up to Marcus, helping the boys put their suitcases in the trunk of his car. "You're a bastard, Marcus. How could you take my babies away from me?"

"How could you eat on crap that doesn't go on a plate? How could you deceive us? How could you lie to me? How could you pretend that you love me, when in fact you were loving your got damn clients?"

"That's not true, Marcus. I do love you. Please, Marcus, don't do this to me."

"Don't do what to you, Josephine? Tyler, Kyle, get into the car and close the door. You did this to yourself. Now I see why we weren't having sex as often as I wanted to. You were too busy fucking other women. That's why you got so upset with Destiny."

Josephine made the mistake of slapping him again for bringing up Destiny's name, and she found herself lying on the ground.

"Bitch, are you crazy? You were the one who made me run to her. You were the one who got upset with her, because she didn't want your trifling ass. I want a got damn divorce, and I want you out of my house. Take whatever your nasty ass came with, and leave that which you didn't buy," Marcus said angrily.

"I'm not giving you a got damn thing, and I'm not leaving this house!"

"I think you will if you don't want your precious little important friends involved in this scandal that's about to rise."

"You wouldn't do that to me! They haven't done anything to you, Marcus."

"I know. That's why I said I'm divorcing you,

and I want you out of my house, and do not take anything that does not belong to you. I'll be back in one week, and I hope you're gone. See how it feels when the tables turn? You're always snapping on me, and telling me to get out of your house. You must have forgotten that you moved in here with me, and that it was I who put you through school, and it is I who wants you the fuck out of here. Oh, by the way, don't even ask for visitation rights to my sons."

"Marcus, please, you can't be serious?"

"Were you when you trotted your proud ass over to William's house and told him what Destiny did? I suggest that you not try the slapping-me-again thing. I'll kill your ass this time."

"How did you find out about that?"

"You didn't think that Destiny was going to let you get away with that, did you? She called because she thought that I might want to know why you came in all bruised up the day that you said you fell. I just didn't say anything to you about it because I had already done enough to hurt you."

"Marcus, please let's not do this. I know I've done some undesirable things, but I never thought in a million years that we would ever get a divorce. I can't do that, Marcus."

"Like I said, if you don't want other people involved in this mess that you've created, I suggest that you have your crap out of my house in one week."

"Where am I going to go, Marcus?"

"I don't give a damn. I just want you out of my house in one week or else your little friends' husbands or wives will be getting a copy of that video. What would make you record some crap like that anyway?"

"I didn't do that. I don't know who did it."

"Payback is a motherfucker, ain't it, Josephine?"

"You know who did this to us?" she asked.

"No, I don't, but it doesn't take a genius to know that this has Destiny written all over it."

"I'm going to kill that bitch. You just watch and see."

"I don't think you're going to want to do that either. If it was her, she sent me two copies of the DVD, remember—one for you, and one for me. So my guess is that she has copies for other people also. I suggest you get over it and get on with your life. I got to go, my sons don't want to sit in the car while I converse with a trifling whore like you. You got one week to be out of my house. . . . One week, Josephine, and that's all."

"Can I at least say good-bye to my sons?"

"Go ahead, and make it quick."

Josephine walked over to the passenger side of the car and opened the door. She looked at her sons, but they refused to acknowledge her. "Mommy's so sorry for what's happening. I didn't mean to hurt you two or your dad, but I promise that I am going to make things right between us again. I love you two."

Josephine reached into the car to touch Kyle, who was sitting in the front seat, and he leaned over to ward off her touch.

"Honey, please give me a hug. I promise to straighten things out. I promise."

"Dad, please let's go!" Kyle said to his father. Josephine moved away from the car. She didn't want to upset her sons and husband more than she already had. She watched as they drove away. She held her tears until she went back inside the house. She screamed, cried, kicked and fell on the floor, but that did not change the fact that her husband and kids were gone.

Josephine picked up the phone and dialed Michelle's number. She hoped Leon didn't answer the phone, because he might not call her to the phone. Luckily, Michelle answered. "Hello," she said, chewing on a piece of bubble gum.

"Michelle, this is Josephine."

"I know who you are. I got caller ID too."

"Michelle, somebody filmed that last party, and they sent Marcus two copies of it."

"What the fuck do you mean somebody filmed the last party? If Leon gets ahold of that crap, he'll kill my black ass," Michelle whispered into the phone.

"Who's that on the phone, Michelle?" Leon asked.

"Baby, it's Josephine."

"Oh yeah, I forgot to tell you that she called you last week while you were sleeping."

"I know. She told me when I got to work."

"Josephine, I don't care what you do or how

you do it, but you better keep my name out of that mess."

"What do you mean, Michelle? We're all in this together."

"Take it how you see it, Josephine. You started it, so you fix it. You know that if Leon finds out that I was doing what I did with those other people, he is going to kill me."

"Michelle, listen, I didn't call you to scare you. I just wanted you to know what is going down, and I want you to keep an eye out for Destiny."

"What makes you think she had anything to do with it?"

"I'm not sure if she did, but she called me about a week ago and mentioned something about the things that I do when Marcus isn't home."

"You're the one who wanted to invite other people into the group."

"What other people?"

"The guy that did the work on your basement."

"Oh no! What if it was him? Do you think they know Destiny?"

"Hell, I didn't know him. How am I supposed to know if he knows Destiny?"

"Marcus and the boys left."

"What do you mean they left?"

"They packed their suitcases and left."

"You let him take your boys?"

"I didn't have a choice. He threatened to expose me to the OPS."

"That's fucked up."

"That's not the fucked-up part. He told me to be out of the house in a week."

"How is he going to put you out of your own house?"

"It's his house, Michelle."

"And? Who gives a damn? Can't you get half of everything, and get custody of the boys?"

"Michelle, do you have a brain in that tall, skinny body of yours?"

"Do you have one in yours? I'm not the one in trouble here, you are," Michelle said; then she blew a big bubble and let it pop.

"Michelle, you obviously don't seem to think that there's a connection with you here. Marcus said that he'd expose you, me and everybody in the video."

"Michelle, get your ass off that phone and start dinner. You know how long it takes you to cook a meal," Leon said.

"OK."

"Michelle."

"What, Josephine?"

"Don't take this thing so lightly. We don't know who did this. I don't want you to get into trouble with Leon."

"OK, Josephine, but I got to go."

"Bye." Josephine hung the phone up and went to the kitchen to clear away the lunch that was still on the table.

Josephine wished that she could take back everything that had been going on for the past year. She hated that she ever met Parnell; he was the one who told her to turn to the same sex to get the satisfaction that she wasn't getting at home. She loved her husband, and what he did in bed. She just had an attraction to women, and Parnell was the one who told her to experiment, to see if she liked it. Josephine and Parnell quickly became very close friends. Josephine hoped that Marcus would take the time to calm down, and come to his senses, and come back home. She didn't know how she was going to stop Parnell from getting involved in this, unless Marcus filed for a divorce with a different firm. But knowing Marcus, if he was serious, he was going to file at the firm where Parnell worked to expose him.

Josephine wanted to warn Parnell, but Parnell hated discussing things at home around his wife and kids. Had she not allowed people into her home while her husband was gone, she wouldn't be going through the things that she was going through. She wanted to hurt everybody who had something to do with her husband finding out about her. She wished that she hadn't been in the kitchen singing, while the mail person was delivering that package to her husband. She wanted to die from humiliation. That video had important people on it, and she knew if it got into the wrong hands, some could lose their jobs. If she was sorry for anything in her life, she was sorry for messing with Destiny. She couldn't wait for tomorrow to try and stop things from becoming worse than what they were. She called William, even though he had told her to never call again.

"Hello, may I please speak to William?" she asked the woman who answered his phone.

"May I ask who's calling?"

"Josephine Riley."

"Hold on, I'll get him for you," she said.

William came to the phone. He was upset that Josephine had called. "Look, Josephine, if you're calling to ask about Destiny again, I have no way of getting in touch with her."

"William, this is a matter of life and death."

"Once again, I have no way of getting in touch with her, and I don't want to. So whatever it is that you need to talk to her about, you need to hire a private detective or run an ad in the local newspaper. She's an avid reader."

"William, please, this is a matter of life and death. Destiny is in a lot of trouble, and she needs my help," Josephine lied.

"Well, if she needs your help, I'm sure she'll be contacting you soon." William hung up his phone.

"Who was that, honey?"

"Destiny's therapist that I told you about."

"Why is she calling you?"

"She's looking for Destiny, but I keep telling her that I don't have any way of getting in touch with Destiny."

Josephine wanted to call Parnell, but she'd just have to wait until tomorrow. If his office got one of the videos, she knew that he would call her. She didn't have anything else to do, so she began to pack her things. She cried while she put her things into neat little piles. The ringing of her phone startled her. Josephine answered the phone, and the screaming voice on the other end made all the blood drain from her brain. She nearly fainted at the sound of Michelle screaming for her to help her. Leon snatched the phone from Michelle. "I knew your trifling ass was no good. You been fucking my woman, for how long now? That's the reason why that bitch loves you so damn much. That's the reason why she didn't mind working all night long with you. I knew no fucking shrink's office stay open that late at night. When I get through kicking her ass some more, you can come pick this bitch up," Leon snarled into the phone.

Josephine could hear Michelle begging him not to hit her anymore. Josephine dropped her phone, and fell to her knees, crying. "Please don't let anybody else have a copy of that video," she sobbed into the carpet. "Oh, what am I going to do if everybody else gets a copy of it?" Josephine was scared. She hung up the phone and it rang again. She looked at the caller ID. It was Marcus calling from his cell phone.

"I dropped a copy of that video off to your little friend Michelle's house a little while ago. Did you get a call from her?"

"Marcus, why? Leon is over there probably killing her."

"Do you think I give a damn? Is it bothering you that one of your many lovers is getting the crap beat out of her?"

"I thought that this was between you and me. You told me that if I didn't want any trouble, get out of your house, and give you a divorce and the kids, and I agreed to that. Why did you do that to her?"

"Do you remember all those nights you claimed that you and Michelle were at the office putting clients' files in order and working on new cases? Well, I put two and two together after watching the video in its entirety. I know why you and Michelle stayed at the office so late. You made a complete asshole out of me and other people. How many people have you deceived, Josephine?"

"Marcus," she cried into the phone. "I'm getting my things ready to pack as we speak. Please don't hurt anyone else with that video. I am sorry for all of the trouble that I've caused you, and if I could take it back, I promise you that I would give anything to do just that."

"Well, you can't!" he challenged into the phone. "You were so careless that you let my sons see that crap, and I've had to comfort them all got damn day long. They're afraid that everybody's going to know that their mother is gay. Do you know how much you've hurt them? Two innocent little boys, waiting for their mother to join them in Disney World, but no, she was too busy throwing a got damn gay orgy. How long have you been bisexual, Josephine?"

"I . . . I don't know, Marcus. It just happened."

"You're telling me that you just all of a sudden decided that you were going to be bisexual? If you knew that you would have rather been with a woman, you should have said so, instead of leading me to believe that you were just a cranky-ass bitch, who didn't want to be bothered with her own husband."

"Marcus, that's not what I'm saying. I—"

"I don't want to hear any more of your lies.

Do you think your mother and father would be happy to know that their daughter with all the degrees is an undercover bisexual, manipulating bitch?"

"Marcus, please don't do this to me."

"Don't do it to you? What about me and your sons? What about us, Josephine?"

"Marcus, I know you're hurting, and you're upset right now, but please don't do this to me. If it'll make things easier for you and the boys, I'll be out of the house by tomorrow, if you promise me that you won't give a copy of that video to anyone else," Josephine begged.

"Naw, you got one week, and I don't plan on giving a copy of it to anyone else. I didn't like the idea of talking to Michelle and having her lie to me."

"Marcus, baby, I'm so sorry for all of this, and I promise that I'll be out of your house, and I'll give you the divorce and full custody of the boys."

"If they want to see you, we'll make some type of arrangements for that. In the meantime, don't bother us."

Josephine rose early the next morning. Her eyelids were heavy from the lack of sleep. Her nerves were on edge, because she was afraid that another one of her friends was going to call her, screaming down the phone the way Michelle had.

When the phone did ring, the caller had blocked his or her number. Josephine was afraid to answer, but she had to, because it could be Michelle calling from a pay phone.

"Hello," Josephine's shaky voice said into the phone.

"How's things going so far, Mrs. Riley?" Destiny asked.

"Destiny, why are you doing this to me and my friends?" Josephine asked.

"Ah, have we humbled ourself? Is this real or what? Do you remember how you waltzed into William's house and ruined my life in that one single moment? As far as your friends go, I haven't decided on what to do with them."

"Destiny, I don't want to fight with you anymore. I want this thing to end here and now, please?"

"Please, my ass! You took away everything from me. Well, not everything—life does go on. You didn't think about how William would react to what you told him. Did you? To be perfectly honest with you, Josephine, I don't see why it bothered you so much that Marcus gave up a little of that good crap, because he doesn't possess what you want. So why did you get so damn mad, when you were eating fur berry pie?"

"Destiny, please. I have sacrificed a lot since Saturday. I don't think I can take much of this any longer."

"Then, bitch, kill yourself! I went through a whole fucking lot too! William threw me out! You tried to figure out how to fuck me on the side! You talked about my momma, even though I didn't give a damn. Now you want me to leave you alone? Beg, bitch! Do something spectacular for me to make me stop—otherwise, don't expect anything but more grief."

"Destiny, what do you want from me?"

"I want my life back! Can you give that back to me, Josephine? Can you?"

"Destiny, I may not be able to give you William back, but I am so sorry that I made him go away."

"Like I said, if you want this crap to stop, you need to do something spectacular to prove it."

"I don't know what you want from me, but if it's any consolation to you, I lost my husband, my children and my home."

"Hmm . . . let me see, does that make a difference to me? Hell the fuck no! Beg, bitch, or do something spectacular. See ya."

"Destiny, wait. . . . Destiny, Destiny." Josephine sighed. "How in the hell am I supposed to get in touch with her?"

Marcus dropped his sons off at school, then went to the law firm that Parnell worked in. When Parnell saw Marcus walk into the office, he almost jumped out of his skin. Marcus looked at Parnell and didn't see the man that Parnell thought he was; instead, he saw the man in the video moaning and groaning from another man pleasuring him.

"Good morning, Marcus," Parnell said, with his hand extended.

Marcus looked at Parnell's extended hand

and refused to touch it. "Good morning to you too," Marcus said.

Parnell was offended by Marcus's rudeness, but he didn't question him. "How's Josephine, and what are you doing here?"

Marcus thought that Parnell would have gotten the I-don't-want-to-be-bothered-with-you attitude when he didn't shake his hand, so Marcus became annoyed with him. "What's it to you? Don't you have better things to do, like attend parties without your wife?"

Parnell got the message then. He hurried out of Marcus's face, and to his office to call Josephine. He peeped through the door of his office in time to see Marcus meeting up with Romel.

Josephine recognized Parnell's office number. "Josephine, what in the hell is Marcus doing down here in my office?" Parnell whispered into the phone. "I spoke to him, and he was so rude to me. He asked me if I had any parties to attend without my wife. What did he mean by that, Josephine?"

"Parnell, you don't have anything to worry about. I would have called you yesterday, but you know how you are."

"Your husband just asked me a question that aroused my concern, and if you know something about that, you should have called me yesterday."

"I would have, Parnell, except you told me not to call you at your home on the weekend."

"Josephine, stop with the bull crap. Your husband is in this office. The lawyers in this office specialize in family practice you know, things like divorce. Did he find out about the party, Josephine? Because if he did, then that means that my family is in jeopardy."

"Yes."

"What the fuck did you just say?"

"Parnell, he knows about everything."

"How in the hell did that happen, Josephine? What does he know about me?"

"Somebody brought a camcorder to the party and filmed it."

"Josephine, please tell me that you are lying!"

"Parnell, there's no need for you to get all excited over this. This is between Marcus and me. He's not going to bring you up or anyone else that's in the video."

"How do you know that, Josephine? Hold on a minute." Parnell put the phone down. The secretary had tapped on his door and walked in. She handed him an envelope. It was addressed to him, but it didn't have a return address on it. "Thanks," he said to the secretary. "Can you close the door all the way for me?" Then he returned to his call. "Josephine."

"I'm here."

"That was the secretary. She brought in some mail for me," Parnell said as he tore the envelope open. He pulled out the pictures of himself with a man in an awkward position and he nearly fainted. He dropped the phone.

Josephine could hear him rustling with the phone, and she started to wonder if something was wrong. "Parnell . . . Parnell, are you still there?"

"Josephine, someone mailed me copies of pictures of me on that night. Wait, there's a letter attached. Hold on while I read it." Parnell read the note and started to sweat.

*Parnell,*
*One would have never guessed that you liked to toss salad, but from the looks of these pictures, they seem to tell a different story. How could a man as handsome as you, with a wife and kids, enjoy the forbidden? Do you think that it would be appropriate for you to keep this information from your pretty little wife? What would she think of her big, tall, handsome husband in such a compromising position with another man?*
*Your Friend*

Josephine waited patiently while Parnell read the letter. She could hear Parnell's breathing change from normal to rapid, and she knew that whatever was in that letter had upset him.

"Josephine, I thought you said that I didn't have anything to worry about."

"Parnell, I'm sorry. Let's just wait and see what happens."

"You're sorry? I got a wife and kids—not to mention my damn job to worry about if this crap gets out here."

"Parnell, Marcus is in that office because he's divorcing me. He took the kids, and he wants me out of the house in one week."

"OK, but what does that have to do with me? You're the one who allowed this crap to happen, and you better figure out how to stop it."

"Parnell, I don't think Marcus sent you those pictures."

"Well, who the hell sent them?"

Josephine said, "Destiny."

"I don't give a fuck who had something to do with it, but you . . . you better not let this crap reach my doorstep."

"Parnell, I promise you that I'm not going to let that happen."

"Who filmed it?"

"The construction workers."

"How do you know that?"

"It's a hunch. I better get off the phone so that I can call them, and, Parnell, I'm really sorry."

"I am too," Parnell said. He hung up the phone and interlocked his hands together. He didn't know what he would do if this thing got out in the open.


Josephine called Hakim, and just as she had predicted, Hakim told her that he had no knowledge of what she was talking about. She just hung up on him.

Then her phone rang, startling her. She didn't know why every time the phone rang, it scared her. She looked at the caller ID, but she didn't recognize the number. "Hello."

"Hello," the muffled voice said.

"Look, if this is a prank call, please stop it."

"Josephine, this is Michelle."

"Michelle, are you OK?"

"No, I'm not. I'm in the hospital."

"Which hospital, Michelle? I'm on my way."

"No . . . no, please don't come out here. Leon might hurt you too."

"Is he there?"

"No, he just left, but he said that he's coming back."

"Didn't you call the police on him?"

"Are you crazy? Do you know what he would do to me if I told the police that he did this to me?"

"Are you crazy, Michelle?"

"I'm not telling on my man. If I hadn't been doing that crap with y'all in the first place, I wouldn't be laying up in here with three broken ribs, two missing teeth and two black eyes."

"Michelle, you should have reported his ass to the police. I would have helped you in any way that I could."

"Josephine, you've done enough. Leon loves me. He wouldn't have done this to me if he didn't. He was just mad at me for what I did with you and those other women."

"Michelle, he doesn't love you if he has to put his hands on you. He could have just walked out on you or forgiven you if he loves you so much."

"You don't understand, Josephine. I love Leon."

"I do understand, but he didn't have a right to put you in the hospital. He could have killed you."

"But he didn't. He said that he was sorry for doing this to me, and that when I get out of the hospital, he's going to make it up to me."

"Michelle, you need to think about that.

What if he kills you the next time something happens?"

"He ain't gonna kill me, because he loves me, and there isn't going to be a next time."

"Michelle, girl, you better—"

"I got to go," Michelle whispered into the phone.

"Michelle, wait."

"I got to go, Josephine. I just heard Leon talking to the nurse. Bye."

Michelle hung up the phone just before Leon walked into the room. He had a small bouquet of flowers in his hand. Michelle smiled when he handed them to her.

"Damn."

"What, baby?" Michelle asked.

"Don't smile. You don't look so good with those two teeth missing. When they say they gon' fix that for you?"

"I got to go to the dentist when I get out of here tomorrow."

"I hope so," Leon said. "Did anybody come back in here trying to get you to change your story?"

"No, baby, and if they did, I was going to tell them what I told them when you brought me in."

"That's right, baby. You got robbed and jumped on. That's what you stick to. And baby?"

"What?"

"I promise that when you get out and go to the dentist, I'm going to make up for beating . . . I mean doing this to you. I love you, though."

"I love you too, pookie."

"OK, baby. I'm out of here. I'm gonna go home and clean that mess up that we made, and, baby, I'm gonna buy you a new glass table too."

"OK, pookie," Michelle said. She covered her mouth before she smiled this time.

Leon kissed her on the forehead, and then he left. "Stupid bitch. She better be glad that I didn't kill her ass, and I am not buying a got damn glass table. If the bitch hadn't been screwing around on me with another woman, I wouldn't have threw her ass through it," Leon mumbled under his breath. "If I ever catch Josephine's dyke ass, I'm fucking her up too. Turned my innocent woman into a got damn dyke, but I bet that bitch got her head straight now."

"Excuse me, did you say something?" a man waiting for the elevator with Leon asked.

"Hell naw, I wasn't talking to you," Leon snapped at the man.


Rosalee hadn't been feeling good, and going to work every day didn't make things any easier for her and Audrey. Rosalee hated that she hadn't told Destiny that she had a fifteen-year-old sister the last time she had seen her. Had she not let her pride get in the way, she and her daughter wouldn't be living from check to check, but Rosalee tried to make Audrey as happy as possible.

Audrey was her baby, she helped Rosalee

with the house chores, and she stayed by her mother's side when she didn't feel good. Rosalee had refused to go to a doctor to see why she had gotten sick all of a sudden. Audrey was concerned with her mother being sick one minute and fine the next. Rosalee kept telling Audrey that she couldn't afford to go to the hospital, because they didn't have the money. Audrey had to trust her mother's word when she told her that she was going to be all right.

Audrey came home from school one day and prepared dinner for herself and her mother like she usually did, and she completed her homework and house chores. By the time Rosalee would have been getting off work and on her way home, Audrey had set the table.

She reheated the food, then waited. An hour later, Audrey knew that something was very wrong. Her mother was never late coming home from work, and Audrey didn't know who to call or where to begin looking for her mother. Thirty minutes later, Audrey remembered that she could have called her mother's job. She could barely see the numbers on the phone from the tears that seemed to come, no matter how hard she tried to stop them. She waited for someone to answer the phone at the factory.

The phone rang several times before someone answered it. Audrey asked if her mother was going to be working overtime. The person on the other end of the phone placed her on hold, and when the next person came to the phone, he told her that her mother had to be rushed to the hospital earlier in the day and that he had called the number listed for emergencies, but that number had been disconnected. Audrey wrote down the address to the hospital and the directions that the person on the phone gave her. She went in the money that her mother had saved up for emergencies and took enough out for bus fare. Audrey arrived at the hospital an hour before visiting time was over. The front desk gave her a visitor's pass and the room number. Audrey didn't know why her mother was in the hospital. She rushed into her mother's room, and touched her mother's face. Rosalee opened her eyes slowly.

"Mom, what's wrong with you?"

Rosalee was too weak to talk just above a whisper. "Baby, the doctors don't know yet, but Momma's going to be all right," Rosalee whispered.

"Mom, when are you coming home?" Audrey asked.

"Honey, Mommy has some test that she needs to take."

"What kind of test?"

"I don't know right now, and as soon as I find out, I'll let you know."

"Mom."

Rosalee could barely open her eyes, but she tried hard to let her baby girl know that she was awake. She was just too weak to talk. She moved her head slightly up and down to let Audrey know that she heard her.

"Mom, I can see that you're too tired to talk, and visiting hours will be over in a little while.

I'm going to let you get some rest. I'll be OK, and I know to go straight home. I'll tell Ms. Jones that you are in the hospital, and, Momma, you know she'll keep an eye on me." Audrey leaned over her mother and kissed her on the cheek. "I love you." Audrey knew that her mother could hear her, because she could see a tear running down the side of her face. "Mom, don't cry. Ms. Jones will keep an eye on me. It's going to be OK." Audrey kissed her mother again and eased out of the room.

Audrey took the right buses home and went straight to Ms. Jones's apartment. Ms. Jones was the landlady, and she and Rosalee were very good friends. When Ms. Jones opened her door, Audrey fell right into her arms and cried.

"Chile, what's the matter with you?" Ms. Jones asked.

"Momma's in the hospital, and she told me to tell you so that you'll know to keep an eye on me," Audrey said. She hugged Ms. Jones tighter and cried harder.

"Chile, you know I don't mind, but you got to stop all that crying. What them doctors say wrong with her?"

"I don't know, and Momma couldn't really talk."

"Well, you go upstairs and get you some clothes for school tomorrow, and lock your momma's door, and come on back down here with me."

Audrey did as she was told.

"Ms. Jones, do you think my momma is going to be OK?"

"Honey, chile, your momma is a strong woman. She gon' be OK. Now go and get cleaned up. Audrey?"

"Ma'am?"

"Did you eat anything?"

"Yes, ma'am."

"All right. Now gon' in there and get cleaned up, and don't stay up too long. You got school in the morning."

"Yes, ma'am."

It was hard for Audrey to stay focused in school, and she barely ate her lunch. As soon as her last class was over, she ran the two blocks to her house. Ms. Jones was waiting on her so that they could go to the hospital and see her mother. Once they arrived at the hospital, the doctor thought that Ms. Jones was Rosalee's mother, and he gave her the bad news. Rosalee had uterine cancer, and because it hadn't been detected in time, it had spread to both ovaries. Rosalee had been to surgery. They had to remove her entire uterus and both ovaries. She had six months to live, if that long.

Ms. Jones took the bad news well, but she didn't know how to break it to Audrey. She didn't know what she was going to do with Audrey, but she did remember Rosalee mentioning something about an older daughter. She just had to wait until Rosalee was well enough to tell her how to get in touch with Destiny, just in case something happened to Rosalee.


Two days after Rosalee's surgery, she was feeling much better, and was able to talk more without getting tired. She explained to Audrey what Ms. Jones already knew, but she couldn't bring herself to tell her daughter that she had six months to live, if that long. Rosalee wanted to tell Audrey about Destiny, but she felt like now wasn't the right time. She needed to get in touch with Destiny first before she told Audrey, just in case Destiny didn't want to have anything to do with her. Looking at Audrey made Rosalee wish that she could have been a mother to Destiny. She felt guilty for letting her daughter down, and if she had six months left to live, she wanted to reconcile their relationship.

Rosalee thanked Ms. Jones for watching Audrey, and she promised to make it up to her when she got out of the hospital.

# 8

Hakim was finally taking Destiny to meet his sister. He had also invited Eric to come along, but Eric was swamped with homework. Destiny didn't know if she wanted to dress conservative or sexy. She called Eric one last time for his advice. "Boo, knock them off their feet, dress a little bit of both. Wear a sexy top and a conservative skirt, and wear some of those stiletto heels. They make those long legs of yours look outrageously beautiful." Destiny decided to wear a low-cut burgundy satin dress, which fit snugly around her waist and flared out at the bottom, and a pair of silk burgundy-colored sling-back stilettos. She went to the bathroom and made her face up.

She double-checked her hair to make sure that all of the hairpins were still in place. She picked up her matching purse, and went to Eric's to ask him if he liked the way she looked.

"You look good enough to eat," he said.

"You like?" she asked.

"No, baby. I love."

She kissed him playfully on the cheek and said, "I'm glad that you like the way that I look. Maybe you can help me out of this dress when I get back."

"I'd like that, so hurry back."

Destiny went back to her apartment in time to get Hakim's call telling her that he was waiting downstairs for her.

"Hey, you look really great," Hakim told Destiny as he held the truck door open for her to climb in.

"Thank you. You look great yourself."

"Thank you. I want you to enjoy yourself tonight. My sister and her friends have gatherings that I usually don't attend very often, and I thought this time would be perfect for you to meet her, and the rest of the gang."

"Hakim, are you taking me to a party?"

"Nooooo . . . well, it's a small one. Trust me, it's nothing really big. My sister and her friends have been getting together once a week forever. You'll enjoy yourself."

"You don't think I'm overdressed, do you?"

When Hakim and Destiny arrived at Jasmine's, she greeted Destiny and introduced her to everyone there.

"Destiny, this is Jayla." Jayla waved.

"You met my good friend? This is Karen."

"Hi," Karen said, "Nice to meet you."

"This is Stormy."

"Girl, you look fabulous. It's about time we finally get to meet you. Jasmine said that Hakim speaks highly of you."

"Thank you, and you look fabulous yourself."

"Where are Toya and Samantha?" Hakim asked.

"They're home fat and pregnant," Jasmine said.

"Sis, where's Troy?"

"He's out with the fellas. Remember, this is ladies' night."

"Then maybe I should meet up with him and leave Destiny here with you all, since I'm a man."

"You will do no such thing. You can party with the girls every once in a while," Stormy said.

"I guess."

Destiny felt relieved when Hakim decided to stay. She was already feeling uncomfortable meeting Jasmine and her friends for the first time.

"Excuse me for saying so, but y'all may think I'm crazy, and drunk, but Destiny and Jasmine look a lot alike. Is that a coincidence or what?" Stormy asked.

"Stormy, shut up, will you?" Jayla asked.

"Are you dating her because she looks so much like your sister?" Karen asked Hakim. "I mean, she does look like Jasmine."

"We're not dating. We're just friends," Hakim said.

"If I were a real man, I sure as hell would date her. Honey, you are beautiful, and we're going to have to share beauty secrets," Stormy said.

Destiny blushed at Stormy's comment. "I don't mind telling you my secrets, but you have to share yours with me too."

"Baby, that's not going to be a problem."

Stormy pulled one of his business cards out of his purse and handed it to her.

Destiny tore off a piece of an old receipt that she had in her purse, and wrote both her cell and home numbers on it and handed it to Stormy.

After a few more drinks, Hakim was helping Destiny climb into his truck. Once she was secured in the seat belt, he handed her the plate of food that Jasmine had fixed for her.

"I had a ball. I like your sister and her friends," Destiny said, slurring her words.

"They like you too."

"Hakim . . . is Stormy a man?"

"Didn't you pay him any attention, when he said, if he was a real one, he'd date you?"

"Oh yeah, he sure is pretty as hell," Destiny said.

"I can't be the judge of that, but he does make a pretty woman."

"Ooh, somebody got turned out at Josephine's party."

"There you go. Next time you want somebody to do your dirty work for you, call Stormy."

"OK . . . OK, I quit. I got something for you and your friends for doing that for me."

"Is that right? I forgot to tell you that Josephine called me a few days ago."

"She did? What did she want?"

"She asked me if I knew you, and if I would ask you to please stop, and she said that she doesn't want to fight with you anymore, and she's sorry for what she did."

"Oh, she did, huh?"

"Yeah. So what you got for us?"

Destiny took four envelopes from her purse and handed them to him. "Just a little thank-you for you and your friends."

"How sweet. So what is it?"

"Wait till you open yours and see."

"OK. Thanks again."

"You're welcome, and tell your friends that I said, I thank them too."

"I sure will. Now come on and let me help your drunk ass to your apartment."

"My ass isn't drunk, I am. And I'm not going to my apartment, I'm going to Eric's, so I can tell him all about your sister and her cool-ass friends."

"OK, I'll walk you to his door."

"Thank you, Hakim . . ."

"You're welcome, Destiny." Hakim walked her to Eric's door and waited for her while she fumbled with the keys.

"Crap, what am I thinking? This is Eric's apartment," she said, and knocked on the door.

Eric opened it.

"She's wasted," Hakim said.

"I can tell. I hope she enjoyed herself."

"She did, and guess what?"

"What?" Eric asked.

"My sister's friends think that she favors my sister. Maybe I better look into that."

"Thought I was playing, didn't y'all? I told you she looks just like you."

"Eric, Hakim, both of you is full of crap. I'm going to bed," Destiny said as she lay on Eric's sofa.

"Hey, man, take care of her. I'm tired. I got to go. Tell Destiny I'll call her in the morning."

Eric closed and locked his door. He walked over to where Destiny was lying, picked her up off the sofa and carried her to his bedroom. He undressed her and pulled the covers up over her; then he put the plate that she brought back with her in the fridge.

Eric climbed back in bed with Destiny, who had turned over on her side, and was still sound asleep. He rose up on one arm and watched her as she slept. He kissed her softly on the mouth, and continued to admire how beautiful she was. Eric knew that he was falling in love with Destiny, and he wondered if she was falling for him too. He wished that she hadn't come back drunk, because he wanted to make love to her tonight. For the past couple of days, he had been too busy with homework, so they hadn't spent a lot of time together. He looked down at her and hoped that one day she'd give up the whole let's-be-friends thing.

Eric lay back on his pillow and pulled Destiny close to him. The warmth of her body aroused him, and as much as he tried to resist her, he couldn't. Eric turned her on her back and climbed on top of her. He entered her and made love to her.

Destiny woke up with a slight headache. She eased out of bed to keep from waking Eric. She found her purse and hurried to the bathroom, and took out a thin packet that contained her birth control patch. She had taken it with her last night, because she had forgotten to put it on after she got out of the shower, and she was having so much fun at Jasmine's, it slipped her mind to put it on again. She went to the kitchen and made herself a bowl of milk and cereal. After she finished the cereal, she went to the bathroom and brushed her teeth. She felt a trickle of moistness on her thighs. She wiped, and she realized that Eric had been there.

She rushed back to his bedroom and jumped on the bed, causing him to wake up. "You took advantage of me while I slept last night, didn't you, Eric?"

"Baby, I tried so hard to resist you, but you looked so damn good in and out of that dress that you had on, I couldn't help myself. The raging dickster took control of my body and he made me take you."

Destiny smiled and said, "The dickster? Who in the hell is the dickster, Eric?"

"Him," Eric said, pointing to the bulge underneath the bedcovers.

"Slay the dragon first, and come back so I can meet the dickster."

Eric jumped out of the bed and playfully said, "Watch out, world, here comes the dragon slayer. Keep that thing warm," he said, pointing to the space between her thighs. "The dickster doesn't like it cold, he likes it hot."

"Go brush your teeth, goofy," Destiny said.

Eric went to the bathroom and grabbed his toothbrush and toothpaste. He noticed the plastic wrapper in the trash bin. He picked it up and read the writing on it. Eric's heart sank. He had been irresponsible last night when he made love to her without using a condom. He realized that he could have gotten her pregnant, and he wasn't ready for a baby.

"What's taking you so long?" Destiny hollered out from the bedroom. "You wet the nookie last night, now you're taking your time to come play in it?"

"I'm coming, baby," Eric said. He dropped the wrapper back in the trash bin and hurried to the bathroom. He realized that he had just gotten a reality check, and now he needed to be more careful about the way he did things. "What did you just say?" he asked Destiny.

"I said you wet the nookie last night, and it's ready for you to play with it now."

"How did you know what I did last night?" Eric asked.

"I was wet this morning when I woke up, and you better be glad that I remembered to put my patch on this morning. Next time you sneak some nookie, you just might fertilize an egg."

"I thought about that this morning when I went to the bathroom. I saw your empty wrapper in the trashcan and it scared the crap out of me."

"Well, next time you better make sure that the nookie is protected before you go sneaking off into it."

"You're not mad at me for that?" Eric asked.

"No, baby, but I will be if you don't wet it some more."

"Here comes the dickster." Eric leaped on Destiny and kissed her playfully on the mouth. Eric knew that he had fallen in love with Destiny; he was just waiting for her to admit that she was in love with him too.

Derrick had thought long and hard about looking for Rosalee, and finding out who his child was. He had a lot of regrets now. He found himself thinking about Destiny a lot because she reminded him so much of his Rosalee. At one point he thought that she could possibly be his daughter, because she didn't just look like Rosalee, but she looked a lot like his own two children as well. He thought about the day that Destiny had brought lunch to him and Hakim's crewmen. One of his own crewmen had asked him if Destiny was his daughter, and he had said no. The crewman told him that he was lying, because she looked a lot like him, and Derrick told him that Destiny was his son's friend. The crewman laughed and said, "You better check that out before he gets too serious about her." Thinking back on that day made Derrick want to look for Rosalee even more.

He finally got into his car and drove to where he knew she had last resided, and a neighbor gave him a different address. The neighbor told him that Rosalee only came around on occasion before her parents had passed away, but she was almost sure that he could find her at the address that she had

given him. Derrick got back into his car and
drove to the address that the old neighbor had
given him, and for a minute he sat outside the
building, wondering if he should go on or give
up. He walked up to the building and looked
for her name on the doorbell. She lived on the
second floor, according to her bell. He rang
the bell, but got no answer. He tried again, and
still he got no answer. Ms. Jones heard the bell
ringing and she peeped out the window.

"Can I help you?" she asked.

"Yes, ma'am. I'm looking for Rosalee Symone."

"She's not available. May I ask who you are?"
Ms. Jones asked, because she was afraid that he
had come to take Audrey away.

"Yes, ma'am. I'm an old friend of hers," Derrick said.

Ms. Jones thought that maybe he had heard
about her being sick and in the hospital, so she
told him which hospital Rosalee was in. She
gave him her room number. When he arrived at
the hospital, Rosalee was asleep. She looked a
lot older than he would have recalled her to be.

He didn't want to wake her, so he sat in the
recliner beside her bed. He watched her sleep,
and he could see the same features in her that
he had seen in Destiny. Derrick felt the same
feeling that he had when he first saw Destiny.
Rosalee finally opened her eyes after an hour.
When she saw Derrick's face—even though
the medication that she was on had her drowsy
all the time and blurred her vision—she knew
that she was looking at Derrick.

"I didn't think that I would ever see you again, and not under these circumstances. How did you find me here?" Rosalee asked.

"I wouldn't have bothered you under these circumstances, but I have a lot on my mind, and I went to your parents' house. A neighbor told me that both your parents passed, and . . . well, I'm sorry to hear that. She gave me your current address."

"So what made you look me up now?"

"I know it's been a long time, Rosalee, and I could have found you a long time ago, but there are things in my life that I thought I'd put behind me, but I guess it's time to face them," Derrick said.

"But why now, after over thirty years, Derrick?" Rosalee asked.

"I don't . . . Guilt maybe."

"What have you got to feel guilty about? You walked out on me and your daughter before I gave birth to her. Now you're feeling guilty and you want to make it up to her, or are you feeling sorry for me, because I have six months or less to live?"

"Rosalee, look, I'm sorry about that, and no, this don't have anything to do with what's going on with you. You said my daughter?"

"Yes, your daughter. The one that you abandoned before you ever gave her a chance."

"I was married, Rosalee, and scared as hell."

"You think I wasn't scared? You think it was easy to tell my parents that I had gotten myself pregnant by a married man, and have them constantly criticizing you? I couldn't take the fact that you left me while I was pregnant, Derrick, and I did the same thing that you did. I abandoned our daughter too."

"Rosalee, I didn't believe that the child was mine after you started seeing another man."

"I was already pregnant, Derrick. I was three months pregnant when I met him. I had just found out myself when I told you. Had you not been so selfish, things wouldn't have ended the way that they had."

"If you had only trusted me, Rosalee, things would have been different."

"So I was supposed to sit at home alone and wait on you to get away from your wife and two kids whenever you could? I was lonely, Derrick. I wanted someone to sleep next to every night, just like you had someone to go home to every night. I wanted to wake up next to the man that I had fallen in love with, and that was next to impossible, because you were married," Rosalee said, choking on her words. She coughed hard, and it took her a while to catch her breath back.

"Rosalee, I know that you're angry with me for walking out on you, and hell, I'm angry with myself. I didn't know how to accept you being with another man, and I know that I had a wife at home, but I didn't feel the same way about her that I did you."

"Speaking about your wife, where is she now?"

"We divorced a long time ago."

"So what made you come looking for me now?" she asked Derrick.

"You said you had a girl, right?"

"Yes. I had daughter."

"Where is she now?"

"I don't know. We don't talk, but I do plan on making up to her before I leave this world," Rosalee said.

"What happened between the two of you?"

"I told you that when you left, I abandoned her too. She doesn't want to have anything to do with me."

"I'm sorry that the both of us were real stupid and abandoned our daughter, but I don't think it's too late to make up to her," Derrick said.

"I hope not, Derrick. I waited until I found out that I'm terminally sick, to want to have a relationship with my own daughter."

"Rosalee, we all make mistakes. I sure made one when I left you alone with our daughter. I feel bad about this, because I don't even know my own daughter's name."

"I was just thinking that. We're sitting here talking about her and yet you've never met her, nor do you know her name."

"So what's her name?"

"Destiny."

Derrick almost fell out of the recliner. "You're kidding me?"

"No."

"Rosalee, I am so ashamed. My son met this girl—well, she's a woman—and her name is Destiny. She brought us lunch one day at the work site, and I couldn't help notice that she looked so much like you. At first, I thought that she just looked like you, but then I looked at her standing side by side with Hakim and I had the strangest feeling that she was your . . .

I mean our daughter. I told my son later that night about you, and I should have just asked Destiny when I had the chance to, who her mother was, but I didn't know how to."

"You're telling me that my daughter is dating her own brother?"

"No . . . no, they're not dating."

"That's good to know. So how do you think you're going to break the news to her?"

"I was just thinking that maybe we could get together and tell her. When are you getting out of the hospital?"

"In another week, I hope, but I don't think we should do this together. It may be too much for her to handle. I think one at a time would be better. I also have something else to tell her, along with trying to get the two of us back together."

"What's that, if you don't mind me asking?"

"I have another daughter. She's fifteen, and her name is Audrey."

"Wow. Destiny doesn't know that she has a sister?"

"No, and I can't give you or anyone else a reason why I didn't tell her about her sister," Rosalee said, with tears in her eyes.

"I wasn't there for Destiny, Rosalee, but I promise that if Audrey needs me, I'll be there for her."

"But she's not your daughter."

"That's obvious, Rosalee. All that I didn't do for Destiny, I can do for Audrey."

"Thank you, Derrick." Rosalee cried.

"Rosalee, what's wrong with you?"

"I have cancer, and the doctor said that I only have six months to live, but they don't know me like that. I'm a fighter, and I refuse to die in six months. My daughters need me," Rosalee said, crying harder.

"It's going to be OK, Rosalee."

"I hope so, Derrick. I am not ready to die just yet."

"Rosalee, you OK?"

"I'm OK. I just hurt so badly. The pain is unbearable at times, but the nurse should be in here in a minute to give me something for it."

"Then if you're all right, I'm going to leave now."

"Derrick, take care, and it was nice seeing you after all this time."

"I promise not to stay away for so long."

"That's nice, but it may be too late."

"I wish you wouldn't talk like that."

"I wish that I didn't have to."

"Well, I'll see you soon. This is my business card with my home, cell, work and pager numbers on it. Use them if you need me or anything."

Rosalee was glad that Derrick had found her, and deep down inside she knew that the family reunion wasn't going to be that long for her, because she had six months or less to live. She pushed the call button for the nurse to come and give her some morphine for the pain that she was in, so she'd fall asleep.

When Audrey got to the hospital to visit her mother, Rosalee was awake, but she was slightly sluggish from the morphine. Audrey sat in the recliner, and could smell the faint scent of a man's cologne. "Mom, you had a visitor today?" she asked.

"Yes, baby. Momma had a visit from an old friend. We talked about a lot of old things," Rosalee said. Her words were a little sluggish, but she was determined to tell Audrey about Destiny.

"Old things like what, Momma?"

"Like when he and I dated. I got pregnant."

"Momma, my daddy came back?"

"No, sweetie. Your father didn't come here today."

"You said that you two talked about when you dated and you got pregnant. That's with me, right?"

"Audrey, sweetie, Momma has something to tell you, and I don't want you to be angry with Momma."

"OK, Momma."

"Audrey, you have an older sister. Her name is Destiny. She and I didn't get along, so I didn't tell you about her, and I never told her about you."

"Momma, I can't get angry with you for not telling me that, but why now?"

"I can't hold things back from you and expect you to understand them as they happen. Honey, I chose to tell you now, because Momma may not be here much longer."

"Don't say that, Momma."

"I don't want things to be the way that they

are, but, honey, we don't have control over things like life and death."

"But it's not fair."

"I know, baby. It's what you do with the time that you have on this earth that makes the difference in your life."

Audrey tried really hard not to cry in front of her mother, and Rosalee didn't expect her not to. When Audrey did cry, Rosalee made her get in the small bed beside her. They wept together.

"Momma, when can I meet Destiny, and how old is she?"

"You can meet her real soon, and she's twenty-seven."

"Twenty-seven. Momma, she may not want to be bothered with me. She's grown."

"You just leave that up to me, honey."

"Momma, things are going to be OK," Audrey said to her mother.

Rosalee had held on to consciousness for as long as she could. The pain medication that she was on had finally taken its toll, and before she closed her eyes, she said, "Sweetie, I know . . . I know."

Audrey kissed her mother, then went home. Ms. Jones was waiting at the door for her. "How's your mother feeling today, baby?"

"Momma told me that I have a big sister, and that she won't be here too long. She said that she wants me to meet her, and I don't mind except she's grown. Momma should have told me this a long time ago. Ms. Jones,

I'm mad at Momma, but I don't want that to make her go away."

"Hush, baby. Your momma gon' be OK, and so is you and your sister."

"Momma must be carrying a lot of guilt around with her, Ms. Jones. She don't need to. I promise that I won't be mad with her anymore. I just want her to come home."

"I know, sweetie and she will."

"That's what I told Momma," Audrey said.

"Now, chile, you go on in the bathroom and clean yourself up, and go in the kitchen and eat before the food gets cold."

"Yes, ma'am."


Rosalee finally woke up from her drug-induced sleep. It was late, but she needed to talk with Derrick.

"Hello, Derrick."

"Hello, Rosalee."

"I really don't know how to approach Destiny, and I'm so afraid that she'll reject me, and I don't want that to happen again. I know that this is a lot for you to handle, but do you think you could kind of talk to her, and tell her that I am very sorry for what I did to her, and ask her to please come visit me?"

"I'll do that for you."

Derrick didn't want to wait until tomorrow to tell Hakim what he had found out. He called his son, but got no answer. An hour later, Derrick's phone rang. It was Hakim.

"Dad, you called?"

"Yes."

"What's up?"

"I found Rosalee."

"That's good to hear. So how was it?"

"She's not doing so well. In fact, she's in the hospital."

"What's wrong with her?"

"She has cancer, and six months to live."

"Damn . . . oops, excuse me, dad."

"You're a grown man. Um . . . what I'm about to tell you may change how you feel about me."

"How's that? You've already explained to me who Rosalee was to you, and that the two of you have a child together, and now you just told me that she's dying from cancer. What could you tell me that could possibly change the way I feel about you, Pops?"

"Well, son, I guess you're right. Say, can I ask you a few questions before I tell you what this call is for?"

"Sure, Dad."

"Have you ever slept with Destiny?"

"No, Dad. I kissed her once, but there was no chemistry."

"Why did you stay friends with her?"

"Because I like her."

"Hakim, what if I told you that Destiny is your sister?"

"What if you did? What are you expecting me to do?"

"Nothing."

"So you're saying that she is?"

"Yes."

"Man, get out of here. Where did you get that from?"

"I told you that I finally met up with Rosalee. We talked and she told me that she had a daughter, and that her name was Destiny. I was shocked at the news, but more so, because I knew who she was talking about."

"So what are you going to do? Whew . . . I'm sure glad I didn't sleep with her," Hakim said.

"So am I. If you had, it would have been all my fault. So you think Jasmine will be OK with learning that Destiny is her sister?"

"Dad, come on, you know how Jasmine is, but she'll get used to it. You know."

"Hakim, you sure you're OK with this?"

"Dad, I can't change your past, and I already love her like she's my little sister. Say, guess what she did for me and my crew?"

"What?"

"She's sending us to Jamaica."

"She is?"

"Yep."

"That was nice of her, but what did you do to get such a nice gift?"

"I went to a party for her."

"Oh, that must have been some party?"

"You don't want to know."

"Probably don't. Hakim?"

"Yeah, Dad."

"There's one more thing that I have to tell you, and then I'll let you go."

"What's that, Dad?"

"Rosalee has another daughter. She's fifteen, and I promised Rosalee that since I wasn't in

Destiny's life, I'll be there for her other daughter if something happens."

"Man, you learned a lot in one day."

"You can say that again. I want to make it up to Destiny, but it seems like she's a headstrong young lady. I am going to talk to her, and if she decides that she doesn't want anything to do with me, I'll have to deal with that. Had I not been so selfish, things wouldn't be the way that they are now."

"Dad."

"Yeah, Hakim."

"Is Rosalee's other daughter, your daughter too?"

"No. As a matter of fact, I didn't ask her who the father was."

"So how do you know that she's not your daughter?"

"Hakim, have you been listening to anything that I've told you? I can't be her father too, because I left Rosalee when she was pregnant with Destiny."

"Oh yeah, that's right. Sorry. Dad?"

"What's up?"

"I got a plan."

"Here comes trouble."

"No, Dad. I think this is a good way to get things out in the open. Just give me a few days to set something up before you talk to Destiny."

"I guess I don't have a choice. I was going to ask you for her number."

"Sure, but give me a few days to set something up, and we'll all get to meet one another as family. I bet you that I won't be wrong. A family reunion always brings families together."

"All right, Hakim, I'll give you a couple of days to pull this thing off, but what about Rosalee? She'll still be in the hospital in a couple of days."

"Who knows? We just may get lucky and she'll be released. If not, we'll take the reunion to her."

"Hakim?"

"Yeah, Dad."

"Thank you."

"You're welcome."

"Talk to you in a few days, then," Derrick said to his son.

"All right, and, Dad, thanks for trusting me to handle this. Talk to you later."

Josephine had finally moved all of her belongings out of Marcus's house. She hadn't seen or heard from Marcus or her sons in a week. She'd been served with the divorce papers two days before, and she decided that she wouldn't protest it, because she didn't want to hurt anyone else. She had been to the hospital to visit Michelle. Michelle's battered face and body made Josephine feel sorry for her.

Josephine hated Destiny, but she saw no way to get even with her, without hurting more people. She hated Leon just as much, and she decided to pay him a visit when he got off work.

She returned to the small two-bedroom apartment that Parnell let her rent in one of his rental properties. She hadn't had a chance to buy much to go in the small apartment, except a bedroom suite and a few other things. Josephine couldn't believe that she had gone from living in a big beautiful home to a small two-bedroom apartment. The apartment was decorated nicely, but she missed her home, husband and kids.

When she finished cleaning and unpacking, she went to see Leon. Once she got to the apartment where he and Michelle lived, something within her told her to turn around and go home, but she couldn't. She rang the doorbell and Leon buzzed her up without asking. Josephine walked the two flights up and knocked on the door. Leon said, "Come in, man, it's open."

"I'm not a man," Josephine said.

"I was expecting a friend of mine, not you, but you sure was fucking my woman like you are a man."

"I didn't come here to argue with you," Josephine said. She didn't pay any attention to the malice in Leon's eyes as he walked over to the door and locked it.

"I don't know why you would have the got damn nerve to come over here at all. You've been sleeping with my woman, who, I'm sure by now you know, is in the hospital—thanks to you."

"That's why I'm here. You didn't have to do that to her, and you need to turn yourself in."

"Or what, bitch? You came here to take me down to the police station?"

"No. I came here to convince you to do the right thing."

"Was it right for you to have sexual relations with my woman? Y'all bitches weren't paying me to let y'all carry on like that."

"You talking like we are some hoes or something. You don't own Michelle."

"Let me guess, because the bitch gave you some pussy, do you?"

"I just came here to tell you that what you did to her was wrong, and you need to be locked the fuck up for it." Josephine turned to walk out of the apartment, but she turned around and said, "And you need to clean this nasty-ass apartment up before your bruised and battered woman, whom you could care less about, gets out of the hospital." She turned to walk out the door again, but before she could open it, Leon pounced on her. He grabbed her around the neck.

"Bitch, I'm waiting on Michelle to get out to clean up this mess. That's what she was here for in the first place," Leon said, holding her tight around the neck as he dragged her to the bedroom.

"What are you doing? You better let me go!" Josephine screamed out.

Leon slapped her hard, and that made Josephine grab the side of her face, where he had hit her. "That's the same thing that Michelle should have said to your trifling ass, but she didn't. Now shut the fuck up and don't say a word if you want to live." Leon went to answer the knock at the door. Whoever it was,

Josephine heard Leon tell him that they'd get together later, because he had some business to take care of.

"I don't know what you think you're doing. But I'm not Michelle, motherfucker. I will call the police," Josephine cried out.

Leon ignored her, and ripped off her clothes.

"Stop!" Josephine screamed.

"Did Michelle tell you to stop?" he asked, and then he slapped her again and undid his pants.

"What do you think you're doing? Stop!" Josephine screamed.

Leon wasn't trying to hear her. He stood behind her and pushed her on her knees, then entered her. Josephine screamed from the pain that seemed to split her back in two. "You like it like this, bitch?" Leon asked as he ripped into her anus. "You wanna be a man? Why you crying like a bitch?"

"Please . . . please . . . please stop this. You're hurting me," Josephine said in gasps.

Leon ignored her, tearing into her deeper, harder and faster. Just before he released his semen, he felt her go limp. He came and let her limp body fall to the floor. He kicked her in the side as he walked by her. He went to the bathroom and cleaned himself up. After that, he went to the kitchen and got himself a beer, then went to the living room and turned on the television. He waited for Josephine to regain consciousness. By the time he'd finished his third beer, he heard her stirring in the room.

Leon got up from the sofa and went to where she was. She was trying to put her ripped clothes back on, but she froze in her tracks when she looked up and saw Leon. "Please, I don't want any more trouble. I just want to get out of here."

"I don't want anymore either, and that's any more of you either." He walked over to the dresser and took out a pair of Michelle's jogging pants and a T-shirt. He handed them to her. "Here, put this on, and Josephine?"

She didn't look at him when she answered.

"Don't even think about telling anybody about what just happened here today. Michelle brings her work home, and I got everybody's address that's in that video, not to mention the little stories I've heard Parnell make up about his senior partner, Romel, or isn't he the boss at that law firm?"

The first thing Josephine had planned on doing was to go to the police and make out a report on Leon for rape. When Leon mentioned spreading the mess that she was in around, she quickly forgot all about the police. She put the jogging pants and T-shirt on in a hurry, snatched up her torn and ripped clothes and walked out of the apartment as quickly, and painfully, as she could. She opened her car door with the keyless remote, climbed in and never looked back. She locked her doors and started her car. She had been in such a hurry to get away from Michelle and Leon's building that she hadn't noticed the pain that she now felt.

Josephine drove as safely and quickly as she could to her new apartment. She rushed into it and stripped off the clothes that Leon had given her to put on. She went to the bathroom and drew herself a hot bath. She slid to the bathroom floor on her knees and cried. She waited for the tub to fill up and stepped into it. She rinsed the dried blood from the back of her legs and inner thighs. She poured half the bottle of body wash on her towel and scrubbed her body until her skin burned. After she finished bathing, she went to bed.

Marcus had moved back into his house one week after Josephine had moved all of her things out. It hurt him deeply that things had come to this, because he loved Josephine, but he couldn't forgive her for what she had done—and with whom she'd done it. Marcus had calmed down a lot since he'd last seen Josephine, and he wanted to know that she was all right. He called her cell phone.

Josephine answered as soon as she saw his number. "Hello."

"I just called to let you know that I'm going to make some kind of visiting arrangements between you and the boys as soon as possible."

"I would like that. I miss my babies, Marcus, and I know that there is nothing on this earth that I can do to take back what I did, but I do want you and the boys to know that I am very sorry."

"Thank you" was all Marcus could bring himself to say. He had thought that if he heard her voice, he would find some kind of compassion and allow her to at least come back home to be with the boys. Hearing her voice again, and hearing her say how sorry she was, only made

Marcus remember how much of a deceptive person she was.

"I know it's late, but can I at least talk to the boys?" Josephine asked.

"I'm sorry, but they've already gone to bed."

"Since there's no school tomorrow, do you think it would be OK if I stopped by the house to see the boys?"

"Let me talk to them first, and maybe we can arrange a mutual place to set up a meeting."

"Marcus, why are you treating me like this?"

"Why did you treat me the way that you were treating me?"

"I—I . . . Marcus, please, we don't have to do this."

"I didn't do anything to you, you did it to yourself. I have to go." Marcus took the phone away from his ear and gently placed it in its cradle.

"Marcus . . . Marcus," Josephine screamed into the phone. "Why are you doing this to me?" She redialed their home number several times, but Marcus ignored the calls.

After she finally got tired of Marcus not answering her calls, Josephine got dressed and drove to their home. She rang the doorbell, beat on the door; and screamed out for Marcus to let her come back home. Marcus ignored her; then he called the police. When they arrived at the house, Marcus had her taken away for trespassing on private property. As the police dragged her away, Josephine screamed out all kinds of obscenities at Marcus. "You son of a bitch. If you were a real man, none of this crap would be happening. You dirty mother-fucker, you will get yours. . . . You will get yours. You just wait and see!"

"Ma'am, you're going to hit your head if you don't bend down to get in the car," one of the responding officers said.

"I don't need to ride in a got damn police car. I can drive my own got damn car back to wherever you're taking me. Now take these handcuffs off me, and I'll leave."

"Sorry, ma'am, I can't do that, and I can't let you take the vehicle."

"What do you mean, you can't let me take the vehicle? It's my damn car."

"Well, ma'am, your husband just showed my partner proof that the vehicle is in his name, and he doesn't want you to take it."

"Oh, I don't believe this crap. Marcus, you're not right. You no-good bastard."

"Ma'am, I'm going to have to ask you one more time to get in the car, before I put you in it."

The police made her get off the property and told her that if Marcus called them back because she had returned, they were going to arrest her. They gave her the option to leave by squad car or on her own two feet.

"I can't believe that he is doing this to me," Josephine said to one of the officers.

"He just wants you off his property, ma'am. I suggest you go home, and not back there. Otherwise, you're going to end up in jail. Have

a nice night," the officer said as he watched
her walk down the street.

Hakim had a hard, yet easy, task to do. He
had to get two families together, and Destiny
was the link. He'd been up all night trying to
come up with a plan. He decided that he'd give
a dinner at his house and introduce Destiny
into the family, but first he needed to get her
back together with her mom, because Derrick
had said that Rosalee was very ill. He planned
to do that by having a family barbecue at his
house. Hakim even thought that it would be
good for his own mother and her friend to
come. Hakim called his dad and got Rosalee's
information at the hospital. Then he called
Destiny. She had just come in from Eric's, and
he told her that he had something important
for her to do, and he'd pick her up by three.
Then he called Rosalee's extension at the hospital and introduced himself to her. He told
her about his plans to bring Destiny out there
to see her, and Rosalee didn't know what to
think of that, but she was glad that he was
giving it a try.

As planned, Hakim picked up Destiny and
drove her to the hospital. Surprised by where
Hakim had brought her, she asked whether
Hakim was playing a joke on her. Hakim answered no, and told her that he wanted her to
meet someone. When Hakim got the passes, he
took Destiny to her mother's room. He tapped
lightly on the door before entering. Destiny

gasped when she saw her mother's worn face; all the anger and resentment that she had been feeling all these years went away. Rosalee was asleep. Destiny turned to Hakim, who wrapped her in the comfort of his arms. He held her tight, and said, "Destiny, it's about time you face your mother. I know that this is hard, but things shouldn't be the way that they are."

Sobbing, Destiny asked, "How did you know about my mother?"

"I kind of want your mother to explain that to you."

"Hakim, how could you do this to me?"

"Destiny, let go of any anger that you have, because your mother needs you very much."

"I knew that one day this time would come, but I didn't know that it would be like this."

"Now that it has, there's nothing that you can do about your mom's illness, but you two can salvage what's left and make the best of it."

Destiny walked over to where her mother lay. She was still a beautiful woman, but her face looked worn. Destiny gently grasped her mother's face and held it in her hands, like a mother would do to a daughter. "Mom . . . Mom, wake up."

Rosalee's eyes opened slowly, and when they focused on the person in front of her, they filled with tears. "I know I'm not dreaming, because I feel your hands on my face," Rosalee said in a whisper.

"No, Mom, you're not dreaming. I'm here, and I'm . . ." Destiny choked up on her own tears.

Rosalee reached out and pulled her daughter to her bosom. "I'm so sorry for the way that I walked out of your life, baby."

"Mom, it's OK."

"Mmm . . . mmm." Hakim cleared his throat.

"Oh, Mom, this is Hakim, a very close friend of mine. And, Hakim, this is my mother, Rosalee."

"We've met over the phone. I'm glad that you brought my daughter out here to see me."

"It was nothing, ma'am," Hakim said.

"How about you call me Rosalee?"

"I will."

"Destiny, there's a lot of things that I need to tell you, and I hope that I have enough strength to stay awake to get it all out."

"Destiny, I'm going to go back to the house so that you and your mother can talk. Call me when you're ready for me to pick you up," Hakim told Destiny before he got up to leave.

"OK, and Hakim?"

"Yeah."

"Thanks again for doing this for me."

"It was nothing. I'll see you in a little while."

Destiny pushed the chair close to the side of her mother's bed. "Let me begin with how sorry I am for taking so long to come to my senses. I've always wanted a relationship with you, Mom, but I was angry, and I'm sorry for that."

"Baby, you don't owe me any apologies. I'm the one who should be apologizing. I don't know why I got so scared of having a child alone. I was very much in love with your father, who, by the way, is a wonderful man. He, too, is sorry that he wasn't there for you."

"Mom, you're talking like you've recently talked with my father."

"I did. Destiny, your father came here and we talked. At first, I didn't know why he'd come, but when he began to talk, I realized why."

"Why did he come, Mom?"

"He came, because he said when he first saw you, you reminded him so much of me, and it scared him. He was afraid to ask you any questions, and he decided to find me for answers."

"Who is he, Mom?" Destiny asked.

"Your father's name is Derrick."

Destiny's eyes bucked wide. "Mom . . . you talking about Hakim's dad, Derrick?"

"Yes, honey. I hope you're not angry with me for keeping that from you. I had forgotten all about his two children."

Destiny smiled. Now she knew why Eric always said that they looked like sister and brother, and why she and Hakim weren't physically attracted to one another. "I'm not angry. I've given up all the negative emotions."

"Well, there's more to the story," Rosalee said.

"OK."

"You have another sister."

"I know. I met her already. Hakim took me to meet her, but he didn't mention any of this."

"I don't think he knew at the time that you were his sister, and I'm not talking about Jasmine. You have a sister named Audrey."

"Mom . . . I wish you would have told me this a long time ago."

"So do I. I hate that it had to come to this for me to reconcile with you, but—"

"It's OK, Mom. I told you that I want to know everything, and I want to get everything out in the open before I leave here today. I want to know why you're here."

"I have cancer. I wasn't going for regular checkups, and this is the result of me neglecting my health. The doctors said that I have six months to live, but I don't believe them."

"Mom, does Audrey know that you're this sick? Does she know about me?"

"Yes, and I told her all about you too."

"Where is she now?"

"She's with a neighbor."

"Do you think I can meet her today?" Destiny asked.

"If that's what you want."

"Yes, it is."

"I'll call Ms. Jones and have her send Audrey here."

"How's she getting here?"

"She knows how to take the bus."

"No. Tell her to take a cab."

"OK." Rosalee called Audrey at Ms. Jones's house and told her to take a cab to the hospital right away. Audrey got scared and asked her mother if everything was all right. Rosalee assured her that it was, and she told her that she had a surprise for her. When Audrey got to the hospital, she knew right away who Destiny was.

She stood there and faced an older version of herself.

"Come over here, I don't bite," Destiny said, with her arms outstretched.

Audrey walked over to Destiny, and into her arms. Destiny hugged her as if she had known her all her life. "You're very pretty," she told Audrey.

"So are you," Audrey said shyly. "I've thought about you, and what you'd look like. I'm glad to meet you."

"I'm glad to meet you too. I hope that we can spend some time together to get to know each other better."

"I'd like that."

Destiny, Audrey and their mother talked for hours, until the visiting session was over. They took a cab back to Destiny's place.


Audrey went home with Destiny that night. Destiny called Eric over to meet Audrey. He told her that he'd be over as soon as he finished up an assignment from school that he was doing.

"I like your apartment," Audrey told Destiny.

"Thank you. Are you hungry?"

"Not really. Ms. Jones just made dinner."

"Well, how about dessert?"

"I'd like that."

Once Eric had completed his school assignment he went straight over to Destiny's place.

"Fine, when my friend Eric comes, we'll

go out for ice cream. Hey, that must be him at the door."

"Hi. Boy, you sure do look a lot like your sister."

"Thank you," Audrey said, smiling.

"Eric, this is Audrey, my own little sister. Audrey, this is Eric, my very best friend in the whole wide world."

"Didn't she just sound like a little girl?" Eric playfully asked Audrey.

Audrey just smiled and shook her head.

"You don't have to be shy around us, Audrey. I want you to be comfortable and feel free to ask as many questions that you want answers to."

"I'm all right, Destiny. I'm just a little overwhelmed at finding out that I really do have a big sister."

"And another one, and a brother," Eric added.

"Eric, shut up. She just met Hakim, and just today I found out that he's my brother too."

"I knew. I kept telling you that the two of you were related."

"Shut up, and let's take Audrey out for ice cream."

"Audrey, did she tell you that she's very bossy?"

"No."

"I thought you were about to say that you can tell. I thought you were on my side?"

"She's my sister. I got to help her."

"Now see that's what I'm talking about. Now, Eric, shut up."

Eric walked over to Destiny and pulled her into his arms. He kissed her on the forehead, saying, "I'm very proud of you. You're growing."

Destiny squeezed Eric tight. "Only because I have you."

Eric wiped a tear from her face and said, "Let's go."

The three of them ordered their desserts, then sat at a booth and talked while they ate. Destiny fell in love with Audrey.

"I got an idea."

"Destiny, when you get an idea, it usually means trouble."

"Come on, Eric, every idea that I come up with isn't always bad."

"OK. What is it?"

"Audrey, how would you like to go shopping tomorrow?"

"I—I . . . I guess."

"Audrey . . . just say yes, because it hurts her feelings when she wants to do something for you, and you don't accept."

"Eric, you always got something to say."

"Tell me it's not true, then."

"Whatever."

"See, I told you. Her feelings are hurt now."

"They are not."

"OK. I'd love to go shopping."

"Good. Shopping it is. You can have whatever you want. I don't care."

"Destiny, don't spoil her or I'll get jealous," Eric said, joking.

"You sure you two aren't in love?" Audrey observed.

"Hey, watch it. We're very close friends," Eric said, but his heart said that they were very much in love.

The way Destiny looked at Eric, when he said that they were just close friends, made Eric believe that she was just as much in love with him as he was with her. It was just a matter of time before she faced the truth.

"Well, if everybody's all done here, we can go to the house and watch some movies. Audrey, do you want to do that?" Destiny asked.

"I don't care what we do."

"Good, movies it is then. Eric, you got popcorn at home?"

"No. You popped the last pack."

"OK, then we'll just have to go get some."

When they got back from the store, the three of them cuddled up on Eric's sofa and watched movies until Audrey could no longer keep her eyes open. Destiny walked her back to her apartment and put her to bed. Then she went back to Eric's. They embraced for a long time, and then he kissed her passionately on the mouth, before walking her back to her apartment. "I'll see you in the morning," he said, then turned and walked back to his place.

Destiny climbed into the bed, next to Audrey, and watched her sister as she slept. She looked so peaceful, sleeping. Destiny soon found herself overwhelmed with so much emotion, she began to cry. She got out of bed, went into the living room and called Eric. She needed to talk to him. She needed a shoulder to lean on. She and Eric talked well into the night about the possibility of Destiny taking full custody of Audrey if something happened to Rosalee. First, though, she needed to discuss that with Rosalee and Audrey. Before they ended their conversation, Eric told Destiny that everything was going to be all right. Destiny told Eric that she hoped so. Eric blew a kiss through the phone, saying, "It will. Just be patient."

"I am. I miss you."

"I miss you too. Go to bed and get some sleep."

"OK. Talk to you tomorrow." Destiny hung up the phone reluctantly.

Destiny didn't remember feeling sleepy or falling asleep, but she was a little tired from not being able to go to sleep. *Eric must be down here,* she thought, because she smelled breakfast cooking. She looked over to the other side of the bed, and Audrey was not there. Destiny slid out of the bed and went to the kitchen. "Ooh, that smells so good."

"We know," Eric said. He was on the other side of the fridge, looking in the cabinet for the maple syrup.

"What are you two doing?" Destiny asked.

"Making you some breakfast," Audrey said.

"No, we're making *us* breakfast," Eric said. "Just sit at the table, and we'll do the rest, but first go and brush your teeth."

"Eric, shut up," Destiny said, turning and walking out of the kitchen and to the bathroom, where she washed her face and brushed her teeth.

"Hurry up, slowpoke, didn't you say that you wanted to go shopping today?"

"Eric, be patient," Destiny said while she brushed her teeth.

"Yeah, I said that to you last night, copycat."

After Destiny finished brushing her teeth, she went back to the kitchen and joined Audrey and Eric at the table for breakfast.

After breakfast they headed out for shopping. "Are we taking your car or mine?" Eric asked.

"I like your truck better, and, Eric, I need to talk to you about my car."

"Oh boy, that sounds like trouble," Eric said.

"It's not, but we'll talk about it later," Destiny said.

The three of them climbed into Eric's truck. He drove them to the mall.

"What's this place?" Audrey asked.

"It's a shopping mall," Destiny answered.

"I've never been to this mall before," Audrey said, looking around.

"Well, let's go inside. I want you to shop till you drop," Destiny said; then she looped one arm in Audrey's and the other in Eric's.

"Any particular store you want to go in?" Destiny asked Audrey after a moment.

"I don't know," Audrey said.

"Let's try this one," Destiny said, pointing to one of the stores that she shopped in a lot.

"OK, girl, start shopping," Destiny said.

"I don't know what to get."

"Well, I can see that you're going to be shy, so I'll help you out," Destiny told Audrey.

"I'm going to look around while you two shop," Eric said.

"We'll find you, and I promise that we won't be long," Destiny offered.

"Yeah, whatever," Eric replied, laughing and leaving.

"I know that we're just meeting one another, honey, but when Destiny does something for a person, she goes all out. So there's no limit to what you can have today. OK, honey?"

"OK," Audrey said, picking out several outfits and accessories to match.

"Come on, let's pay for this stuff and put it in the car, and let's do some summer shopping, since it's just around the corner."

Audrey followed her sister to the checkout counter. Destiny and Audrey took the bags and walked out of the store, over to where Eric was waiting.

"Destiny, thank you," Audrey said sincerely.

"Baby sis . . . you don't have to thank me for anything. Crap . . . oops, I didn't mean to curse, but, Eric, can we go and get Momma something?"

"I don't care, and I'll even go with you this time."

Destiny smiled at him and wrapped her arm around his waist. They bought Rosalee the prettiest gowns and robes that the store had, and then they picked out a pair of house shoes.

"Momma's going to really like those things. They are so pretty," Audrey said.

"So are you," Destiny replied.

"Destiny, are we going to see Momma now?"

"Yes, but first we better drop your things off at home."

"I got something for you too," Audrey told Destiny. When they made it back to Rosalee's apartment, Audry went to her room and came back with a picture of her and Rosalee in a frame. "This is for you."

"Thank you. It's beautiful."

"Maybe one day you, me and Momma could go and take some pictures together."

"Oh, I'd love to," Destiny said.


Eric went up with Audrey and Destiny to visit Rosalee. She was weak, but she enjoyed their company. Rosalee liked Eric a lot. She could sense that what he felt for Destiny was more than just friendship, and she sensed the same from Destiny.

Destiny and Audrey kissed their mother and left.

"Aren't you glad that you listened to me?"

"Yes."


Audrey hugged and kissed Destiny and Eric on the cheek before she went into her house.

"I'm proud of you and your family getting together, and I'm very proud of you for forgiving your mother," Eric said.

"Thank—"

Eric put his finger on Destiny's mouth to silence her. "You don't have to thank me for that." Then he leaned across the seat and kissed her.

"It's a habit."

"Lose it. It's a bad one."

# 9

Destiny picked Audrey up from school, just as she had promised to do. First they went to visit Rosalee at the hospital, but she wasn't feeling well. So they went back to Rosalee's apartment, and she and Audrey cleaned the house and threw out a lot of things that Destiny planned to replace for them. She called Hakim and Eric to come help with the bigger things that were too heavy for them to carry. After they finished cleaning the place, Destiny and Audrey went shopping for new things.

"Did y'all go see ya' momma today?" Ms. Jones asked.

"Yes, ma'am, but she was too tired, so we didn't stay very long."

"Is she getting any better?"

"She said that she is, but she's tired a lot from the pain medication."

"Does she know that y'all done threw all of her things away?"

"Kind of. Destiny asked her yesterday if it was

OK if she redecorated the apartment before she came home."

"She's coming home?"

"The doctor said she should be getting out by the end of the week."

"That would be good, but I'm going to miss having you down here with me."

"I can always come down and keep you company," Audrey said.

"I sure would like that, but it seems like I'm going to be up there with you and your momma so that I can make sure she takes her medication right."

Destiny picked Audrey up from school again, and they went to visit Rosalee, who was feeling a lot better than she was yesterday. The doctor had put her on a lower dosage of the pain medication that she had been on, and now she seemed to have more strength.

Destiny and Audrey were leaving just as Rosalee's doctor was coming in to talk with her.

"Hello, Ms. Symone. How are you today?"

"I'm feeling better than I was yesterday."

"I think that's because the dosage of pain medication you were on was too high. So how's the pain?"

"It's better, but I wish it would go away."

"I wish that I could make it go away for you, but, unfortunately, I can't. I tried to get here earlier to tell you about your test results, but I got pulled into a meeting."

"Were they good or bad?"

"I hate it when I'm asked that question, especially when I have to bring some news to a patient."

"It's not good, is it?"

"I'm afraid not. The cancer has spread throughout your body, that's why you're having so much pain."

"Oh."

"Rosalee, do you mind me asking you if you had regular pap smears?"

"I don't mind, and no, I didn't. I wish that I had now, because I know now how important they are. What if the cancer goes into remission?"

"I certainly hope that it does, but if it doesn't, Rosalee, the best thing for you to do is to change your eating and living habits, take your medications and start the radiation treatments."

"Am I still going to be released on Friday?"

"Yes. You'll be out of here soon. The next three days are going to come by quickly, and you'll be out of here."

"I hope so. I'd rather be at home dying than here in the hospital."

"I am so sorry that I didn't have better news to tell you."

"Thanks, Doc. . . ."

"You're welcome. I'll see you on Friday to discharge you."


For the last couple of days, Hakim had been planning his surprise dinner, and once he got it together, he went to the grocery store to purchase the items on his list. He was picking through the steaks for the best ones to purchase, when someone tapped him on the shoulder. He turned around, and he didn't know what to say to her, but he could tell from the expression on her face that she was very angry.

"Hi, Hakim."

"Hi, Candice."

"I haven't heard from you since you fucked me, and I wonder why?"

"I told you what I was about when you met me."

"Is that right? You didn't seem like that when you were eating this," Candice said, pointing to her crotch.

"I'm sorry, but that must have been one of the other guys that you picked up. I don't eat crap that I didn't cook or order from a restaurant."

Candice looked a little puzzled. She was sure that Hakim had been there, but maybe it was the guy the week after him. So she played it off and said, "That's not the issue here. The issue is, you fucked me and stopped talking to me. You haven't answered any of my phone calls, text messages or voice mails. Why?"

"Obviously, if I didn't answer any of your calls, I must have been busy, or perhaps I'm not interested anymore."

"You're a cold son of a bitch, but you won't be after this baby is born and I take your ass to court for child support. Ooh, don't look so interested now." Candice laughed. "I'll see your black ass in court, Daddy."

"Yeah, well, that's the one thing I'm not going to worry about. I didn't strap it up for nothing. I'll see you in court whenever you're ready, and oh yeah, don't forget to bring your real baby's daddy. I am not the one."

"Fuck you, Hakim. You are my baby's daddy and we'll see about that crap in, ooh, seven months."

"You got my address and phone number. I'm not hiding from you, and I'll be glad to go in front of a judge, if it'll make you feel better, but if I were you, I'd save myself the embarrassment."

"I got you."

"Well, I had you, and you're nothing to brag about."

"Like I said, I got your bitch ass."

"Damn, she made me forget my wine . . . ugly ass."

Hakim carried the bags into the house and put away the food. He called Destiny, Jasmine and their father and invited them all over for dinner on Friday. He asked Destiny to bring her mother and sister so they could meet Jasmine also.

Michelle had been home for several days, and already Leon was treating her like she was dirt. Michelle wished a million times over that she had told the police the truth. Leon fussed at her almost every day about not having a job and being able to help support them. She hated it when he fussed, so she went out looking for a new job. He had started to drink heavier, and he drank almost every day. His verbal abuse toward her had gotten worse, and eventually he started hitting her for the smallest things. He slapped her when she made white rice, and he'd asked her for chicken- flavored rice. He hit her another time because she made grape Kool-Aid, and he had wanted cherry Kool-Aid.

Michelle was too afraid to tell anyone about the abuse she was experiencing. She snuck and called Josephine, but she had to hang up quickly, because Leon had come out of the bathroom sooner than she had expected.

"Did you make my lunch for work tonight?"

"I had to make you some tuna, because we don't have any more of that sliced turkey meat."

"You waited until the last got damn minute to tell me that we ain't got no damn meat for a sandwich?"

"I forgot, Leon," Michelle said, backing up from Leon.

"You know damn well, I ain't taking no funky-ass tuna to work with me."

"Leon, I made what we had."

"And that just had to be some funky-ass crap that smells like your ass sometimes."

"Leon, baby, I could fry you some chicken right quick."

"I ain't got the time to wait on you to thaw out no got damn chicken," Leon said; then he rushed her. He grabbed her by the hair and pulled her close to him. He let her hair go and slapped her so hard that she fell to the floor. "All you had to do was tell me that we didn't have anything else to make a damn sandwich with."

Michelle stayed on the floor, holding her face. "I won't do it again, Leon. I promise."

"If your trifling ass had a damn job, I could afford to buy me a lunch, but naw, you here laying around like the lazy bitch that you are."

"Leon, I went out today looking for a job, and I called a lot of the numbers in the paper. I should be getting a call from one of them real soon, baby."

Michelle got up after Leon walked away from where she was. "Fucking bastard. I hate him," she mumbled under her breath. She didn't know where she was going, but she knew that she wasn't staying there with him for too long, acting as his punching bag. She went to the bathroom to see if her face was bruised. She had a handprint where he had slapped her. She bit down on her bottom lip until she drew blood. She stood in front of the mirror and cried.

"I got to leave out of here in two hours. Get your ass in there and thaw me out some of that chicken to take to work for lunch."

Michelle went to the kitchen and took out a pack of chicken wings and thawed them. She cooked Leon half the pack so that he wouldn't have any excuses to hit her again. Leon left for work.

During his lunch break he noticed that there weren't any condiments to put on the chicken. He became very upset and called home to tell Michelle to remember how he liked to eat his chicken. Michelle apologized as many times as she could before he got off the phone. Leon ate the chicken and bread. He drank the Kool-Aid, which she'd made for him, and decided that she had made the wrong flavor. He got upset with her for that.

When he came in from work the next morning, Michelle was still asleep. He checked the microwave to make sure that she had made him some breakfast, but he was still upset about the condiments and the Kool-Aid. He reheated his breakfast and ate. He went to the fridge for some Kool-Aid, and there wasn't any more. He was furious. He looked around the kitchen and saw the Kool-Aid pitcher sitting in the dish rack. He stormed out of the kitchen, to the bedroom; he dragged Michelle out of the bed by her hair. Michelle didn't know what was going on, and before she could catch a glimpse of Leon, she prayed for her life.

"You forgot to put something in there for me to put on that dry-ass chicken," Leon said, holding a handful of her hair in his fist.

"Baby, that chicken wasn't dry. Leon, I just forgot to put catsup and hot sauce in your bag. That's all."

"You made me cherry Kool-Aid, and I wanted grape."

"Leon, you just got upset, because I made grape Kool-Aid and you wanted cherry."

"Did I ask you any mothafuckin' thing?"

"No . . . but—"

"But my ass," Leon said before he slapped her in the face.

Michelle screamed for him to let her go, but

he wouldn't. She tried to protect herself, but he kept hitting, punching and kicking her, until she didn't move anymore. She lay on the floor unconscious.

"Michelle . . . Michelle . . ." Leon said her name, but Michelle didn't move. "You can play dead, all you want to. You wouldn't be down there if you didn't fuck up everything. Stupid-ass wannabe dike. Get the fuck up before I kick you some more." Michelle still didn't move. Leon got down on the floor and roughly turned her over. There was blood coming from her mouth and nose. He shook her, but she didn't move. He noticed that she had a lump on the back of her head when he turned her over. Leon got up and knocked down a picture on the wall, broke a lamp and turned the furniture over in the living room. Then he went to the bedroom and pulled the drawers out of the dresser; next he threw the contents all over the room, then called the police. They sent an ambulance over for Michelle. The ambulance took her back to the hospital, while the police listened to the story that Leon had to tell.

They asked Leon how he had gotten the scratches on his face and arms. He told the police that he had gotten the scratches at work. When they asked where he worked, he said at a scrap metal yard. When they asked if he had done that to Michelle, he told the police that he found Michelle lying on the floor, unconscious, when he came in from work. The police wrote everything down, but they didn't believe

Leon's story. They were going to see if the neighbors had seen or heard anything. One neighbor told them that it was impossible for an intruder to come into the building, because a visitor had to be buzzed in.

Another told them that they often heard Leon fussing with Michelle a lot lately. When asked if it was easy to get into the building, the neighbor said the same thing that the other neighbor had said. Leon had tried to make it look like someone had come into the apartment and robbed and beat Michelle. The police told Leon that they'd get in touch with him in a few days. They had to go to the hospital to see if Michelle could tell them what had happened to her.

Leon locked the door and quickly went to his car. He drove to the hospital to see what Michelle was going to tell the police. When he got there, he had to wait for the police to leave her room. He asked the nurse in the emergency unit if Michelle was conscious, and the nurse told him that she was. She asked Leon to go to the waiting area, and someone would come and get him when the police left. Leon went to the waiting area, as the nurse had instructed. After thirty minutes the two officers that had come out to their apartment came to the waiting area to get Leon. Leon thought that they were coming to tell him that he could go and visit with Michelle; instead, they place him under arrest for assault and battery.

Leon tried to get the police to take him to see Michelle, because she had the story wrong.

He tried to convince them that he wasn't the one who did that to Michelle, but the police had a written statement from Michelle, telling them everything that Leon had done to her. She admitted that he had jumped her before and had put her in the hospital. Leon insisted that he found her lying on the floor, bleeding, when he came in from work. He begged them to just let him go and see her, and she'd tell the truth.

Leon saw Josephine coming in the door and he cursed her and called her all kinds of names. He told her that it was her fault that Michelle was in that hospital bed all busted up. Josephine ignored him and told him that she was going to press charges against him now for what he had done to her. He screamed out to her that she didn't have any evidence. She told him to think again. She really didn't have any evidence, but she thought that he would be too scared to bother her to find out. Josephine rushed to the emergency department to see what he had done to Michelle this time. She cried when she saw Michelle all bandaged up; and Michelle's face was so swollen, Josephine barely recognized her.

"Michelle, I hope you told the truth this time."

"I did, Josephine."

Josephine listened to Michelle, but she sounded different when she talked. It sounded like she whistled with each word that came out of her mouth. "Why do you sound funny?" Josephine asked Michelle.

"That bastard knocked all my got damn teeth out. He's going to pay for doing this to me."

"Did you tell the police about the last time?"

"Hell yeah, I did."

"Where are you going to stay?"

"Hell, I don't know."

"I got an extra room, if you want to stay with me."

"I don't mind, as long as I don't have to go back to him."

"Are they going to admit you?"

"I won't know until my X-rays come back, and I hope not—because I need to go to the dentist and get my mouth fixed. I'm getting it fixed with the money the bastard keeps under the mattress."

"You want me to take you back over there to get your things?"

"Hell yeah. The police said he might be in there until tomorrow afternoon, if they give his ass an I bond. If not, somebody got to bond him out."

Michelle's X-rays came back, and the doctor told her that she was lucky, because nothing was broken this time, but her gums were busted up pretty good. Michelle was released, and Josephine drove her back to the apartment. She didn't have her keys to get in, and she had to get the maintenance man to let her in. She took all the money that Leon had under the mattress, and she packed all her clothes in garbage bags. She and Josephine took them down and put them in Josephine's trunk.

By the time she made it back up the stairs, the phone was ringing. It was Leon calling collect to ask her to forgive him again. He promised that if she didn't press any charges, he'd make it up to her. He told her to take the money under the mattress to his sister so that she could bond him out—he needed bond money. Michelle told him that when he saw that money again, it would be in her mouth. She needed to get her teeth, which he knocked out, replaced. Leon threatened to jump her again if she spent his money, but Michelle told him that she wasn't going to worry about that. She told him to check his background while he was in there, and remember what the last judge had told him about hitting on women. She finished packing the things that she wanted, locked his door and left.

She took his money, which had been under the mattress, out of her purse and counted it.

"How much is it?" Josephine asked.

"It's thirty-five hundred dollars," Michelle answered.

"Where in the hell did he get that money from?"

"There's no telling," Michelle answered. "Does my face look real bad?"

"Yeah."

"My cell's ringing." Michelle dug her cell phone from her pocket. "Hello."

"My brother wants me to pick that money up that's under the mattress so I can bond him out."

"Is that right, Shanequa?" Michelle asked.

"Yeah, he told me to call you so I can come get it."

"Tell your brother that whatever is left after I go to a dentist in the morning and get my teeth—which he broke and knocked out—fixed and replaced, then he can have what's left. Tell him I already discussed this."

"I'm not telling him crap, and I'm coming over there to get his money," Shanequa said angrily.

"OK, my keys are under the mat in front of the door, and since you want to be a smart-ass, tell your brother I don't think there's going to be crap left. And you, don't call my phone again!" Michelle pushed the end button and stuck the phone back in her pocket.

"That was his sister asking for the money that you took?"

"Hell yeah."

"Michelle, my apartment isn't all that big, but it's nice. Parnell let me rent it out. He said I can stay or find something bigger if I want."

"You don't think Marcus is going to let you come back home?"

"No. He already filed for a divorce and is trying to find a mutual place for me to visit the boys."

"Damn, that's cold. All of this time I been sitting in this car, and I'm just not recognizing that it's not yours. Whose is it, and where's yours?" Michelle asked.

"Marcus took it away from me, and this is mine."

"Get the hell out of here!"

"No, he took it."

"Josephine, don't tell me that you were making all that money, and you put it in the bank account with Marcus?"

"I'm not that stupid. I got some money saved up. I plan on continuing working as a therapist. I just have to find a place to rent an office in."

"Why don't you go back to the old place?"

"It's already rented out."

"Damn, they don't waste time, do they?"

"Nope, but I'm OK."

"Marcus shouldn't do you like he's doing you. I know he's mad and all, but you two are married."

"Soon we'll be divorced."

"Can't you ask for certain things if you want to?"

"Sure I can, if I want to start a lot of trouble for more of my friends."

"Oh yeah, that's right. I forgot he threatened to tell on everybody."

"He's a hot mess."

"You got something up your sleeve?"

"No, Michelle."

"Do you think it would be wise for you to let me come stay with you?"

"That's my apartment, and whoever I want to come live in it with me is my business."

"I just asked."

"I know, but I'm not going to allow Marcus to dictate my entire life to me," Josephine said; then she burst out laughing.

"I hope Leon's ass is miserable in jail, and I

hope they bust his buttie wide open when he go to the pen," Michelle said, laughing.

Josephine stopped laughing and started to cry abruptly.

"What's wrong with you?" Michelle asked.

Josephine pulled her car in front of her apartment building, and she cried harder.

"Crap, did I say something wrong? Why are you crying?"

"Michelle, if I tell you what happened to me, you have to promise not to tell, because—"

"Because what, Josephine?"

"I . . . What I have to tell you may make you angry."

"Josephine, just tell me what the fuck you broke down crying for?"

"Michelle, I went to your apartment the first time that you were in the hospital, to confront Leon. He invited me in and he started to talk mean to me. When I told him that he shouldn't have done that to you, he ripped my clothes off and raped me anally."

"Josephine . . . Josephine, I'm not mad at you for that. I don't want his ass back. It's obvious that you didn't call the police, because he would have been in jail, but please tell me that you got some proof? I want his ass to be put away for a very long time."

"Michelle, I told you that I didn't want to get anybody else in trouble over that video. He threatened to send it to other people if I told on him."

"I hate that this crap is happening to us. We left that damn video at his place."

"He's not going to be able to give it to anyone else—if he doesn't get out of jail."

"Right. He hasn't got any bond money, and I bet you he's not thinking about that video. Will you take me back there tomorrow to get it?"

"Sure I will."

"Josephine, his ass is going to pay for that crap he did to you, and I'm going to make sure of that."

"How will you do that, Michelle?"

"Leon got a record for domestic violence. The judge told that bastard that if one person presses charges against him, he was going to jail for a very long time."

"Are you going to press charges against him?"

"You think I ain't? He shouldn't have done that to you." Michelle broke down crying herself. She was so mad at Leon for doing what he did to Josephine. "I have to go back."

"Back where, Michelle?"

"Back to my place."

"You're mad at me?"

"No . . . no, I'm not mad at you, Josephine. I got to go back, because if he calls collect again, I need to be there to answer the phone."

"For what, Michelle? You are mad with me for telling you that."

"Josephine, please, I'm not mad at you for that. The reason that I . . . You know what?"

"What?"

"Let's get the hell out of this car first and go in the house; then I'll tell you what I was getting ready to say."

Josephine helped Michelle take her things

up to Josephine's apartment. She was so curious over what Michelle had to say, Josephine tripped up the stairs twice, trying to hurry up and get her things in the house. Once they got everything out of the car, Josephine said, "OK, that's it. Tell me why the hell you wanted to go back there."

"I don't have to go back there. I can forward all of the calls from our phone to your phone. You do have a house phone, don't you?"

"Yes."

Michelle forwarded her phone calls to Josephine's number. "Just watch and wait. His dumb-ass family is probably going to call too, but you know that they can't get your number from doing that?"

"No, I didn't."

As soon as they finished putting her things away in the closet, and fixing the extra covers that Josephine had on the floor for Michelle to sleep on, the phone rang.

"Wait, before you answer that. Look at the caller ID," Michelle cautioned Josephine.

"I don't recognize the number."

Michelle ran over to the phone. "It's him. Get your small tape recorder."

Josephine had to remember if she brought the thing with her, and then she remembered putting it in the kitchen drawer. She ran to the kitchen and got it for Michelle.

Michelle accepted the collect call from Leon.

"Michelle, where you been? My sister came to get the money for me. I don't have a bond, but I go to court in the morning. They said that I might get a low enough bond to be bonded out. I left thirty-five hundred dollars under the mattress. Give it to her, and where you been?"

"Maybe if you had taken a breath, and let me talk, I could have told you where I been."

"Well, start telling me, and, baby, I'm sorry for hitting you. If it's some money left if I get bonded out, I'm taking my baby out. OK?"

"OK, Leon. I was angry with you, so I called Josephine to come take me home."

"Did she try to touch you, baby?"

"Naw, she didn't try to touch me, baby, but that bitch told me that you raped her in the butt. Did you do that, baby?"

"Why you asking me a question like that, baby?"

"Because if you did, I hope you did it to punish her for what we did, like you punished me."

"Baby, you know that I love you, right?"

"Yes."

"You ain't trying to trick your man, are you?"

"Leon, baby, what I did was wrong, and you had every right to kick my ass. I love you, boo, and I'm by your side, no matter what. Did you rape that ass, baby?"

"Why you asking me something like that? You ain't gon' do nothing but get mad at me, and leave me in this hellhole."

"No, I am not. I miss my man, and, boo, if I could get your ass out tonight, I would. I can't let my man go to prison. I ain't gon' let that happen. Fuck that."

"You mean that, baby?"

"You damn right I mean it," Michelle said, pretending she was crying.

"Baby, why you crying?"

"Because I miss you. I'm coming to get my man in the morning."

"You coming for real, baby?"

Michelle pretended to be crying louder when she said, "Hell yeah."

"OK, baby, I'll tell you what happened."

Michelle pushed the record button down on the tape recorder so she could record his confession. "Tell me what all you did to her, baby."

"She came over here, thinking she could tell me that what the fuck I did to you was wrong. I tried to ignore her, but she kept telling me to turn myself in. I told that bitch that I was sorry. I got mad, baby, and I hit that bitch and knocked her to her knees. I wasn't going to rape her, baby, but I had to punish her for doing what she did to you, so I ripped her clothes off and I tried to rip her ass open, baby."

"OK, baby. Leon?"

"What, baby?"

"Thanks for your confession. I recorded all of it, and, Leon, you're a fucking pervert. It's your turn to be punished."

"My sister's gon' kick your ass. I'm calling them right now, and I want my got damn money."

"You don't have any. Like I told you before, I want my mouth fixed. Bye, Leon."

"You better not hang up the—"

Michelle hung up the phone.

"He's mad, isn't he?" Josephine asked.

"Yes, he is. Let's call the police, Josephine, and get this over with."

"Michelle, what if they say I made him do that to me?"

"Come on, Josephine, you're a licensed psychologist. Why are you asking dumb questions?"

"I don't know. Let's call them and get it over."

The police wanted to take the taped confession, so Josephine and Michelle said that they would come down to the police station and give them a copy of the tape they had just recorded.

# 10

Hakim called one of his favorite restaurants and made reservations for nine people. Trying to prepare the dinner himself had become frustrating. After Hakim got off the phone with the restaurant, he called Jasmine and invited her and Troy out for dinner. Then he called Destiny and asked her to bring her mother, Audrey and the nice little old lady who babysits her sister to the restaurant on Saturday. Finally he called his dad. He had a call on his other line, so he let his father go.

"Hello," Hakim said when he clicked over to the other line.

"I called to apologize to you for acting the way that I did when I saw you in the store the other day."

"Candice, you didn't have to call me for that. You said what you had to say, and I heard you. If I am the father of your baby—which I doubt seriously—I will step up to the plate." Hakim had met Candice about a year ago. When he found out that she had lied about not having any kids—not that it would have mattered to him—he added her to the "three *F*" rules and never saw her again.

"I am positive that you are the father of this baby. I don't know about the rest of the kids that you claim, or don't claim, but you are this baby's father."

"That's the reason why they have DNA tests. When the baby is born, I want you to contact me and let me know. I don't have a problem with taking the test to prove that your child is *not* mine."

"Like I said, you are the father of this one."

"If that's what you've called me for, I got the message. In the meantime I would appreciate it if you wouldn't call my phone again—until you give birth to your child."

"*Our* child, and since this is your baby, I need things, like maternity clothes and extra money to buy other things that I may need throughout this pregnancy."

"Do I look like a fool to you?"

"You look like Hakim."

"I'm glad that you noticed, because I don't see myself giving you crap. I said, have your fucking baby, and call me when you do. Until then, do not call me. Thank you, and good-bye." Hakim hung up his phone while Candice was still on the line.

"I know that two-timing, trifling son-of-a-nothing didn't hang up the phone on me? Bastard. I can't wait to have this baby, and I'm going to take his ass for all he's worth."

* * *

Today was Rosalee's discharge day, and she was excited about going home. Destiny and Audrey had picked her up, and once the three of them made it to the house, Ms. Jones was waiting there to surprise her. She and Destiny had come up with the idea to give her a "welcome home" party. Audrey made the banner that read: WELCOME HOME MOM! WE MISSED YOU. Rosalee noticed that she had new furniture in the apartment.

"Is this the same apartment?"

"Yes, it is," Audrey said.

"It looks so different. Thank you, Destiny. And Ms. Jones?"

"Yes."

"I bet you had something to do with this, didn't you?" Rosalee asked.

"Yes. And stop calling me Ms. Jones. Call me Corrine, after all this time."

"I was just being respectful."

Destiny smiled and said, "Let's eat some of the food that *Corrine* made before it gets cold."

"You cooked?" Rosalee asked.

"Yes, I did. You can't have a party without food."

"Well, then, let's eat. I'm hungry. I didn't care too much for that hospital food, and when they served something good, they didn't give me enough."

"It looks like they didn't feed you at all. You look so skinny, Momma," Audrey said.

"I know, Momma lost a little weight."

After eating and talking with her family and friend, Rosalee had to go to bed. She was weak and tired.

Destiny helped Audrey and Corrine clean up; then she went home.

For a single moment her life seemed to be on the right track. She had her mother in it. She had two new sisters, and Eric was her best friend, but she knew that it was soon going to be shattered when her mother was gone. Destiny wondered when she would ever have a day in her life that she would be happy, and not sad.

"When is it ever going to be Destiny's day?" she screamed out loud.

Josephine and Michelle pressed charges against Leon. Leon denied the charges of rape, but the tape told a different story. Denied bond, Leon was turned over to county jail, where he was to await his next court date. Leon's sisters were waiting outside the court building when Josephine and Michelle came out.

"You two dykes are going to be sorry that you ever fucked with my brother."

Josephine and Michelle ignored her as they walked to the parking lot.

"I got that videotape and the list of names of the people in it," Leon's sister Shanequa said.

"Shanequa, you don't have crap, so you better leave me the fuck alone," Michelle told her.

"Oh, I got the tape, the night you tricked my brother into telling that lie. He ain't raped your ugly-ass dike friend."

"Just ignore her, and let's go get that tape," Josephine told Michelle.

"How you gon' go get something that we already got? Leon hid the tape under the bed, stupid. Now do you believe that I got it?"

"Shanequa, you and your sister, Shaquanda, better get the fuck away from me and leave me alone."

"Leon told us that if y'all press any charges, to send it out, and you know my little brother sell bootleg DVDs, so he know how to make copies."

Josephine and Michelle hurried to the parking lot, where Josephine's car was parked. Once they got inside, they locked the doors.

"Please tell me that they couldn't get back in that apartment and get that video?"

"Josephine, I don't know, but we better go back over there and get it."

"I ain't worried about them. I'll snatch all that purple weave out of . . . What was her name?" Josephine asked.

"Shanequal. She had the nerve to talk crap, with all that purple-ass hair in her head, looking like she just cashed her momma's welfare check, then went to the beauty shop."

"But did you see the other one's hair? She looked a hot mess. What in the hell was she thinking when she let whoever it was put that bright red crap in her head."

"Girl, yeah, and they both had their nails done in the same colors. Tell me that ain't ghetto? Project hoes."

"They live in the projects?"

"Naw, Josephine, but they used to before they tore them all down. They momma ain't never had a job, 'cause she got a check for all them ghetto-fabulous-ass kids of hers," Michelle said; then she started laughing so hard, tears came out of her eyes. Josephine was laughing just as hard.

"Where did you meet Leon at?" Josephine asked Michelle.

"In the damn projects. I went over there one day with a friend that I went to high school with, and he was in the stairwell shooting dice."

"What made you talk to somebody in a stairwell shooting dice?"

"He was fine, and my friend told me that all the girls in the building liked him."

"That made you talk to him?"

"Girl, yeah."

"What is he now?"

"A jailbird."

"But you're in love with that jailbird."

"I was, Josephine, but to tell you the truth, I got tired of Leon a long time ago. All it took was two good ass beatings and I knew that it was time to go. I should have left after that first one. I guess I got stuck right, and couldn't give up the dick."

"That's what's wrong with a lot of women nowadays. They can't give up the dick. Speaking of dick, I sure do miss Marcus. I wish that before we go to divorce court, he'd change his mind."

"Girl, keep going, hurry up."

"Why?"

"That was Leon's mother's car parked in front of his house. Them ghetto-fabulous project hoes drove and beat us here."

"Then that means that they do have the video, and I hope they were lying about having a list of names and addresses of those people," Josephine said.

"I don't know, Josephine. You remember when you told me to redo all of your clients' files? I took them home to do them, even though I knew that I wasn't supposed to."

"Yeah?"

"Those files had all of your clients' names and addresses in them, and Leon was the one helping me with them."

"That doesn't mean that he got their information."

"Josephine, I rewrote that crap, and I'm not even sure if I remember whether or not I tore the old files up and threw them in the garbage."

"I'm not going to worry about that crap right now. I have too much to worry about as it is," Josephine said as she drove home.


Destiny and Eric picked Rosalee, Audrey and Corrine up for the dinner. They arrived at the restaurant minutes before Derrick and Hakim. Jasmine and Troy called Hakim's cell and told him that they were going to be five or ten minutes late. The waitress seated them at the table, which was reserved for them, and offered drinks before she gave them a menu.

"Everybody, thanks for joining me for dinner.

We're waiting for Jasmine and Troy. Everything's on me, so if anyone—except you, Audrey—wants to order drinks, go right ahead," Hakim said.

Jasmine and Troy finally made it to the restaurant. "There they are," Jasmine said, pointing to the table. "Sorry we're late. There was a lot of traffic."

"It's OK, I'm just glad that you two made it. Jasmine, you remember Destiny. This is her mother, Rosalee; that's her sister, Audrey; and that's the babysitter, Ms. Corrine Jones; and that's Eric." Hakim introduced everybody at the table to Jasmine and Troy. He handed Jasmine flowers and a card.

"It's a pleasure to meet you all," the latecomers said.

"Same here," everybody else said.

"Drinks, anyone?" the waitress asked.

Jasmine ordered a glass of Chardonnay. Troy ordered a scotch on the rocks. Everybody else, except Rosalee and Audrey, already had drinks. After Jasmine drank her glass of wine, the waitress asked if everyone was ready to order their food. She took the table's orders.

"What's going on here?" Jasmine asked, looking over at Troy.

Troy hunched his shoulders up and shook his head as a gesture to say that he didn't know what was going on.

"Dad, Derrick, what's going on?" Jasmine asked again.

"Open the card, Jasmine, and read it," Hakim told her.

Jasmine opened the card and read its contents. She closed her eyes for a moment, and everybody thought that she was getting ready to explode. She took a deep breath and said, "Dad, I don't know if I should be mad with you, and, Hakim, I'm going to kill you. Destiny . . ." She paused. "The night that Hakim brought you to my house, did you know that you were my sister?"

"No."

"My friends kept telling me that you looked a lot like me. I didn't think much of it, because I just thought that Hakim was dating you because you reminded him of me so much, but I guess not." Then she began to cry. "I'm happy to have you as a sister, but I'm jealous, because I always thought that I was Daddy's little girl."

Destiny got up from the table, walked around to where Jasmine was sitting and gave her a hug. "I just found out a few days ago myself, and I was hoping that you'd accept me as your sister. As a matter of fact, I just found out that I have a little sister."

Jasmine started to laugh as she hugged Destiny back. "Well, I guess that makes two of us." Jasmine felt relieved when Destiny finally took her arms from around her neck. She didn't want to let her true feelings about being told Destiny was her father's daughter spoil the evening. She didn't know what she was feeling exactly, but she knew it had something to do with Destiny.

"Well, baby, you got a little sister. How about

that?" Troy asked as the waitress returned with the orders.

"Honey, let's just focus on our food, because you know that I have other plans," Jasmine told Troy.

"Maybe you could have canceled that, Jasmine?" Hakim asked.

"Oh, Hakim, I would have, but tonight we're giving Toya a baby shower. I really can't miss that."

"But—" Derrick began.

"Dad, it's OK if she has to go."

"Destiny, I'm sorry that I can't stay that long. I have a baby shower to go to. Maybe we can get together and do something soon?"

"That'll be fine with me." Destiny could sense the change in Jasmine's attitude, but she didn't care. She had a sister, and she was fine with her. She wasn't in the habit of kissing butt to get along with other people, so she went right along with Jasmine's act.

After Jasmine finished half of her food, she and Troy got up to leave. She apologized again for not being able to stay.


"Jasmine, you don't have a baby shower to go to. Why did you lie?"

"Why do you have to ask questions, Troy?"

"That's obvious. I asked because as soon as you found out that Destiny was your sister, you put on a fake smile and your attitude went from happy to 'isn't this a bitch?'"

"Well, Derrick could have told me that he had

a fucking illegitimate daughter in the world, but nooooo . . . he has Hakim do his fucking dirty work for him."

"So you don't like the fact that you have a sister?" Troy asked.

"I was doing fine by my damn self. Thank you very much."

"Well, Jasmine, if you felt that way, why were you sitting at the table acting phony?"

"Troy, just take me home."

"I'm dropping you off at home."

"You're dropping me off? Where the hell are you going?"

"Away from you. This is one of the reasons why we hardly ever do anything together. You're not mad that your daddy got another daughter. You're jealous of her."

"Why the fuck would I be jealous of that?"

"What does that mean? Why are you referring to her as 'that'?"

"Why are you asking me all of these got damn questions? If you like the bitch so much, why don't you go back to the restaurant and be with her."

The rest of the ride home, Troy didn't say anything else to her. When he pulled in front of their house, Jasmine reached over the armrest and turned the ignition off. She snatched the keys out of it.

"I don't know where the hell you think you're going in my car, but it isn't happening."

Troy still didn't say a word to her. He opened the driver's-side door and climbed out. He closed her car door and walked to the garage. Jasmine got out and ran up behind him.

"I asked you, where were you going?"

"If you haven't noticed, I'm not in your car anymore."

"Why can't you ever be on my side for once? How would you feel if your father and brother sprung some crap like that on you?"

"My daddy had another family on the other side of town. When me and my family found out about it, we were teenagers. I love my half sister and brother just like my mother had them."

"Well, that's you and your fucked-up family."

"I'm not mad, though—you are. And speaking of fucked-up, what are you?"

"What are you trying to say, Troy?"

"Just what I said earlier. You're jealous of her."

"Jealous of her who?"

"Your half sister."

"Fuck you, and my half sister."

"Move," Troy said as calmly as he could.

"I'm not moving anywhere."

"Jasmine, stand there if you want to, but when I open this got damn garage door and you're still standing here, I'm not stopping. I'm getting tired of you."

"I'm tired of you too."

"Good, then I'll leave."

"You better come back here tonight or else."

"Or else what, Jasmine?"

"You'll see."

"And you're not crazy either."

"Yeah, well, tell your bitch that I said hello."

"Jasmine, right about now, I wish that I had a bitch. She sure as hell wouldn't be like you." Troy got in his car and pulled out of the garage.

Jasmine watched Troy as he drove off. She hated it when he acted like she was the one in the wrong. She hadn't asked her father to have another daughter by some strange woman. Then she thought about Destiny's mother and how sick she looked. "Oh well," Jasmine said out loud. She rolled her eyes when she thought about Destiny.

*First the bitch starts to date my brother, and now she's my sister. What is this world coming to? I don't like her, and I don't have to like her. Waltzing her ass into my life like I want a sister. I was doing OK without one.* Jasmine started to cry, and she wanted someone to talk to, so she called Stormy.

"Hey, Stormy," she said, sniffling into the phone.

"Hey, boo, what's up with you? You sound like you're upset."

"I am."

"About what?"

"That girl that Hakim brought over to my house with him."

"What about her?"

"She's my father's daughter."

"I told you that! Honey didn't I tell you that y'all looked a lot alike?"

"Stormy, please stop it."

"What's wrong, Jas? You don't seem too happy about her being your sister. And by the way, how did you find out that she was?"

"My trifling brother decided to invite me and

Troy—who, by the way, got upset with me and left tonight—out to dinner with her and her family. He got one of the waitresses to bring me a card, telling me that she was my sister, with a dozen roses—like that was supposed to soften the blow."

"Jas . . . sweetie, maybe you need to think about this before you decide that you don't want her to be in your life. You have to remember, sweetie, that neither one of you asked for this. She probably doesn't know how to deal with this either. Sweetie, just give it a chance. It will all work out with time."

"I don't have the time to welcome a new sister into my life."

"You seemed to like her a lot when she came to your house with Hakim."

"That's before I knew that she was my father's daughter."

"I'm glad that you said that, because it's not going to change. She's your father's daughter, as well as you are, and, sweetie, you just have to find a way to deal with that. Tell me this, why don't you want to get to know your sister?"

"I don't have a reason to like that expensive hoe."

"Whoa . . . a hoe is a garden tool, and that wasn't nice of you to say."

"I'm just not feeling her, Stormy. She can have my brother and my dad, but I don't want to be bothered with her."

"Well, Jas . . . it's your choice. I just think that you should give it some time before you regret something."

"I'll think about that."

"One more thing—where the hell did Troy go?"

"I don't know, and I don't give a damn."

"What the hell is wrong with you, for real, Jasmine? Your man leaves you for what, and you don't give a damn?"

"I'm tired of him blaming everything on me. Whenever something goes wrong in our fucked-up relationship, he blames me for it."

"You two need some quality time, baby."

"We don't need crap. He's the one who's always gone, not me."

"Jasmine, you spend so much time at that beauty shop, I wonder sometimes, when do you have time for your man?"

"When does he have time for me?"

"You know what, Jasmine? You need to lie down and get some rest, because you're upset, sweetie. Once you're rested, I want you to call me back—no matter what time it is."

"OK, I'll talk to you later."

Jasmine wasn't trying to hear what Stormy had told her. She was tired of people trying to give her advice on things that were happening in her life. She didn't know what Troy had meant when he said that she was jealous. What was she jealous of? she thought. Just because Destiny had on an expensive outfit and shoes didn't mean that she was jealous of her or any-body else, for that matter.

Jasmine watched at least three movies before Troy came in. She stormed out of the den to the bedroom, where he was undressing.

"Where the hell have you been all this time, Troy?"

"I decided to rejoin your family to finish having dinner."

"You went behind my back to be with them after we left?"

"I'm tired and full. Your sister said to tell you that she hopes the two of you can get together real soon."

"Well, you should've told her that I'm not interested, since you made it your business to go back. What gave you the right to go back there?"

"Me . . . I gave *me* the right to go back there. I'm going to bed now. Are you done talking to me?"

"Hell naw! Do you know how that makes me look?"

"Like the damn fool that you've been acting like for a minute now."

"You know what?"

"No, I don't know what, but I know who. I know who is going to bed. Me. We are done talking about you and your family and whomever else you may think you want to talk about." Troy pulled the covers back on the bed, climbed in and turned over on his side.

Jasmine looked at his back. She felt like getting a knife from the kitchen and stabbing him with it. She snatched a pillow off the bed and went back to the den.

# 11

Leon ignored the fact that his mother had told him not to call her house collect until the weekend came. Leon, however, had to make sure that his younger brother, Leonard, got that videotape from his sisters, who would forget the house was on fire if you mentioned hair weave and fake nails.

"Ma, this Leon on the phone," Leonard hollered out to his mother.

"Is he calling collect?"

"Yeah, Ma."

"Hang up my damn phone. I told that boy to call on the weekends only. Hell, he can wait till tomorrow. I didn't put his ass there. Hang up my damn phone."

Leonard didn't pay his mother any attention, and he accepted the call anyway, to see what his brother wanted. "Man, hurry up and talk before I get in trouble. Ma told me not to accept this call."

"Boy, shut up with your big-headed ass."

"At least I ain't locked the fuck up."

"Leonard, shut up. Did Shanequa and Sha-quanda come back yet?"

"Nope. 'Dizzy' and 'Dizzier' aren't here yet. What happened in court today?"

"Them bitches pressed charges against me. Look, tell your stupid sisters that I said to give you that videotape and list of names and addresses. I want you to make copies of it and send it to some of the people in it."

"How am I going to know which ones to send it to?"

"I'll call tomorrow, so Momma won't be fussing. I want you to mail them five at a time," Leon said.

"Boy, you accepted that damn call anyway?" Leona asked, walking by.

"Naw, Momma, dang, you told me not to."

"Boy, who you think you talking smart to? I'll dang your ass all right," Leona said as she walked past her youngest son and slapped him upside the head.

"Man, she plays too much. She better be glad she my momma."

"Boy, shut the fuck up. You know Momma will tag that ass. She from the jets," Leon said, laughing.

"You better watch yo' ass while you're in there. Smart-assed punk."

"Keep on, and I'll tell Momma that you accepted this call."

"OK . . . OK, you want me to get a videotape and list of people from the dumb twins and make copies of it to mail to people? Who's paying me to do this crap? You locked the fuck up."

"Dude, who you think gon' pay yo' lil' ugly ass? Me. I want you to go over to my guy lil' D's crib and tell him that I said to give you a stack for me. Buy whatever you need for the videos and pay for the postage. Keep two for yourself, and put the rest up. Tell him that I got him when I get out of this joint."

"OK, man. Hey, big bro?"

"What's up, baby bro?"

"You awright in there?"

"Yeah, I won't be in here for long. As soon as that video starts to get out, so will I."

"OK, man. I got you."

"Say, lil' bro?"

"Wassup?"

"Be cool, dude. Don't let Momma know what you're doing for me. Tell her that it's a school assignment or some of your bootleg movies you're making a copy of to sell."

"OK, man. I better get off this phone before Ma starts trippin' again."

"Awight, lil' man. I'll be home soon, you just watch and see." The brothers hung up.

"Boy, I better not find out that that was your brother calling here collect on a Friday, 'cause if it was, I'm gonna beat your ass. You ain't paying no bills around here, but you sure as hell keep them name-brand gym shoes on your feet."

"That's because you know I sell them bootleg movies, Momma, and I do give you money."

"That don't mean I put it on the phone bill."

"Man, you're a trip."

"Who you calling a trip? Boy, I'll slap fire from you. I'm ya' momma, not yo' no-good-ass daddy. Speaking of his no-good ass, when was the last time you saw him?"

"Uhm . . . the other day."

"He still looking bad?"

"Yeah, Momma, the man's on crack. How do you expect a crackhead to look?"

"Boy, if yo' mouth ain't as smart as his was. It ain't smart at all. Keep it up and you gon' be just like that crackhead daddy of yours," Leona said to her baby son.

"I don't think so. That's why I'm still in school making straight A's."

"And Momma is proud of her baby too." Leona walked over to Leon and grabbed his fat cheeks in her hands and kissed her son. "Keep up the good work so you can take care of yo' momma, baby."

Leonard looked at his mother curiously, and he wished that he could have shared this with her: *Get up off yo' fat lazy ass and get a GED. Go to college or become a nurse's assistant. Take care of yourself. Get off the government-housing program, and see what it feels like to own your own crap. Momma!* His mind screamed out, but he knew better than to say something like that to his mother, because Leona didn't play. She could fight, and she would kick your ass. Instead, he said, "I am, Momma . . . I am."

"And don't be like yo' lazy-ass, locked-up brother either. Damn jailbird."

"Momma, what time is Shanequa and Sha-quanda bringing your car back?"

"Why, you ain't driving it."

"How am I going to learn how to drive if nobody teaches me? What was the purpose of getting me a learners permit if you wasn't?"

"Boy, go in there and do some homework or a science project or something."

"Momma, when they coming back for real, though?"

"Them two cows should have been back here with my car. They better quit playing with me, before I hand 'em some."

"Is their cell phones back on?"

"Did you pay their bills?"

"I guess that means no, then?"

"Leonard, you're smarter than I thought."

"Momma, I be right back. If their dumb as . . . oops."

"Boy, you gon' make me beat that ass just yet."

"I'm sorry, Momma, I didn't say the whole word. But if they come back, tell them to wait for me before they go back out. I'll be right back."

"Boy, where you going?"

"To the store."

"Bring yo' momma a pop back."

"What kind?"

"A ninety-nine-cent two liter, boy."

"OK." Leonard walked out the door. He slammed it behind him. He wasn't going to the store, he was going over to lil' D's house to get the money for his brother, and the store was in the opposite direction. "Damn, she gets on my last nerve."

"Boy, I want you to slam my damn door like that again. I dare you," Leona screamed out after Leon.

As soon as he got to the corner, his sisters were driving up in their mother's car. He flagged them down. Shaquanda pulled the car over to see what he wanted.

"Shaquanda, run me over lil' D's house for Leon."

"For what?"

"I just told you for Leon, dang."

"Momma told you to stop saying dang, because it sounds like damn. Keep it up and I'll tell her you keep saying it."

"And I'll snatch that ugly-ass weave out yo' head."

"Now you gon' cuss. I ain't taking you nowhere."

"Wait till Leon call home tomorrow, and I tell him that yo' trifling butt didn't take me to get the money to pay for his stuff."

"Boy, get in, and you better hurry up and get whatever you got to get from lil' D, so I can take Momma her car back." Shaquanda drove the two blocks to lil' D's house. Leonard hopped out and took the stairs two at a time to the second floor, where lil' D lived.

"What's up, lil' Leon?"

"Nothing much. Leon told me to come over here and get—"

"I know, lil' bro. Here, I already got it waiting for you. You can count it if you want to."

"Naw, that's OK. Thanks, dude."

"Awright. That's my guy, and he knows I got his back."

Shaquanda started to blow the horn. "I got to go."

When Leonard got back in the car, Shaquanda snapped on him. "Boy, I told you to hurry the fuck up. Ain't anybody got time to sit in front of a got damn drug house. The police might be watching this crap."

"Girl, shut the hell up, and let's go. You act like I was up there for a long time. Run me to the store to get Momma a pop."

"I ain't running you nowhere. Get yo' ass out and walk to the store."

"Come on, Shaquanda, take me to the store so I can get Momma a pop."

"Nope."

"Wait till you ask me to loan you some money to get your nails done again. I'm going to tell you to wait on your social security check, and I hope you need a fill-in."

"Girl, take him to the store," Shanequa said. "You know how you get when you need a fill-in."

"You was doing fine sitting over there with your mouth shut. Keep it that way."

"Whatever," Shanequa said as she twisted a finger with a two-inch nail on it in front of her sister's face.

"Boy, get out and get Momma a pop and hurry back or you will be walking back home. And can I get a big bag of chips?"

"Me too," Shanequa said.

"Yeah, whatever."

"Boy, come back without those chips and yo' butt will be walking home."

Leonard went into the store and got the pop and two big bags of chips for his nagging sisters.

"Come on, boy. Hurry up so I can take yo' momma back her car."

"For what? She already got her groove on."

"Boy, shut yo' mannish ass up. How you know what Momma be going to do?" Shanequa asked.

"Let me out this damn car. Y'all ain't that stupid, or is all that red and purple weave messing with y'all brains?"

"Watch and see if I don't tell Momma what you said about her."

"Where the hell have y'all been in my damn car?"

"Momma, we went to court for your son, and to his house, and on the way home, we ran into yo' dumb son, and he wanted me to take—"

"She took me to the store to get your pop," Leonard said before Shaquanda told their mother that she took him to lil' D's house. He knew that Leona would have kicked his butt if she found out that they had been to a drug spot.

Shaquanda got the message, and she didn't say anything else.

"You put gas back in my car?" Leona asked.

"Yeah, Momma."

"Just because you're nineteen doesn't mean that I won't knock that weave off your head. You better watch the tone of your voice when you're talking to me."

Shaquanda frowned her face up, then turned

her bottom lip up at her mother when she turned her back. She rolled her eyes and went to her bedroom and got on the phone.

"Momma, can you take me to the store later?" Leonard asked his mother.

"For what, boy?"

"I got to get some stuff for my science project."

"Yeah, let me finish my dinner and we can go."

Leonard went to Shaquanda's bedroom and asked her for the DVD that she got from Leon and Michelle's apartment.

"Look in my bag over there." She pointed to the bag that was hanging on the closet door, then started conversing with whoever it was on the other end of the phone.

Leonard got the DVD out of her bag and went to his room. He locked his door. He put it in his computer, clicked on the DVD player and looked at what was on the DVD. He understood why Leon didn't want their mother to know what he was doing. Leonard was only sixteen years old, and the stuff that he saw on the DVD was sickening to him. He thought that maybe if he were older, he'd understand what was going on.

A knock at his door startled him, and he quickly closed the program. "Boy, if you want to go to the store, you better come on."

"OK, Mom, let me turn my computer off."

Leona took Leon to the office supply store, where he purchased two 24-packs of rewritable DVDs and a case of padded envelopes to mail the DVDs in, so they wouldn't break or scratch.

"Boy, you got everything you need, because I'm not coming back outside."

"Yeah."

"What kind of science project you got to do?"

"I'm showing the different ways people alter things by recording stuff and changing it frame by frame."

"That sounds interesting."

"It is."

"Well, I hope you got everything that you needed, because I told you that I'm not coming back outside. I'm eating my dinner and going in my room."

"I heard you, Momma, dang."

"I should reach over there and smack that word right out of your brain."


Leon called his mother's house as soon as he was able to get a chance to use the phone. He had Leonard read off the list of names and addresses, and he told Leonard which ones to mail a copy of the DVD to. He had to mail a total of fifteen copies, one with a letter. After Leon finished giving Leonard instructions on what to do with the DVDs, he asked to speak with his mother.

"Hey, Ma, what's up with you?"

"No, the question is, what's up with you, Leon? Did you rape that lady and beat Michelle like they say you did?"

"Ma, I did what I did for a reason. If you knew what Michelle did to me, you'd understand, but anyway, Ma, I might be able to get house arrest—"

"Wait a minute, boy. I know you ain't trying to ask me if you can come back here to be on house arrest? You can go back to your own place."

"Man, Momma, you can't help me out?"

"I am. I let you call my house collect. I ain't got enough room for you, and I don't want my phone line tied up with no house arrest box hooked up to it."

"Momma, you got four bedrooms. How come you don't have enough room?"

"One for me, one for Shaquanda, one for Shanequa, and one for Leonard. That's why the people gave you your own low-income apartment. You should have thought about what you were doing before you did it."

"Momma, how come you can't give a brother a chance to get his crap together?"

"Boy, you better watch yo' mouth. You had all the chances in the world to do right, but you chose to do what you wanted to do. Call your friend lil' D. Let him help you. I told you that if you go to jail one more time for hitting on a woman, don't ask for my help, because you ain't got no business hitting on a woman. And then you have the audacity to rape one— boy, is you crazy?"

"Forget it, Momma . . . forget it. Will you at least keep the rent paid on my apartment if I can't get house arrest at home?"

"Yeah, its thirty-three dollars, right?"

"Yeah, Momma."

"OK, is that all you want?"

"Yeah."

"Well, I'm going to get off this phone, and when is your next court date?"

"Next Friday."

"OK, maybe I'll come this time."

"I love you, Momma, and tell my sisters and baby brother that I love them too."

"I guess you got religious up in there too?"

"Bye, Momma, I got to go."

"You take care of yourself, and remember, you can't do wrong to people and not expect to pay for that wrong."

"I know that, Momma. I'll talk to you soon. I love you."

"I love you too, son." Leona got off the phone.

Leonard addressed the fifteen envelopes with the names that Leon had him check off the list. He couldn't mail them until Monday, because the post office had closed hours ago.

# 12

"Hey, girl, what's up? Long time, don' see," Jasmine told Michelle when she walked into the beauty shop.

"Girl, I been through some crap. It's time for a new me," Michelle said, trying to keep the empty spaces in her mouth covered with her top lip.

"What you need a new look for?" Toya asked. She was too big from her pregnancy to do hair, so she was doing nails.

"I got to find me a new man. Leon locked up."

"What the hell the project kid don' did now?" Jasmine asked.

"Girl, he raped the lady that I work for."

"Tell the whole story," Stormy said.

"What whole story?"

"Girl, you know his two lil' sisters don't hold hot water too good, and the juicy crap they came up in here and told was a big bucket of scalding hot water."

"What did they tell y'all? Them two young-ass, weave-wearing, ghetto-ass project hoes make me sick."

"They said that Leon got a DVD of you and some other people doing each other and he kicked your ass. That's why you trying to hide them gaps in your mouth?"

"Stormy, you keep up too much crap."

"I didn't tell them girls to come in here and tell your business. They did that on their own. Now you better apologize with your snaggle-toothed ass before I call those ghetto-ass project hoes."

"I'm sorry, but you can't believe all that stuff they say."

"Enough about you, I just found out that I have a new sister," Jasmine said.

"Get out of here. Is she older or younger than you?"

"She's younger, and I don't like her."

"What's her name?" Jasmine asked.

"Destiny."

"Destiny!"

"Yes, that's what I said. How do you want your hair done?"

"In a weave wrap," Michelle said. She didn't want to alarm Jasmine, but she needed to know if they were talking about the same Destiny.

"What about a perm?"

"Yeah, that too. What does your sister Destiny look like?"

"She looks a lot like me."

Michelle pictured Destiny, and then Jasmine; sure enough, she could see the resemblance.

She couldn't wait to tell Josephine about this. Maybe Jasmine would tell her where Destiny lived, since she didn't like her. "Why don't you like her?"

"Because I didn't ask for a sister, that's why." Jasmine started relaxing Michelle's hair, and Michelle kept asking questions about Destiny to make sure that they were talking about the same person.

"So what is it about her that you don't like?" Michelle asked.

"I don't like the prissy way she looks."

"Prissy? What do you mean 'prissy'?"

"Damn, Michelle, don't you know anything? Prissy, as in she had on very expensive crap. I wouldn't be dressed in expensive clothes just to meet and have dinner with someone. She got up from the table and hugged me, like I needed to be hugged. Bitch!"

"What kind of car does she drive?"

"I don't know. I didn't see it."

"So you don't think the two of you can get along?"

"No, Michelle. I wouldn't mind it if she stayed away from me and my family." Jasmine did Michelle's hair, and Michelle rushed back to Josephine's to tell her what she had just found out.

When Michelle got to Josephine's, Josephine was sitting at the dining-room table talking on the phone. Michelle waited patiently for her to end her conversation with whoever it was on the other line.

"I got an office. . . . I got an office! I can start back to work as soon as I pay the month's rent and security deposit."

"That's wonderful, but guess what I just found out?"

"What?"

"Do you remember the shop where I get my hair done?"

"Yes."

"Jasmine, the girl that does my hair, just found out yesterday that Destiny is her half sister."

"Get the fuck out of here."

"No, I'm serious, and get this—she doesn't like her."

"Oh, really?"

"Yes, really. You know what that means, right?"

"No, but I'm sure you're going to tell me."

"That means we can find out where she lives, and get her to stop sending out that DVD. You and I both know . . . ooh crap."

"What?"

"I must be the dumbest person on the face of the earth right about now."

"Why do you say that?"

"I remember meeting Jasmine's brother, Hakim, at the shop once, about two years ago, and he owned a construction and remodeling company with his dad. . . . Got damn it, Josephine, you said that Marcus found the company that remodeled your basement? The guy that finished your basement is Jasmine's brother, Hakim, and Byron invited the guy that he met and started dating to the party. I heard that Hakim and Destiny were about to date. One of those men had to tell Destiny, you can figure out the rest for yourself."

"My guess is that they found a way to film the party and took the pictures. That's where that empty camera box came from," Josephine said.

"So what are you going to do?"

"About what?"

"About Destiny."

"I'm not going to do anything yet, but you can keep going to the shop to get more information on her. I guess if any more of those DVDs pop up, I can go and talk to her."

"You take crap too lightly, Josephine. That bitch has ruined your life and mine. What else do you need to wait for her to do?"

"Michelle, please."

"OK, you're right. I'll just wait and see what happens next or who gets hurt next."

Josephine wanted to tell Michelle to go to her room and shut up, but she wasn't a child, so she went to hers instead.

Eric usually studied on Sundays, but today he was going over to Rosalee's with Destiny. Rosalee wanted to talk to her, because she felt things were going to turn for the worse for her. She told Destiny that she had sensed some animosity from Jasmine. On the way to Rosalee's house, Destiny told Eric about wanting to trade her car in or sell it for something else. Eric ignored her, since he drove her almost everywhere she went.

Once they made it to Rosalee's apartment, Audrey greeted them.

"Hey, big sis, Mom's in her room, and she's expecting you, but I don't think she feels too well."

"I know, but how are you, little miss?"

"I'm doing OK," Audrey said.

"Well, when I'm done talking to mom, can we talk?"

"Sure."


"Destiny, you look pretty as usual."

"Thank you, Mom. You look pretty yourself."

"Audrey helped me bathe, and get dressed. Destiny, I asked you to come today, because I wanted to ask something of you. You can say no if you don't feel like you can handle what I need to ask of you."

"What is it, Mom?"

"Will you take Audrey, and look after Corrine, if something happens to me?"

"Mom, you didn't have to even ask me a question like that. I would do anything for you."

"Anything?"

"Anything, Mom."

"Good. Then I want you to watch that other sister of yours."

"Mom, you already ask me to do that," Destiny said.

"No, honey, I'm not talking about Audrey.

I'm talking about that Jasmine, girl. I saw the look of evil in her eyes that night. She doesn't like you."

"I know, Mom. I saw that too, and that's why I got up to hug her. I wanted her to know that no matter how she feels about me, I have nothing against her."

"I wasn't sure if you noticed that or not."

"Yes, I did. Now, enough about Jasmine and me. What made you ask me if I would take Audrey?"

"I wasn't really truthful to you or Audrey, but I didn't want to worry Audrey. I know you're strong enough to handle things better. The doctors told me that my cancer had spread to more of my vitals organs, and I don't have six months to live. They cut that time in half, and it could be even less."

"Mom, are you sure?"

"Yes."

"I can have someone else check you out for a second opinion, if you want?"

"No, sweetie, I'm tired of all the testing and the poking. This is all my fault. I didn't have to be in this predicament. I wasn't taking care of myself, and I hope that you do. I didn't have the patience to have a pap smear done on the regular. I hope that you do, because you know your grandmother had cancer too, but it was in remission."

"Granny didn't tell me that she had cancer."

"If she didn't, that's because she made it a point not to put too much pressure on you, because she didn't want you to worry about anything."

"I'm glad that she was that way, because I do worry about things—like you, Momma."

"Sweetie, if you'll just take custody of your sister, and watch over Ms. Corrine for me, I will be more than happy, and I won't worry so much."

"Momma, you don't have to worry about those two."

"I have a last will and testament, which they gave me at the hospital, and, of course, you know that I don't have much, but my two babies and Ms. Corrine. If she heard me calling her 'Ms.,' she'd have a fit. In the last will and testament, I have named you as Audrey's legal guardian. I am forever grateful that you came back into my life, but it shouldn't have had to be like this."

"Some things happen for a reason, Momma, and I'm not saying that my coming back into your life now will change what's happening to you. But I'm here, and I plan on making the best of whatever time you have left."

"You always had a sweet side to you. Who brought it out?"

Destiny smiled as she thought about Eric. She owed all that to him.

"Eric. I'm so glad that I have a friend like him."

"The way you broke out in that smile, you're more than friends, but you're only fooling Destiny."

"And just what do you mean by that, Mother?"

"Destiny, I can see the love you have for that man all in your face. He loves just as much."

"Momma, I like Eric a lot, but I'm not ready to be in a relationship right now."

"Don't tell that to me, tell him and your heart."

"He already knows."

"Then why does he try so hard to make you see that he's in love with you?"

"What makes you say that?"

"You'll figure it out one day."

"Oh, Momma, that's not fair."

"OK, you're right. That's not fair to keep something like that from you. Destiny, he goes out of his way to make you happy, sweetie. Don't you see it?"

"Momma, I'm scared of being in another relationship."

"I bet you that he's just as scared, but I can tell that he has your best interest at heart."

"How do you know that?" Destiny asked, smiling.

"I can just look at him with you, he's happy. Why don't you give him a chance to make you happy?"

"Maybe one day."

"Well, you better not let some other woman come along and take your good thing away from you."

"Momma, I'll beat her down."

"For what? You just said in so many words that he's not your man. So why would you be worried about him meeting another woman?"

"Momma," Destiny said as she giggled. "You

think you can see what I feel for Eric. He's a great friend. I love talking to him, because he's also a good listener."

"He must be very good in bed, because you're not going to allow another woman into his life."

"Momma, you should be ashamed of yourself."

"No, Destiny, you should allow yourself to love again. No matter what the other guy you were with did to you, that does not mean that all of them are the same."

"You think so, Momma?"

"I know so, sweetheart. Give him a chance."

"OK, Momma, but just not right now."

"That's up to you, sweetie, but remember, love doesn't wait forever."

"I got you, now you get some rest. I'm going to talk to Audrey."

"Are you going to let her know that she's going to live with you if something happens to me?"

"Do you want me to? Or would you rather tell her, and she and I discuss it?"

"I guess you better tell her first, and then I'll talk to her."

"Yes, Momma."

"Destiny?"

"Yes, Momma."

"I know you don't want to hear this, but I do have some insurance, enough to cover my funeral. Audrey knows where it is?"

"I'm not ready to discuss that just yet, Momma."

"I understand, but soon, OK?"

"Yes, Momma, soon." Destiny let her mother rest.

Eric and Audrey were playing a video game.

"Hey, Eric, do you mind if I talk to Audrey for a minute?"

"No, go ahead. I'll play the game."

"Audrey, let's go in your room and talk."

Audrey got up and followed Destiny into her room.

"Sweetie, Mom wanted me to talk to you, because she isn't feeling too well. Mom doesn't know exactly how much longer she's going to be with us, and I know that you can already see that, right?"

"Yes."

"She asked me, if something were to happen to her, if I would take care of you. I don't quite know how to ask you what I'm trying to ask, so bear with me."

"If you're trying to ask me if I want to stay with you, the answer is yes."

Destiny sighed deeply, then said, "That was easy. How come I can't be a big girl like you?"

"You are. I know that Momma is very sick, and I understand that she isn't going to be around for long, but there's nothing we can do to change that. It scares me a lot, but I know that we're going to be OK."

"You're very mature for your age, and I'm very proud of you."

"And I'm glad that I have a sister like you.

You came into my life at the right time, and I'm grateful for you, Destiny, and so is Momma."

"I feel the same way about the two of you, and I hate that I took so long coming back to Momma."

"Destiny."

"Yeah?"

"What about Ms. Jones? She's always been good to me and Momma."

"You don't have to worry about her, sweetie. Momma already asked me to look after her too."

Audrey smiled. She walked over to her sister and hugged her around the waist. "I love you, Destiny."

"I love you too, Audrey."

"Do you think that you could come spend next weekend over here with me and Momma?"

"If that's what you want, honey, I sure can."

"Thank you."

"Anytime."

Audrey dried her face, then she looked up at Destiny. "Well, I better go back in there and finish beating Eric. He really doesn't know how to play that well."

"OK, sweetie, I'm going to check on Momma." Destiny dried her own face and went to check on Rosalee. She chuckled at what Audrey had said about Eric. Destiny knew that Eric was just letting Audrey beat him in the video game that they were playing, because Eric was really good at playing those kind of games. She went in her mother's room and stood close to her bed. Rosalee was sound asleep. Destiny tiptoed back out.

"Is she all right?" Eric asked.

"Yeah, she's sleeping. You ready to go?"

"Are you?"

"Not really, but I need to talk to you about some things."

Audrey came over and joined the conversation.

"I know . . . I know, you have to go. Maybe next weekend you can come with Destiny and spend the night too," Audrey suggested.

Eric looked at Destiny for an answer.

"You can come. It'll be like we're camping out," Destiny joked.

Eric looked at her again, only this time he looked puzzled. "Camping out?"

"Yeah. You can bring those sleeping bags," Destiny said, smiling.

"Sounds good."

"Audrey, we're going to get ready and go. I have a few things that I need to look into."

"I'll see you two soon, right?"

"You know you will, and be ready to get whipped. I let you win this time."

"Oh, sure you did. I beat you fair and square," Audrey said as she walked them to the door, then locked it behind them.


After she and Eric were secured in his car, Destiny started to cry.

"What are you crying for?"

"I wasted so much time being angry with my mother, and now she's dying. What am I going to do, Eric?"

"Baby, there's nothing you can do, except enjoy the time that you have left with her."

"I know."

Destiny leaned over the armrest and laid her head on Eric's shoulder. He always knew the right things to say to make her feel good again.

"Does that mean that you'll stay friends with me, and help me raise her?"

"Do you have to ask me questions that don't make sense?"

"I guess that means that you will."

"Yes, it does, Destiny."

"Eric."

"Yes?"

"I want to go looking for a house."

"A house?"

"Big enough for you, me, Audrey and Corrine."

"When you say 'me,' does that mean we'll share the same bedroom?"

"Nope, but we can sneak into each other's rooms."

"I'd like that too, but I would rather be sleeping in the same room with you." Eric wasn't worried about sleeping in the same room with her, because in time he was going to be married to her—he was sure of that.

"So you think that could work?"

"What? Me and you being roommates, and sneaking about the house together?"

"Yeah."

"Yes, I think it can."

"Well, when you get out of school on Monday,

maybe we can drive around and look at some houses?"

"How about you come to my place and go on the Internet while I'm in school and make a list of houses to look at, so we won't be riding around for nothing."

"I can do that, and I can also come to your place now and let you network with me."

"I can do that," Eric said as he smiled mischievously.

# 13

Leonard got up for school early. He showered and got dressed and stuffed five of the padded envelopes in a plastic bag to take them to the post office for delivery, as Leon had instructed.

"Boy, what you getting out of here so early for?" Leona asked, then yawned.

"I got to set my science project up, so I'm leaving out early."

"Oh yeah, I forgot you said you had a science project to do."

"Why are you up this early?"

"Hell, I heard footsteps in my house. Boy, you almost got beat down up in here."

"OK, Momma, lock the door for me," Leonard said. He snatched his jacket off the back of one of Leona's dining-room chairs and headed out the door.

"Boy, the next time you leave you raggedy-ass crap hanging on the back of my chair, which I paid an arm and a leg for, I'll throw it in the garbage can."

Leonard was halfway down the stairs when he hollered back, "OK, Momma, but it isn't raggedy."

"Go to damn school, with your smart-assed self."

Leonard was already closing the hall door behind him as his mother was making her last comments. He took the bus to the post office, dropped the videos off and got a money order for one hundred dollars to mail to Leon for the commissary.

He used the same transfer to get to school. He wasn't really sure of how the videos were going to help Leon get out of jail, because raping someone was a serious charge, but he knew that they were going to cause a lot of trouble for the people that Leon told him to mail them to. Leonard only hoped that he didn't get into any trouble for them.

After school he was going to visit his brother in jail to let him know that he had mailed his packages off. This way he wouldn't call the house collect and make Leona mad.


Josephine got up early. Before she went to court, she tried to eat something, but she was too nervous. She knew that her marriage was over, because Marcus hadn't tried to get back with her. She hadn't seen him since the night she went over to the house and Marcus called the police on her. She hoped and prayed that she would get visitation rights with her sons today.

Michelle asked if she should come along for

moral support, but Josephine declined, fearing that her presence would upset Marcus even more. Josephine didn't know what to expect when she got to court, but she certainly hoped that Marcus would have a change of heart and be more forgiving, when it came to the boys. She knew that they were probably not with him, but she hoped that there was a slim chance that they would be.

Once she reached the courthouse, she almost puked. She was so afraid of the finality of this day that she immediately became sick to her stomach. She took several deep breaths before she entered the building. She took the elevator to the courtroom, and as soon as she stepped out of the elevator, the first two faces that she saw were Marcus's and Romel's. Romel worked at the law firm that Parnell worked in, and she knew that he was a good lawyer. She knew better than to mess with him.

"Hello, Mrs. Riley."

"Hello, Mr. Washington," Josephine spoke back, and rushed into the courtroom. She felt herself sweating through the material of her navy blue pin-striped jumpsuit. She felt what little food she had consumed from the night before rise up in her throat again, but it just wasn't enough for her to throw up.

Romel and Marcus walked into the court-room. If one didn't know exactly who they were, it would have been easy to assume that they were partners. The way that they were dressed made Josephine feel that her casual dress and low-wedged heels tagged her as a little farm girl fighting a very high-profile businessman. She had to take more deep breaths to keep from getting sick and passing out.

Marcus was calm and collected, while she was visibly perspiring. Once their case was called before the judge, Josephine walked up to the defendant's side of the bench. She listened as the judge read out of the files pertaining to her case. When asked if she wanted to protest anything, Josephine said no.

The judge must have read her mind when he granted Marcus full custody, but he gave her visitation rights. Marcus didn't protest that either, because he knew that the boys did miss her as much as she did them. After court was over, she met Marcus and Romel in the hall.

"Thank you for allowing me visitation."

"You're welcome. You can pick them up from school, and have them home by eight. And Josephine?"

"Yes," she said, choking on her tears.

"Don't take my boys around your perverted-ass friends or you will regret it. Understood?"

"Yes, Marcus."

"Eight o'clock," he said again.

Josephine picked the boys up at two forty-five on the dot. She stood outside her car, because she knew that they wouldn't recognize her in a new car, since their dad had taken the car that he bought for her.

"Mommy," Tyler said as he ran into his mother's arms.

"Tyler! Oh, baby, Mommy missed you so much."

Kyle was a little hesitant at first, but that big hug that Josephine had just given Tyler made him rush over to his mother. He rushed right into her arms, and she opened them. She held both her boys as tight as she could. She wanted to cry, but she didn't want them to cry and feel sad.

"Mommy missed you too, baby," Josephine said, holding back tears.

"I miss you too, Mommy."

Marcus watched from a distance as Kyle and Tyler met their mother. It hurt him a great deal that things had to be the way that they were, but he couldn't forgive her for sleeping with not just one woman, but several of them. He noticed that Josephine had a new car, and he wrote down her license plate number. He watched as the boys climbed into her car while Josephine used her cell phone to make a call.

"Mommy, whose toys are these?" Tyler asked.

"They're for you and your brother."

Josephine called her apartment to see if Michelle was still there. When she answered the phone, Josephine politely asked her if she didn't mind going somewhere else for a couple of hours, because the boys were coming over. She told Michelle that she felt that Marcus was going to be watching her, and she knew he was going to ask the boys if she was at her place while they were visiting. She didn't want to risk that.

Michelle told Josephine that she understood, and that she didn't mind going out for a while.

Michelle didn't know why, but she missed the bed that she shared with Leon. She grabbed her purse and jacket, and took the bus to the apartment, hoping that his loud-ass sisters weren't there. Once she got there, she remembered that she had told his sisters where the spare key was.

"Damn," she said under her breath.

"Hi, Ms. Michelle," the maintenance guy said.

"Hey, John. John, I gave my keys back, because I was mad at Leon. Do you think you can let me in?"

"Here yo' keys is. I kept them just in case, because I knew you'd be back."

"Thank you, John." Michelle took the keys and went inside the apartment. "Whew . . . what's that smell?" She walked into the kitchen, and the garbage had rotted. She tied the bag and took it to the Dumpster. Once she finished putting things back into place, she put clean sheets on the bed and lay in it for a nap. She jumped up quickly to put the chain on the door—just in case his sisters came back to the apartment. Once she felt safe again, she went back to the bedroom and returned to bed. She fell asleep, watching television.

Leon called his mom's house to talk to Leonard, to make sure that he had mailed the videos. Leonard told him that he had a day ago. Leon gave Michelle's cell phone number to Leonard, to see if anything had changed. Once he got off the phone, Leonard didn't want to get involved in what Leon was doing. He threw the number in the garbage can.

The next day Parnell went to work and found Romel waiting for him in his office. He didn't like the look on Romel's face, but he figured that it had something to do with a case that Parnell had taken from him by mistake.

"I know you're upset that I'm working on that case now, but it was purely a mistake, Romel."

"Parnell, that's not why I'm in your office. What is this?" Romel handed Parnell a copy of a handwritten letter. He read it, then said, "I don't know what the hell this is all about, but somebody is playing games."

"You think somebody is playing games, Parnell?"

"Romel, I'm not gay, and I never said any of those things about you, man."

"Parnell, I want your resignation on my desk as soon as possible."

"Romel, wait a minute. I don't know who's doing this or why, but I didn't say those things. I'm a married man. Why would I . . . Never mind. I'm not gay, and I know you're not firing me—"

"No. I'm trying to give you a chance to resign."

"Man, come on. Your firm is one of the biggest and the best. Where am I going to find another job like this one? I don't know who wrote that letter, but if you give me a few days, I promise that I will find out."

"There's nothing to find out. Like I said, I

want your fucking resignation on my desk as soon as possible. Do I make myself clear?"

"What the fuck is going on? How do I know you didn't do this crap to me, because I'm friends with Marcus's wife?"

"I don't give a fuck who you're friends with, but you need to clear out this office and haul ass out of here."

"I'll sue the crap out of you, Romel. Who the fuck do you think you are?"

"The question is, who are you?" Romel held the video up for Parnell to see. "You see this? It has you and Marcus's wife on it, with the same sex. Does your wife know about it?" Romel walked out of Parnell's office and slammed the door behind him.

Parnell snatched his phone up and called Josephine. "Bitch, what the fuck is going on?"

"What are you talking about?"

"I just got fired from this firm, because some-motherfucking-body sent Romel, who happens to own this got damn law firm, a letter telling him how I want to fuck him, and a fucking copy of that got damn video. This is all your got damn fault, Josephine. I know that I shouldn't have gotten involved with your trifling ass. What do you do with people's personal information, keep it lying around your office for all to see? That's the only way I can think of that a person could send a letter to my boss."

"Parnell, wait a minute, please. I didn't send that letter or the video. I don't know what the hell is going on, but I will get to the bottom of it. I'm sorry that that has happened to you, and

I think that that's Michelle's fault about the address thing. She was doing some work for me, and I think that she let my friends' and clients' information get into the wrong hands."

Parnell sat at his desk in tears, typing up his resignation. He didn't have much to take from his office. When he picked up the picture of his wife and kids, he couldn't hold back the tears that stung his eyes. He wiped at them and tried his best to keep his composure as he walked out of the law firm. He didn't know what he was going to tell his wife about losing his job. He couldn't go straight home. He stopped at the club where he and the rest of his friends in the video went, but he changed his mind. However, if anyone in there saw a grown man crying, they wouldn't think anything bad about it.

His wife greeted him at the door, and he could see that she had been crying too. "What are you crying for?" he asked.

"You could have told me that you wanted to be with a man instead of me."

"I don't want a man. I want you, and my kids."

She stepped aside and let him in the house. "If you don't want a man, what the fuck is this, Parnell?" She slapped him in the face with the video.

Parnell caught the video before it fell to the floor. He took it to the den to watch it. He put it on and saw himself doing something that he now regretted. He stopped it, and went to look for his wife to talk to her. She was in the kitchen sipping on a mug of coffee.

"Baby, let me explain what you saw in that video."

"How can you explain that, Parnell? Why are you here this early?"

"One thing at a time," he said sluggishly.

His wife flung the mug of coffee at him, and he ducked a little too slow. The mug slapped him in the chest; coffee spilled down it.

"Got damn it, that was hot. You're stupid. Why would you throw hot coffee on me?" he asked while he ripped his clothes off.

"Why would you throw your ass up in another man's face? Was it hot too?"

"Maybe if you had been more . . ." Parnell stopped in midsentence, because he knew that he had just put his foot in his mouth.

"If I had been more what, Parnell?" she screamed at him.

"Look, I shouldn't have said that, Sasha. I didn't mean it. I swear to you that I didn't mean it." Parnell walked over to her and reached out to touch her.

"Don't put your fucking hands on me. Don't you ever touch me again. I was a fool letting you bring Josephine and all those people to my house for a dinner party, but at least I can say that nobody got naked up in here," she snapped at him.

"Sasha, please let's talk about this before the kids get home from school."

"I sent my brother to pick them up for an early dismissal, so we have the rest of the day to talk."

"You told your brother about the video?"

"I told my whole got damn family about it. That's the reason why I'm still here talking to your ass."

"What do you mean by that, Sasha?"

"My momma said that maybe you're confused. My father said that you were just experimenting, but he didn't approve of it. My brothers, they just want to kick your fucking ass, but I said nooooo . . . let me see what he has to say about this mess. So what do you have to say for yourself, Parnell?"

"Sasha, all I can say is that I made a mistake. I don't want to lose you or my daughters for one mistake."

"You expect me to believe that you just did that crap one time?"

"Sasha, yes. It happened that one time," he lied.

"I want you to tell me the got damn truth, or I'm going to call my brother and tell him to keep my daughters away from you, because you're a liar!" she screamed out.

"Sasha, I'm not lying to you."

Sasha walked over to him and slapped him with all of the strength that she could muster up in the palm of her right hand. "You want me to believe that was your first time ever being with a man?"

Parnell grabbed where Sasha had slapped him. He really wanted to hit her back, but he was trying to save his marriage. "Sasha, you can believe what you want to believe, but it was. I swear."

"You want me to believe that was your first

time—the way he was riding your ass. You are a lying-ass bastard, and you still didn't say why you're home early."

He couldn't bring himself to tell her the truth, so he lied again. "I left early, because Romel and I had a dispute over a case that I took over."

"When are you going to start telling the truth, Parnell?"

"I am, Sasha. What more do you want from me?"

"I wanted a husband who isn't bisexual, or whatever you are. And I wanted him to at least tell me the truth so that I could decide whether or not this marriage is worth saving."

"So what are you saying, Sasha?"

"I called your job when I got the video, and I was told that you no longer worked there. I looked at that mess again, because I had to know if you were enjoying yourself, and from what I saw, you were. Now, here you are lying through your teeth about everything. Why, Parnell? That's all I want to know."

"I don't know what else to tell you. I just know that it won't happen again."

"I don't know that, since you couldn't tell the truth about anything, thus far."

"I didn't lose my job, Sasha. I resigned," he lied.

"Why did you resign, Parnell?"

"I don't want to go into that right now, Sasha. I'm trying to resolve one issue with you, and you're bringing up another."

"No, you know what you're doing. You're avoiding the issue."

"If you're going to ask and answer the questions for me, then I'm done here."

"You think so, Parnell?"

"I can't think right now, Sasha. All I can say is that I was wrong, and that it won't happen again. I believe that I was drugged that night at Josephine's party."

"Parnell, Josephine had just given a party when her basement was finished, and I asked to go to that party with you. Why wasn't I invited to either one? Because of the type of party it was, and because you didn't want me to know that you are gay. Also, why don't you look drugged in that video?"

"Sasha, please stop asking so many questions, and let's work on the first one."

"I don't need any answers from you. You couldn't tell the truth if it slapped you in the face. I'm not staying in this bull crap–assed marriage." Sasha pressed her brother's number on the speed dial on her cell phone, so he knew to come get her.

"What are you saying, Sasha?"

"I'm saying that I'm leaving you."

"Sasha, please let's not go through this. I made one fucking mistake, and you're going to leave me for it?"

"Put yourself in my shoes, Parnell. If that had been me with my head stuck between Michelle's or Josephine's legs, you would have had a got damn fit, and I'm sure it would have been over."

"But that didn't happen, and I wouldn't

leave you, Sasha. I would try to work things out with you. Sasha, please don't leave me. I need you. I need my daughters."

"No, what you need is some counseling. You're sick, and you make me sick. How am I going to explain to two teenagers that their father is gay?"

"Keep the girls out of this, and I'm not gay. I made a fucking mistake. I was drugged. I don't even remember that fucking night."

"You are such a fucking liar."

Parnell tried to hold her again, but Sasha snatched away from him.

"Don't put your nasty, filthy hands on me. You have betrayed me, and the worst part, you did so with a man. I can no longer trust you or any of your friends, especially Josephine. Oh, by the way, I called her house, and I was told that she no longer resides there. Mmm . . . Marcus must have gotten a tape too, huh?"

"Sasha, if you give me a chance, I promise to make this go away. I can't lose my family. I can always get another job, but you have to give me a chance to show you, OK?"

Sasha ignored Parnell and went to answer the door. "Get the girls' things and I'll get mine," she told her brother. He followed her to where the suitcases and bags were.

"Sasha, come on, baby." Parnell grabbed her arm as she walked past him.

"Get your damn hands off my sister." Sasha's brother snapped at Parnell.

"I'm trying to talk to my wife."

"I'm not your wife anymore. I want a divorce,

and I'm filing for it soon. I suggest you get ready, because I'm asking for every got damn thing you got."

"Sasha, wait. Let's not go through this, please?"

"'Let's not go through this'? Let me see? Was that you, with your ass up in the air, butt-fucking-naked, getting your brains screwed out by another man?"

"Sasha, I told you that I was drugged that night, and I didn't realize what was going on."

"You know what, Parnell? You must still be drugged, or you think I am now, because you are lying. I will be back for the rest of my things, and I'll see your ass in court, if it isn't up in the air for another man."

Parnell watched his wife walk out on him. First he lost his job, now his wife. He didn't know how he was going to cope with losing everything, but he knew that whoever was sending out that video had to be stopped. He called Josephine again, and she told him that she knew it was Destiny. Michelle was trying to find out where she lived so that she could go talk to her. Parnell insisted that she tell him Destiny's whereabouts as soon as she found out, because he wanted to talk to her also.

Destiny was running late. She had promised Audrey that she'd pick her up, and they would go shopping for a gift for Rosalee.

"What's the rush, boo?" Eric asked.

"Eric, it's already two thirty-five, and I promised Audrey that I would pick her up from school, and take her shopping to buy Rosalee something for Mother's Day. Which happens to be the day after tomorrow."

"I'm sorry, baby, but you can't blame all of this on me."

"I'm not, but if you had kept that thing in your underwear, I wouldn't be late. I got fifteen minutes to pick her up."

"OK, baby, you got time. I'll see you later, and don't drive that truck like a bat out of hell. It's not that Jag you traded it for."

"I know," Destiny said as she rushed out to go pick Audrey up from school. She was in such a hurry that she didn't see Parnell sitting in his car across the street from where her truck had been parked.

He watched her as she drove off. Thanks to Michelle's going to the shop for another hairdo, and talking about Destiny like a dog to Jasmine, she found out where Destiny was living. Parnell wanted to watch her for a while to make sure she lived alone before he took his revenge on her for causing him to lose his wife, kids and job. He took another drink out of the bottle of Martell before he drove off.


Parnell didn't come back to her apartment building until two days later. He figured that since it was Mother's Day she'd be going out somewhere. His hunch paid off. Destiny stepped out of her building with a man, but Parnell didn't recognize him. He knew that he wasn't William. He watched them as they playfully walked to the truck that she had driven off in previously.

He hated her, and he wanted revenge. He looked down on the seat at the silver gun, which he brought from home. One way or another, Destiny was going to pay for all the trouble that she had caused him and his friends. He took a long drink out of a bottle of Martell. He was drunk, and he hadn't showered in days.

Parnell had finished the bottle of Martell before he made it to Destiny's house to spy on her. He had stopped at a store on the way and bought another pint of Martell. He sipped on it while he sat and waited on Destiny and her friend to return. Finally they pulled up. Parnell studied the guy's face, because he was going to be the one that lured Destiny to meet her fate.

Parnell slept well into the morning. He got up from bed and cleaned himself up. He took out a pair of black slacks, a black shirt and a pair of black rubber-sole shoes. After he got dressed, he nervously climbed into his car and drove over to where Destiny lived. He began to sweat profusely. He needed a drink. That was the only thing that could help him feel better right now. He hadn't planned on being so nervous, but he was.

He drove to a liquor store and bought a half pint of Martell. He drank half of it before he reached the building where Destiny lived. Her truck was gone, but he saw the guy that she had been with the day before. He must have been getting ready to go to school or something, because he had a book bag on his shoulder. Parnell quickly put the top back on the Martell, and snatched the gun from out of the glove box. He rushed up on Eric.

"Excuse me," Parnell said.

"Yeah, can I help you?"

"Do you know if there are any vacant apartments for rent in this building?" he asked Eric.

"Um . . . I'm not sure, but I can let you in and show you where the manager's office is. You can talk to him."

"Could you do that for me, please?"

"Sure. Let me throw my bag in the truck."

Once they were inside the hallway, Parnell pulled the gun on Eric. "If you don't want to get hurt, don't call out for help. Take me to your apartment. Now!"

Eric did as he was told. The one time he decided to stop and help someone was the one time that he would get robbed. Eric opened his apartment door and let himself and the man with the gun inside. "Man, look, take whatever it is that you came for. I only have about fifty bucks on me, and it's in my right pocket, if you want to reach in there and get it."

"Shut the fuck up. I didn't come here to rob you. I came here for something else. Where's your bitch?"

"My bitch? I don't have one of those. I live alone."

"If you don't want a bullet in your fucking head, you better stop playing with me. Do I look like I'm playing with you?"

"No, sir, you don't, but I don't know who you're talking about. I live here alone."

"OK, then, where the fuck is Destiny?"

"I don't know. She hasn't been here in a couple of days."

"Don't lie to me, because I am not in the mood. I know the bitch lives in this building, because her fucking sister Jasmine said she does."

"OK, man, look, put the gun down and let's talk about whatever it is that you came here for."

"You think I won't shoot your ass?"

"No . . . no, I don't mean it like that. Man, Destiny isn't here, and I don't know where she is or when she's coming back."

"OK, I see that we got to do this the hard way." Parnell walked over to Eric and slapped him with the butt of the gun. "Where's your phone?"

"On the table," Eric said, holding the spot on his head that was bleeding.

"Call the bitch on her cell phone and tell her that she needs to come home right fucking now. If you want to live, you better get that bitch here, and now!" Parnell snapped.

Eric called Destiny. He told her that something was wrong with his truck, and it wouldn't start. He needed a ride to school right away to take his finals. Destiny told him that she was on her way as soon as she paid for the things that she was on line to purchase at the store.

As soon as she put the bags in the cart to rush home, she bumped into William. Her heart sank, but not like it had when she had seen him at the food court in the mall with his new woman.

"Hey, Destiny. What's been up with you?" he asked.

"Not much, and you?"

"I've been thinking about you a lot lately, and I want you to come home."

"I'm sorry, William, but I don't see why. I saw you at the food court with another woman, and the two of you seemed to be quite happy."

"She's gone. She wasn't like you, baby. I couldn't deal with her. She was a whiner."

Destiny's phone rang again. "Excuse me. Hello."

"What's taking you so long?"

"Here I come now." She closed her cell and stuck it back in her purse. "I'm sorry, William, but I got to go."

"That must have been Mr. Right, huh?"

"Call it what you want, but he sure isn't a Mr. Wrong. Bye. See ya, got to go."

Eric didn't want to call Destiny back to the house, because he didn't want this man to hurt her. He didn't know why he was here or who he was, and with the barrel of a gun pointing at his head, Eric didn't have the courage to ask. He hoped that this was one of those times that Destiny didn't use her key to come in his apartment. He was scared that the man would shoot her on contact.

"Where the fuck is she?"

"She's on her way," Eric said as he looked around his living room for something to defend himself and Destiny with. There was nothing that he could use to help him fend the gunman off. Destiny did exactly what he hoped she wouldn't. She stuck her key in the door, and as soon as she turned the knob, Eric and Parnell jumped up.

"Where the fuck you going? Sit your punk ass down," Parnell told Eric. "Hey, Destiny. Close the got damn door, and don't scream—or he dies first."

"Why are you doing this, Parnell? I can't believe that someone I allowed to handle my personal affairs after my grandparents died would be pointing a gun at me."

"Close the door and lock it, bitch!"

Destiny did as she was instructed to do. "Parnell, what's this about? Why are you here with a gun?"

"You don't know?"

"No, I don't."

"Get over there with your boyfriend," Parnell said, motioning her with the gun. "I'll tell you, but first let me tell you this. If it hadn't been for your half sister Jasmine telling Michelle where you lived, I couldn't have found you."

Destiny looked shocked.

"Don't look so shocked. Jasmine doesn't like you. She said you're too got damn prissy for her, and she has no plans to share you with her father."

"OK, Parnell, but why are you here with a gun pointed at me and my friend?"

"Oh, he's not your man?"

"No, he's just a very close friend."

"That's the same thing. You see, because of

you, I don't have anybody. My wife took the kids and left. I got fired from my job, and my father thinks that I'm a fag."

"What do you mean because of me? I don't have anything to do with you losing your family."

"Bitch, you can't be that naïve. Who sent copies of that video to my wife and job?"

Destiny gasped, and threw her hand up to her mouth. "I didn't," she mumbled through her hand.

"You're a lying-ass bitch," Parnell snapped. He was becoming impatient with Destiny. He cocked the trigger and aimed the gun at her. "Tell your boyfriend what you did, before you die, bitch. And while you're at it, tell him that you love him, so those words will haunt his ass for the rest of his life."

Destiny broke down and cried. She didn't know that things would turn out like this. She didn't want Eric to get hurt, and she didn't want to die. "Parnell, please don't do this. I didn't send that video to your job or wife."

"Shut the fuck up! You're lying. . . . You're lying. You better tell that motherfucker that you love him, because your time is up."

"I love you, Eric, and I'm sorry that—"

"Shut the fuck up, bitch! That's not what I told you to say to him."

Parnell aimed the gun at Destiny's head and pulled the trigger. Eric pushed her hard to get her out the way of the bullet, but it ripped through his hand and hit her.

"Nooooo . . . ," Eric screamed out as Destiny fell to the floor. Blood spilled out of her and covered the front of her chest. Eric scooped her up in his arms and screamed out for help. He didn't care if Parnell shot and killed him, because he had taken Destiny away from him. When he heard the second shot, he waited to feel the pain, and then for things to get dark around him, but that moment never came. He looked over to where Parnell was, and saw him lying on the floor with a hole in the middle of his forehead.

Eric pulled his cell phone out of his pocket and called the police. He couldn't believe that the only woman that he ever loved was gone forever. Destiny tried desperately to open her eyes, but she couldn't. She felt a searing pain in her left shoulder, and all she could do was cry. She heard Eric screaming for her to open her eyes, but she couldn't. She heard the faint sounds of police sirens, and she wished that they would hurry up and come, before she passed out again.


It seemed like it took the medical examiner's office hours to remove Parnell's body from Eric's living room. After they had removed it, and the police had left, Eric cleaned Destiny's blood off him, changed his shirt and went to the hospital to be treated for the gunshot wound to his hand. When he got there, the same police that had left his apartment were at the hospital waiting to question Destiny. She was just coming out of surgery to have the bullet fragments removed from her shoulder.

After she came out of recovery, the police swamped Destiny. The police weren't in her room for long, because she was heavily sedated. They couldn't get much information out of her. They tried to piece together a story from the information that Eric had given them. At first, they thought that Parnell had come to rob Destiny, but then they found out that he was a very prominent lawyer. They needed to know the connection between him and Destiny.

After the emergency room doctors had cleaned and put a cast on Eric's shattered hand, he went to Destiny's room. She lay in the hospital bed, looking peaceful and calm. He imagined her calling out his name for help, and it pained him that he hadn't been there for her. With all of the commotion, he couldn't get to her until some hours later. He bent down and kissed her softly on the mouth, and Destiny slowly opened her eyes.

"What took you so long?" she whispered.

"What difference does it make? I'm here."

Eric saw a smile spread across her face, and a tear ran down her cheek.

"When I heard another gunshot, I thought that he had shot you too."

"No, baby, he shot himself."

"I didn't mean for things to come to this point. Is he going to be OK too?"

"No, baby, he's dead. He shot himself in the head."

"Oh, Eric, what have I done?"

"You didn't do anything. Somebody else did. Somebody else made more copies of that video and mailed it to his wife and job. He lost them both."

"Eric, I remember him saying something about Jasmine not liking me, and that's how he found me. Did he say that, or was I dreaming?"

"No, you were not dreaming."

"My mother warned me to be careful of her. I didn't know that she didn't like me that much, that she would want me hurt."

"Don't worry about her, baby. You're OK, and that's all that matters. Which, by the way, brings about a question."

"What question?"

"Did you really mean it when you said you loved me?"

"I had to say what I had to say. I thought it would have saved me from getting shot, but . . . yeah, I meant it, fool."

"I love you too, Destiny. Will you marry me?"

"Ooh, I heard that."

"What are you guys doing here?" Eric asked.

"The news," Audrey and Corrine said at the same time.

"The news?" Destiny asked, puzzled.

"Yes, the news," Rosalee said.

"Momma, what are you doing out of the house?"

"Just because your momma is sick doesn't mean that she can't get up to come see about her child."

"Well, aren't you going to answer the man, chile?" Corrine asked.

"Answer what?" Destiny asked.

"You know what," Audrey said.

Destiny looked up at Eric, then said, "Yes."

Eric wanted to pick her up and hug her, but he couldn't. "All this time you knew that you wanted me. I don't know what you were waiting for."

"To get shot, so you could ask," Destiny answered; then she burst out laughing. "Oww, this mess hurts."

"So does my hand, but it feels better now."

"I want to be one of the bridesmaids," Audrey said.

"I guess that makes me the matron of honor," Rosalee said.

"What am I going to be?" Corrine asked.

"Something," Rosalee said as she laughed.

"Hey, everybody. We got here as soon as we heard."

"Hakim, Dad," Destiny said.

"Yes, baby girl," Derrick answered.

"How did you know?"

"Jasmine, she said that this is all her fault. She said that she was jealous of you, but that she didn't know that some woman named Michelle wanted your address to hurt you."

"I don't know why she would be jealous of me. I'm not trying to take you or Hakim away from her. I only wanted to be her friend," Destiny said as she began to cry.

"Hey, let's not even go there," Rosalee said. "We got a wedding to plan, and I dare you renege on me. I want to be the matron of honor."

"Who's getting married?"

"These two are," Audrey said, pointing to Eric and Destiny.

"Damn, maybe I should go and get myself shot if it's going to get me a wife."

"Hakim, did you just hear what you said? I know you're not looking for a wife," Destiny said.

"It was just a figure of speech," Hakim said.

"Boy, you should go ahead and get married. It won't kill right away. It'll kill you slowly," Derrick joked.

"So who's the best man?" Hakim asked.

"I don't know. Maybe my brother, but he lives a million miles away."

"What about me?" Hakim asked.

"What if you catch the garter? That means that you got to get married next."

"Destiny, shut up."

"So when is the special day?" Derrick asked.

"We don't know. I just asked."

The whole room burst out in laughter.

"Well, Destiny, you better hurry up and get well so that we can plan your wedding," Rosalee said. "I don't have forever to see you walk down the aisle."

Destiny knew that her mother was right. She wouldn't let her miss her special moment for anything in the world. "As soon as Eric and I can talk alone, we'll come up with a date."

"I guess that means that they're putting us out," Hakim said.

"No, they're not, but I am," the nurse said. "Ms. Symone needs to get some rest."

Eric kissed her. "I'll see you later."

"What are you going to do about the mess in your apartment?"

"Clean it up, but I'll be at yours, if you want me."

"OK, baby."

"Boy, don't be stopping to lend a hand to any more strangers," Corrine said.

"I won't. Anybody need a ride?"

"You know we do," Audrey said.

"Audrey, Momma and you too, Corrine," Destiny uttered.

The three of them turned to see what Destiny wanted. "I love you all."

"And we love you too, and remember, don't take forever, because time waits for no one," Rosalee said.

As soon as everyone left her alone in her room, she called for the nurse to come back.

"Can you give me something to write with, and some paper, please?"

"Sure. I'll be right back." The nurse left her room, then came right back with pen and paper in hand.

"I got a wedding to plan," Destiny said, smiling.

The first thing she wrote at the top of the paper was: *Start a family right away so that Rosalee can have some grandchildren.* Then she thought about having her mother around for that long. Destiny didn't believe what the doctors had told Rosalee. She believed that her mother would be around for as long as she wanted to be. Those doctors weren't God, and they didn't have the power to give or take away life. Then she started on her wedding plans. As much as she hated to, she left Jasmine's name off her guest list, but she definitely wanted to invite Stormy, because she believed that he could help her pull this thing off.

Then she wondered if he liked her—after all, he was Jasmine's friend. But she liked him, and she knew that he had good taste in things.

# 14

Destiny woke up earlier than usual. She missed her man, but today was their wedding day. She wouldn't see him until they met at the church to say their vows. She chose July 9, because it was almost two months after the shooting, and it was just enough time to get everything arranged.

Rosalee had gotten sicker, but she refused to let it show. She was more than determined to be at her daughter's wedding. She wished for the strength to be there when her first grandchild was born, but she knew that each day she opened her eyes, a little more of her strength drained from her body.

She loved the new house that Destiny had bought, and she especially loved the little coach house out back, where she now lived with her nurse. Audrey had moved in the big house with Destiny and Eric, against her will. Rosalee wanted it that way, because she didn't want her baby girl to witness the pain and suffering that she was going through. She had hopes that the cancer would go into remission, but it didn't. It did allow her enough time to be at her daughter's wedding.

Corrine had come over and spent the night so that she could assist Stormy and Rosalee when it came time for Destiny to get dressed. It hurt Stormy that Jasmine couldn't attend her sister's wedding, but Stormy understood why. Jasmine tried to convince Stormy that he was betraying her after all the time that they had been friends. He'd developed a relationship with Destiny against Jasmine's wishes, but their other friends had told Jasmine that she had been the one to betray her own flesh and blood—not Stormy. Therefore, he remained friends with Destiny.

The wedding was beautiful. Rosalee was the matron of honor. Stormy was the maid of honor, and Audrey was the flower girl. Hakim was Eric's best man, and Eric's nephew was the ring bearer. The wedding was small, and most of the guests were friends from the college that Eric attended, and a few people that Destiny knew.

Rosalee held up as best she could during the whole ceremony, but as the day wore on, she became weak and tired. She wanted Destiny to enjoy the rest of her day, and she held out a little longer. Rosalee longed for her bed, but she refused to disappoint her daughter.

"Today is Destiny's day," Rosalee said from where she was sitting during the reception.

"Thank you, Momma. Thank you so much for sharing my day with me," Destiny said.

The DJ put on John Legend's "So High" for the bride and groom to dance to. Destiny followed as Eric led her to the dance floor. Rosalee looked on as she admired her daughter. Destiny looked so happy as Eric held her and they twirled around to the music that filled the room. After the dance Rosalee could no longer tolerate the pain, and her nurse drove her home. Rosalee had told Destiny to enjoy the rest of her day, and she'd be waiting for her when she got home.

Destiny and Eric had put off their honeymoon to be around Rosalee, just in case something happened.

Destiny couldn't believe that almost a month later she was sitting in the same church where her wedding ceremony had been held, looking at her mother lying in a casket.

After the funeral Destiny told Corrine that Rosalee had made her promise that she would look after her. Corrine smiled when Destiny told her what Rosalee had said, and she said, "I knew you and your momma had been plotting and planning. That's the reason why y'all kept insisting how much I would love the coach house if I moved into it."

Destiny smiled, saying, "I need you here more than Momma insisting that I bring you here. I don't know the first thing about raising a baby or what teenagers go through, and you definitely are a part of this family, Momma Corrine."

That made Corrine feel like the grandmother and mother that she always was.

"Chile, when I get through teaching you

how to raise a baby, it'll be a breeze," Corrine said to Destiny.

"Well, I hope you can teach me how to get through the pain," Destiny said.

"Chile, they got all kinds of medicine to numb that pain. That's what made it easy for these teenage girls to keep popping 'em out so doggone fast. Had they not been so quick to numb their hot tails, they wouldn't be so quick to go through all that pain."

"Momma Corrine, I love you, and I don't know what I would do without you, but some of those little hot-tailed girls you talking about just didn't have enough sex education and smarts about themselves."

"You know, Destiny, I think I like that new name you just gave me—Momma Corrine. That fits. Enough about those hot-tailed girls, how you holding up?"

"I'm OK. It's not like she didn't tell me that she didn't have too long to live. I just thought that maybe the doctors didn't know what they were talking about."

"Where's Audrey?" Corrine asked.

"I think she's still sitting in the backyard. She said she needed some fresh air."

"Do you think she's going to be OK?"

"I know she is. You want to know what she told me last night?"

"I guess I do, if you're willing to tell me," Corrine said.

Destiny moved closer to Corrine and laid her head on her shoulder. "Audrey said to me last night that she's glad that you were in her life. She said, 'Destiny, if it hadn't been for Corrine taking on the role of Momma, I don't think I could make it.' I told her that she's just a child, and she has nothing to worry about, because we were going to be there for her. She said that even though you're not our mother, you sure make it easier not to feel the pain of missing her." Then Destiny let all the tears that she had been holding inside flow.

"I will be around for as long as the Man Up Above gives me the air to breathe, and don't you or your sister get to thinking that y'all too big for a spanking, 'cause you ain't. That tree out there growing in the backyard got some nice branches on it." This made Destiny and Corrine burst out in laughter.

Eric stood in the doorway, listening to his new bride and Corrine talking. He had been worried about Destiny and the baby, but now he knew that he didn't have anything to worry about. Thanks to Corrine picking up where Rosalee had left off.

"Now, come on, we still got guests in here, and they probably wondering what done happened to you," Corrine said as she held Destiny's hand and led her back into the dining room, where her mother's coworkers and friends had gathered to reminisce about Ms. Rosalee Symone.


After losing her friend Parnell, Josephine realized that things wouldn't have ever gone wrong the way they had if she had not ventured out into the forbidden. She had found out through Michelle that Leon had sent five of those videos out and was prepared to send out more if she didn't drop the charges that she had against him. After Marcus decided to give her another chance, and allowed her to move back into their home, she decided to give Leon another chance. She dropped the charges, as did Michelle, and Leon was released from jail.

Two weeks later, Josephine was attending another one of her friends' funerals, and Destiny sat off in the distance. When Destiny noticed Josephine looking at her, she walked over to where she was sitting and bent down so that only Josephine could hear what she had to say: "I was your fool, and so was Michelle, but look at where being your fool got her."


Leon had been good to Michelle, just to get her to move back into the apartment with him. He had held a grudge against her and Josephine for pressing charges against him, and for his being locked up in jail for months. Josephine learned that Michelle had come home fifteen minutes late from her new job, which she had gotten because Leon didn't want her to have anything to do with Josephine anymore, and he snapped.

Leon had beaten her so badly, she had to have a closed-casket funeral. He wasn't remorseful during his trial, and he showed no sign of emotions. He sat in court, day after day, and listened as the prosecutor explained to the jury how he had beaten Michelle to death. He listened as the foreman of the jury read the guilty verdict, and even then he didn't bat an eye.

Leon's entire family sat in the courtroom and heard the things that he had done, and for the first time Leona realized that something was really wrong inside of her son's head.

Candice gave birth to a beautiful, blue-eyed, light-complexioned baby girl. She called Hakim out to the hospital to see her. Hakim took one look at the baby, then politely said, "She's a very beautiful baby girl, but she's not my daughter."

Candice became very upset. She told Hakim that she'd see him in court for a paternity test, and when it proved that he was the father, she wanted child support. Hakim didn't have any objections to her request, but he told her that once the test proved that he wasn't her baby's father, he wanted her to leave him alone.

The day finally came, and Hakim and Candice were standing in front of a judge waiting on her to give them the results of the paternity test. Once the judge read the results, Candice burst out crying.

"Your Honor, that can't be right. He is the only man that I was with before I got pregnant."

"Your Honor, I'm not trying to be rude in any type of way, but her daughter has blue eyes and fair skin. She's a very beautiful little girl, but, unfortunately, no one in my family has those traits. Her daughter's father has to be of a different nationality."

"That's a lie, Hakim, and you know it."

The judge banged her gavel on the desk and told Candice to address whatever she had to say to the court, not Hakim. Then she said, "Ma'am, I don't usually get into people's business, but your daughter has no resemblance to this man, and the paternity test proved that he is not your child's father. I suggest that you think about your prior relationships, and find your daughter's father. Good luck in doing so. Court's adjourned."

18 month
3 shots

Jaequese
Hubbard